RESISTANCE TRAINING

USA TODAY BESTSELLING AUTHOR
Kayley Loring

RESISTANCE TRAINING

KAYLEY LORING

Illustrations & Cover Design: Qamber Designs
Copy Editing: Mandi Andrejka, Inky Pen Editing
Proofreading: Jodi Duggan

USA TODAY
BESTSELLING AUTHOR

Kayley LORING

FUNNY SEXY SWEET ROMANCE

This is dedicated to the once-feral black cats who own my heart. That's not a metaphor. They are actual cats with black fur.

AUTHOR'S NOTE

Hi! I'm Kayley Loring and I wrote this book. I love using em dashes. My copy editor loves using em dashes. I have no idea what the difference is between an em dash and an en dash and will probably never figure it out, because I'm too busy coming up with new ways to describe men's butts. I like using em dashes and writing about men's butts more than I like using a lot of commas, semi-colons, and colons. Have a nice day!

CHAPTER 1
BRAD

Fitness Journal—Saturday, March 1

Today's Intention: *1. Continue being relentlessly awesome. 2. Do not Google her.*

THE 4 F'S OF GOOD FORM

FUEL: *5:00 a.m. — Chocolate whey protein smoothie with half a cup frozen blueberries, cup of frozen organic spinach, tablespoon hemp seeds, tablespoon ground flaxseed meal, 5 grams creatine powder, teaspoon MCT oil. *Note: add MCT oil to blended coffee, not smoothie. Use avocado instead. Did not love the mouth feel.*
5:45 a.m. — Three scrambled eggs, two cups sauteed kale, two cups steamed broccoli, half a cup black beans, one cup low fat cottage cheese. Black coffee.
1:00 p.m. — Grass-fed meatballs and zucchini noodles.
6:00 p.m. — Lemon chicken thighs and potatoes. No snacks all day.

FIRE: *Same WHY as always. "Fuck you, high school dicks."*
Listened to Huberman Lab during run.
Metallica instead of Pearl Jam while lifting today.
Gave my favorite client Larry a copy of Can't Hurt Me by David Goggins. He thanked me and told me he already has it but he needs another copy for his yacht. That is the definition of baller. I want to have extra copies of my favorite books for my yacht. And to have a yacht.

FORTRESS: *5:15 a.m. — 3 mile run at a 7:30 pace. Same route as always. Weather's shit, but pace stayed consistent. Didn't think about her at all.*
Leg day at the gym. Fuck leg day. All hail leg day. Deadlift PR — 315 lbs. Romanian deadlifts at 205 lbs 8 reps felt smooth. Strength and sculpting. Dolores told me my glutes are fire and reminded me that her granddaughter is legally separated.

FRACTURES: *7:00 p.m. — Another email from Aubrey Sparks, through the gym website telling me she put Vivian on the wait list for my personal-training sessions. I have not responded. Just like I didn't respond to her DMs on Instagram asking me to reach out to her sister. As if living in the same city as her changes anything. Seriously — how did Aubrey find me? And why now?*
These are not questions I need answered. These questions are weaknesses.
Immediately converted that fracture to fire: Pull-up PR — 20 reps. Perfect form. Pure functional strength. Just me vs. gravity. Recorded for Instagram.
Eight years ago I couldn't do one pull-up. Now I can lift my 6'2" 195 pound body twenty times in two minutes. I have the elite strength of a Navy Seal. That right there is the difference

between the boy I left behind in Seattle and the man I built here.
What got me here? Not getting derailed by feelings.

Just replied to Aubrey and told her I do not have any openings in
the foreseeable future.
Did not ask why now or how she found me.
But fuck.
I'm dying to know what Vivian looks like now.
What she's doing with her life.
But I won't look her up.
Ever.
Vivian Sparks = woman-sized Twinkie.
Not that I couldn't handle it.
My body has not craved Twinkies for eight years. My body will
not crave Vivian Sparks.
Tomorrow's mission: Target my brain's weak desire to know
what Vivian Sparks looks like now. Terminate any thoughts
about her well-being or whether she's on the apps or not.
Decimate mental speculation re: Why now? It's irrelevant.
But fuck.
The truth is Vivian was never a Twinkie.
Vivian was the best chocolate cake, made with love, the icing,
and the cherry on top.
And I never got to taste her the way I wanted to...not the cherry,
the icing, or the cake—and I will never forgive her.
But fuck.
I can't believe she lives here.
Why didn't her sister mention if she's single or not?
Fuck.

CHAPTER 2
VIVIAN

I am genuinely delighted for people who get to live happily ever after with their soulmate or whatever, but why aren't more people talking about how amazing it is to live alone?

Being able to redecorate this little house in my own brand of librarian–cottagecore–boho chic–defiantly messy teenager aesthetic that would drive my ex crazy is objectively awesome. I don't *need* all these pink Himalayan salt lamps, houseplants, antique mirrors, bohemian area rugs, Moroccan-leather poufs, framed graphic prints from Etsy, large crystals that I can't identify, or all of the books I can afford. Especially not the *Official Taylor Swift: The Eras Tour Book* I got on eBay. But I *do* need to have all of these things in my living room while setting the thermometer to a balmy sixty-nine degrees because it makes me deliriously happy knowing how much my ex-boyfriend would hate it.

Being home alone on a rainy Sunday night, doing what I want to do, when I want to do it—this is the stuff my dreams were made of when I was living here with the ex.

And the whole food thing?! I get to eat whatever I want, whenever I want, wherever I want. I can eat donuts while taking a bath at seven thirty on a Tuesday night. I can eat tacos for breakfast while standing over the kitchen sink, listening to a murder podcast and doing Kegels. I can stuff my face with a banana cream pie and then wash it down with a large glass of pinot noir that doesn't pair well with banana cream pie. How could I possibly top this?

By wearing pajamas all day and singing along to my *Fuck U Jeremy Thank U, Next* breakup playlist really loudly to annoy Hairy Styles, that's how.

Hairy Styles is my cat.

This is bliss for me.

Really.

And that's not just the sugar high talking either.

This is the happiest I've been in years.

I almost feel like me again.

I have Taylor Swift breakup song lyrics coursing through my veins. I don't have to wear headphones to listen to my nineties-nostalgia playlists or watch every episode of *Friends* with my office bestie at lunch because I live with an asshole who believes grown-ups should only stream shows with educational value at home. I can have *Pride and Prejudice* streaming on my iPad while listening to Stevie Nicks on my phone and rereading my paperback of *The Secret History*—one of the fifty or so books I had to store at my parents' house because my ex considered physical books to be clutter.

I am free. Free to be me. As long as my cat is cool with everything.

I'm right in the middle of belting out "Stronger" by

Britney Spears when the song is interrupted by a FaceTime call request from my sister.

This is not ideal. I am not mentally prepared to talk to anyone with less than four legs tonight—unless it's one of those amputee cats or dogs. I just want to sing the *Glee* Cast version of "Take a Bow" again, rearrange some of the books on my new vintage bookshelves, then get in bed with Hairy Styles and eat an apple fritter while reading a paperback. I want to leave sugary fingerprints all over the pages and be judged by exactly no one. Then, to relax my brain, I want to watch celebrities do their nighttime skin-care routines on YouTube until I fall asleep. And sleep all through the night, sprawled out starfish-style, taking up the entire mattress. As long as I'm not disturbing my cat.

That was the plan.

But the fact that Aubrey didn't text me first to ask if I'm available to FaceTime leads me to believe that either there is an emergency or she's checking on me again because she thinks I'm depressed. If it's an emergency, then I'm an asshole for not answering. If this is a check-in, then she'll keep calling until I answer and my songs will keep getting interrupted anyway. So, I reluctantly accept the video call. "Heyyyy, girl…!?"

My sister's freakishly symmetrical pretty face is barely recognizable because she's smiling. A lot. With her eyes. And her teeth. And her forehead. Even her ears look like they're smiling. So it's not an emergency.

I should be relieved, but I just felt a new tension knot form in my back.

"Hey, Vivi!" Seriously, I have never seen her smile like this before and I have never heard her greet me so enthusiastically. It's unnerving. She rolls her eyes. "Calm down—nobody died. What are you up to?"

Sus. Highly suspicious, I tell you. But I can't let on that I don't trust this casually upbeat older sister act. "Oh, you know. Sunday-night stuff. I was watching a documentary. And I'm about to start doing meal prep for the week."

"Oh yeah?" She smirks. "By 'meal prep' do you mean you're eating a pie that you were planning to eat tomorrow? And is the documentary about women who sing to their cats, *starring you*?"

"Oh my God—where did you hide the camera?!"

"Hah! I knew it. It's a rainy Sunday night. What else would you be doing?"

"You're an actual witch. I respect it." I set my phone up on top of the book I've placed on the arm of my chair and settle back into the extremely comfortable cushions. "But I can't decide if it's creepy or sweet of you to check what the weather's like in other cities—who does that?!"

"Extraordinarily considerate people who have a compulsive need to know everything," she states matter-of-factly.

"Now I can't tell if that's a humble brag or if you're the most self-aware person I know."

"It can be both. What kind of pie?"

"Banana cream with salted caramel."

"Wow. What's the occasion?"

"It sounded good and I wanted to eat it."

Aubrey blinks once, but she's still smiling. The judgment was there in the blink, I saw it.

"It's Self-Carb Sunday," I add.

"That does sound good," she says, in a tone that is a

subtle and elegant little soul-crushing reminder that I'm not adulting properly.

I moved to Portland a couple of years ago, and even though Aubrey still lives in Seattle where we grew up, her judgey big-sister voice accompanies me wherever I go. Like a hypercritical tube of lip balm or a Stanley travel mug that's supportive but also knows how to do everything better than everyone else. This is how it's been all my life. She's three years older than I am, but I have no memory of my sister ever actually being a child. Or of me not feeling childish whenever I'm around her, even in my mid-twenties.

I sigh dramatically.

Here we go.

"Don't you care about the neighbors hearing you sing?" she asks with genuine concern.

"I only sing really loudly when it's raining super hard. Plus Mrs. Friar is practically deaf."

"Don't cats have super-sensitive ears, though?"

"*Excuse* me. I have the voice of an angel. Hairy is very supportive of my hobbies as long as I remember to feed him and clean his litter box and do whatever else he wants me to do for him."

She giggles, which is weird, because Aubrey never giggles. And she never passes up an opportunity to make fun of my exceptionally wonderful singing voice. She is clearly attempting to make me drop my guard. "I thought you just said Hairy's supportive of your *bubbies*. You know, like, boobies."

"And then you remembered I'm not an adolescent boy from the Elizabethan Era? Are you a little bit drunk right now?"

"No, I'm just really happy that you seem happy."

"I am. I'm so much stronger than yesterday. Now it's nothing but *my* way."

"Are you quoting a Britney song?"

"Am I? I don't know. You don't have to worry about me—I'm great."

"I know. I'm glad."

"Yeah, but you said I seem happy with that condescending tone."

"Well, you just said you're great in that defensive tone."

"Yeah, because you have resting condescension face even when you're smiling."

She sighs. Her sigh is much louder and longer, more mature than the one I produced a moment ago. "Can we start over?" She waves her hand like she's Tom Cruise in a sci-fi action thriller, swiping the mental remnants of our prior conversation away to delete it. "I have news." She's still smiling. She isn't even annoyed that I brought up her resting condescension face. Which is highly sus.

I do some rapid mental sister math and then gasp. "Oh my God!" I pick up the phone with one hand, cover my heart with the other. My heart is genuinely racing all of a sudden. "He proposed!"

"Yes. How did you—"

"The way you're smiling. And I just realized this is the three-year anniversary of your first date! Aubrey—I am so happy for you!"

"Thank you. I can't believe you remember that." She sighs and deflates a little. "Wow. I really wanted to, like, *give* you the news so you'd be surprised like Mom and Dad were."

"Oh, sorry. Tell me now. I'll act surprised—I promise."

"Ugh. That's dumb."

"Shit. I'm an asshole. I ruined your news because I didn't want to talk about me anymore."

"You're the actual worst," she says, smiling.

"Show me the ring, show me the ring! Tell me everything there is to know about everything!"

"Okay, first of all, we are not done talking about you, and secondly...ta-dahhh!" She holds her left hand up in front of the camera, and I can just tell she's been practicing this in front of a mirror and probably already took eleven thousand selfies to post on Insta as soon as she's told all the important people over the phone. Aubrey has wanted to marry Eric since before their first date, over three years ago.

"Wow. Aubrey, it's gorgeous. That is so perfect for you."

"Right?! Mom screamed. And, you know, she's been drinking mimosas off and on since brunch, so then she just burst into tears because she can't believe her first baby's finally getting married, and eventually started moaning about *poor little* Vivi."

"Fantastic. Love that for me." I do not love those two words that have been preceding my name whenever it's uttered by family members for the past few months, but let's move on. "What did Dad say?"

"Dad mumbled something about how Eric could have put half the money he paid for the ring toward a down payment on a house, then said if it was that important for Eric to make me happy then it was a good investment."

"On brand. And sweet." Our parents adore Eric and his

entire family and basically everyone Eric knows and everything he stands for. "They must be so excited."

"They are. I wasn't expecting them to be *that* excited, Vivi. It was so cute. I made them promise not to tell you until I did. I mean, I just hung up with them, like, ten minutes ago." She sighs again. A happy sigh. "It's all happening."

The tip of my nose is tingling and my eyes are getting watery. I have no idea what it feels like to want to marry someone in particular, but I know exactly what it feels like to want someone I love to marry the person she loves, and now it's going to happen. My sister is not a crier, but I can tell she's getting emotional. When she gets emotional she gets really still and clears her throat. It's impossible to tell if she's trying not to cry or if she's trying not to throw up.

"Hey. I won't tell anyone if you vomit," I say, teasing.

"Shut up." She clears her throat. "I'm not crying." She clears her throat again. "There's more; let me talk."

"You're the one who can't talk because she's crying."

She frowns, clears her throat twice, and then says, "I want you to be my maid of honor."

I wait for her to laugh and say *Just kidding—could you imagine?!*

She doesn't. "Did you hear me?"

"Yeah. Wait. Really?"

"Yes, really."

"You want *me* to be your maid *of honor*?"

"Of course I do."

"Are you fighting with Jenna again or something?"

"No. I mean, sort of. She'll be one of my bridesmaids, but you're my sister. I want you to be with me as much as possible. Of course you're my maid of honor."

Well, now I'm crying. "Really?"

"Yes. Why are you so surprised?"

I wipe the tears away, laughing. "I guess I'm getting too hung up on the word *honor* because I don't think of you as thinking of me as honorable."

"Yeah, you're definitely getting too hung up on the word."

We both laugh, and then the tip of my nose gets extra super tingly and I start to detox liquid feelings from my eyeballs. Aubrey stares at me with pink-rimmed eyes, frowning. "Do not make me cry. I'm wearing lash extensions."

"I was going to say—they look really good!" I blubber.

"Thank you," she says, as if she's receiving an award. "Thank you for telling me about magnetic lashes."

"I'm so glad you found the perfect extensions for you!"

"I hope you find the extensions you deserve too, Vivi! Soon."

Wait. Are we still talking about eyelash extensions? I clear my throat and wipe my eyes.

Aubrey clears her throat and widens her eyes.

Now we're just two siblings who are clearing our throats and *not* crying or talking about how I haven't found my soulmate eyelash extensions.

"Okay, well…I'm honored that you want me to be your maid of honor. For real. I would love to. Thank you."

"Thank *you*. I really want it to be a special occasion for you too. The wedding is in June."

"Next June?" I take a sip of wine. That's an unusually reasonable amount of time for someone as impatient and Type A as my sister.

"No, this June."

I almost do a spit take but manage to start choking instead. *"This* June?" I sputter. "June of *this* year?"

"Correct. Three months from now. I'll be sending out save-the-date cards in two weeks, as soon as I've officially locked down the venue I want on Orcas Island. But I've had a group chat going with the owner and the property manager on Facebook for the past few years, and I messaged them, like, five minutes after Eric proposed, so I'm confident they'll be able to accommodate us some weekend in June. And I emailed the local officiant I've been following on Instagram. We're only inviting a hundred and fifty people and I've been editing the list forever. I got this."

I am now realizing she wants to get married before she turns thirty, and I will not say a thing because I am not judging her. "Wow. Okay."

"It has nothing to do with being twenty-nine. Don't judge me."

"I am so not judging you."

"So go ahead and block out all the weekends in June on your calendar."

"I will. Of course."

She slow-blinks at me. "Right. But do it now."

"I'm not going to forget that my only sister is getting married this June."

"I know, but put it in your calendar. While I can see you doing it."

"Yeah, let me put it in my calendar right now, while you can see me doing it." I would call her a bridezilla, but this is literally what Aubrey's like all the time. She's an Aubreyzilla. I'm willing to bet that finally being a bride will make her *less* of a control freak.

I reach for my laptop, which is on the floor, beneath Hairy Stiles. "Sorry, buddy," I say as I slip it out from under him. I make a big show of opening up my browser and entering *ONLY SISTER'S WEDDING TO ERIC!!!* into my calendar for every weekend of June. The only other entry on the weekends prior to these events were *New season of The Bear on Hulu?* And *Upgrade phone?*

Closing my laptop, I say, "When are you going to send me the list?"

"What list?"

"The to-do list. My maid-of-honor duties! Sounds like I should get started, like, ten weeks ago."

She gives me a look, like I'm a toddler asking for the car keys. To be clear, I am a certified paralegal. Very important attorneys trust me to draft legal documents, maintain corporate records, prepare and file documents with regulatory agencies. But my sister can't conceive of me as an adult who is capable of ordering a dozen penis straws online. "Oh, there's no list. For you, I mean. I've got it all under control."

"Um. You've only been engaged for, like, an hour, though, right?"

"Yeah, but I've had the master list in a Google Doc for years and there are spreadsheets, of course. Numerous secret Pinterest boards, and I designed the save the date and all the invitations in Canva ages ago. I've been low-key researching caterers and florists for years. Obviously I've had several dress options on hold. I will send you all the information you'll need to, quote-unquote, 'organize' the bachelorette tea party. It's all good."

"Fine. I'll just check the reviews of all the male strippers in the Pacific Northwest and find the one who is the most punctual and hygienic."

"I said the bachelorette is going to be a tea party!"

"Who said the strippers are for *you*?"

Aubrey laughs. Genuinely. Her head drops forward and her shoulders shake. She even snorts a little. It wasn't anywhere near that funny. "Vivi. Okay, but seriously, I just want you to focus your energy on finding a date."

"You mean a date in June?"

"No, I mean a date for the wedding in June. Someone who will be your date."

Oh God.

Seriously?

This?

I reach for my glass of wine and open my mouth, but before I can tell her Hairy is my plus-one, she says, "A human person who is not your cat who will accompany you to my wedding."

"How dare you. Granny Sparks will obviously be my date."

"Granny Sparks has a boyfriend."

I almost choke on my pinot again. "What?! Since when?"

"Since a couple of months ago. She didn't want to tell you because...you know."

"Because I've been so gleefully involved in a healthy relationship with myself?"

"Because you've been so depressed after getting dumped in the worst possible way."

"Okay. There are definitely worse ways to get dumped. And I am not depressed." I definitely sounded neither depressed nor defensive when I said that.

"You're eating pie and drinking wine at home by yourself while singing to your cat."

"Since when did being an amazing cat mom make a person depressed?"

"Vivian, I'm serious. You've been eating so much pie, and you won't go to that gym I told you about."

"It's not *that* much pie—and what gym?"

"The one I told you about when I was there a month ago. You didn't even look at the website I sent you, did you?"

"For the gym that's not in my neighborhood? Oh my God, I've only gone up *one* size! This is what happens when you're over twenty-five years old. To all women who aren't *you*. It's the natural progression of a woman's body to become more rounded...after eating more and exercising less."

My sister slaps her forehead.

"Hey, I like my curves! I got so skinny when I was with Jeremy, and I love getting my curves back."

"Nobody's telling you to lose weight—they have workouts for curves now!"

"I've been doing them—I lift large forkfuls of pie into my mouth, as many reps as I can until I get fatigued. Wanna see?"

"*Jeremy* is going to be in the wedding," Aubrey blurts out. "And he's throwing us an engagement party here in a couple of weeks—which you do not have to come to. He's going to be one of Eric's groomsmen."

Ohhhh yeah... I can't believe I didn't think of that as soon as she told me about the wedding. I met Jeremy through Eric, not long after he and Aubrey started dating. This is not good. This is not something to look forward to.

Shit. "Well…I mean. June is three whole months from now. A lot can happen in three months. We could all be dead by then!"

She takes a sip of water and a deep breath before saying, "He'll be at the wedding with his fiancée…"

What?

WHAT?!

"What?"

"Jeremy is engaged."

"To Duckface?"

"To the woman he dumped you for, yes."

Wow.

Jeremy Fenton is engaged to Duckface. I did not see that coming. I thought for sure that Jeremy would realize what a stupid idiot he was, leaving me for her. Or that he'd realize what a stupid idiot *she* was for cheating with him while he was still living with me and she was still living with her boyfriend *and* receiving financial support from some married-sugar-daddy situation that originated on Instagram. Or that they'd both realize what assholes they were for secretly seeing each other for an entire year. Or that they would have murdered each other by now since he moved back to Seattle for her, after making me move here for him, because they're both terrible stupid selfish asshole idiots. But I guess that means they're perfect for each other. Good for them.

I reach for the wine bottle that's on the coffee table and empty it directly into my mouth.

A toast to the terrible stupid selfish asshole idiots!

"Are you okay?"

I forgot that I was FaceTiming with my sister. Putting down the bottle and picking up the phone, I say, "Honestly?" I blow out a breath, and not one quippy word follows all that air. "I'm not sure."

"Oh, Vivi…" It looks like so many unexpected genuine words are about to come tumbling out of my sister's mouth, I brace myself. "I hate seeing you like this, and I'm not talking about the barely noticeable extra weight that really and truly looks good on you. I want my wedding to be fun for you. I want you to be as happy as I am. I've been watching you try to fill this void that has nothing to do with Jeremy, and I can't tell if you even realize it or not, and I'm not saying there's anything wrong with being alone or eating pie when you're alone or singing to your cat when you're alone…I just *don't want you to be alone*. You're wonderful, and I think it's been so, *so* long since you remembered how wonderful you are, and I'm so afraid it's all my fault somehow. Please let me help you."

And that's when I remember. I remember that I was never really in love with Jeremy so much as I flung myself into a two-person cult because I got tired of keeping myself busy on the apps. A two-person cult where he was the impossibly handsome, deviously charming cult leader that my parents approved of. And I was the not very devoted follower who had been kind of a mess for a few years and felt she should adhere to his rules about macronutrients and minimalist decor and digital every-thing and the missionary position and cleaning the toilets with bleach and never rewatching TV shows or movies because comfort makes your brain go soft and *oh my God he was a monster*.

I remember that someone else broke my heart years before I met Jeremy. And that guy never even knew my heart was his to break, because *I* didn't realize it until it was too late. And I remember that my sister is marrying the love of her life in three months. And she's worrying about *me*. I have no idea why she feels responsible for Jeremy dumping me, other than the fact that she introduced him to me. But…

"Aubrey." I hold the phone up directly in front of my face. "You're getting married."

"Yeah."

"Let's talk about *you*. I know you don't think I can help you, so just tell me something. Tell me about how he proposed."

Her impossibly symmetrical little face lights up again, and she says, "Okay, I'll tell you, but we will circle back to the gym thing, because I'm buying you an annual membership. For *not losing weight* reasons. This will be my bridesmaid gift to you."

"Uh-huh." I nod in agreement and smile very genuinely as I move super slowly over to the kitchen counter so she can't tell that I'm unboxing the apple fritters. "Sounds fun. Go on."

CHAPTER 3
BRAD

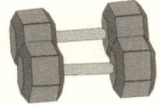

Fitness Journal—Monday, March 3

Today's Intention: Fuck it.

THE 4 F'S OF GOOD FORM

FUEL: *Fuck.*

FIRE: *Shit.*

FORTRESS: *Fuck!*

FRACTURES: *Fuck. It's nothing but fractures this morning. Aubrey Sparks DMed me a photo attachment last night. Here's what she wrote: "This is Vivi after she got dumped by her asshat boyfriend. The one she moved to Portland with. I drove down to see her. She was so depressed. Like she was after you ghosted her. I managed to get a picture of her when she was laughing. I think she looks so beautiful here. It's the first time I'd* *seen her laughing like that in years, and it was because I did my impression of Betty White doing that dance like in the GIF. It didn't last, because I can only do that dance for so long when I'm sober. The only thing that I think would make her truly happy is seeing you again. Because I think that you're the reason she's truly sad. And if it's my fault that you were both hurt, then I don't know that I'll ever be truly happy even though I just got engaged tonight."*

I mean.

Well played, Vivian's sister. Well played.

I might have an opening. What's the point of building this fortress if I don't test it against the person I've been building it for?

Every time that fucking Twilight movie comes up as a suggestion on Netflix my stomach seizes up. That movie will never not remind me of Vivian and everything that happened. I shouldn't be having a response like that. I need to confront this, or else I'm a fraud.

I need to prove to myself that I'm strong and in control in every way that I need to be.

But what if I get one look at her in person and forget why I've been building my fortress in the first place?

This is my entire life.

I can't risk throwing it all away now.

But fuck.

Maybe this is the fire I need to take me to the next level.

CHAPTER 4
VIVIAN

I would have slept through the alarm if Hairy Styles hadn't pounced on my chest. It's a gray, overcast March morning, typical of the Pacific Northwest this time of year. But it feels dark and cloudy inside my brain and body too. It's not a hangover. Not even half a bottle of wine was consumed last night. But I have a serious case of the Mondays and an even worse case of You're Going to Die Alone and Hairy Styles Will Eat Your Dead, Lonely Face.

I start a one-minute timer on my phone app and allow myself sixty seconds to think negative thoughts, so I can purge them.

But also to really enjoy them.

Aubrey was right.

I might be a little depressed.

The first glorious breakup phase, wherein I could rejoice in my freedom, is now over.

Phase Two has begun.

The man I'd moved to Portland with got engaged to

the woman he cheated on me with, while I was busy engaging in food orgies all by myself. The man I'd given up a great job opportunity in Seattle for so he could take a great job in Portland had moved back to Seattle and started a new life with Duckface. While I've been sitting on my gloriously ever-widening ass every night on my new cozy sofa, watching every single movie and show he didn't think I should watch while we lived together. I take comfort in knowing that Duckface surely knows that even the worst episode of *Sex and the City* is better than the best night of sex with Jeremy Fenton.

Okay, if I'm being honest, when he brought his A-game to bed it was pretty great. I wouldn't have moved to a new city for him if it wasn't. I wasn't *that* determined to convince everyone it was a serious relationship.

And I've run out of time to think about why I needed to convince anyone of anything at all, because I have to get to work on time for a meeting with my boss, who I have convinced I am reliable and punctual.

I am one minute late for my meeting with my boss, but he's five minutes late, so it doesn't matter. Traffic in Portland isn't nearly as bad as it is in Seattle, but that's like saying that stubbing your big toe isn't as bad as breaking your big toe. Nobody enjoys being stuck in traffic. Especially when you're stuck thinking about how the asshole you moved to this city with is probably in Seattle driving to work in his Mercedes while listening to NPR and not thinking about what an asshole he is.

The tiny rental house I used to share with him is in the Alberta Arts District, and the law firm I work for as a corporate paralegal is located in the heart of downtown Portland. It's about a twenty-minute drive at this time of day, or four repeat-listens of "So Long, London" by Taylor Swift and one "good 4 u" by Olivia Rodrigo. I bolted out of the house twenty-two minutes before the meeting because I had made the suboptimal decision to hunt for pictures of Jeremy and Duckface on Facebook—an app I had managed to stay off of for over two and a half months —instead of showering or eating.

In the time it took me to get to work, I had gone from promising myself that I'd stay positive, take the high road, and never, ever go on Facebook again to vowing to ruin Jeremy and Duckface's lives to mentally composing an email to Jeremy that expressed my gratitude toward him for leading me to the tiny house I love so much, that is within walking distance of the greatest artisanal ice-cream shop on earth, and wished him love, happiness, and success. When I parked, I asked Siri about voodoo revenge spells, but it gave me directions to Voodoo Donuts instead. Because my iPhone and all of foodie Portland conspires to get me to eat my feelings instead of dabbling in the dark arts.

Well played, Siri.

Well played.

I have every intention of stopping by Voodoo Donuts after work.

When I get out of my morning meetings, I head directly to the break room for a desperately needed protein bar and tea sesh with my work bestie, Marlo. That is when I realize my sister has other plans for me, and her plans are clearly going to be the exact opposite of me going to buy donuts after work.

There are fourteen texts and as many missed calls from Aubrey.

My chest tightens.

But the text that followed the first missed call reads *Nobody has died. Call me back ASAP.*

Perhaps she has important news about a really gross and humiliating thing that happened to Jeremy and Duck-face in public!

But no.

The words *gym* and *personal trainer* and *appointment* jump out at me, the way numbers and symbols float around for Matt Damon in *Good Will Hunting*. Except instead of solving the problems, I want to put my phone in the microwave and walk away in slow-motion, straight to the nearest food truck.

Groaning, I unwrap a protein bar, return to my small office, shut the door, and call my sister back on her cell phone.

She answers before I even hear it ring. "Okay, the gym is called Good Form. I sent you the address. It's in Kenton. That's sort of near you, right?"

"Not really."

"Right, but it's not out of your way or anything."

"It kind of is."

"Anyway, I got you an annual membership—but—I'm also paying for personal-training sessions with the owner of the gym. He's usually impossible to book, but he just had a cancellation, so you have to go tonight."

"I *have* to? I had plans for this evening."

"Really? Do these plans involve other people, or do they involve pastries?"

"They involve other people serving me pastries."

"You need to get out of the house and meet new people in that city that you refuse to move from." She is not wrong about this. She is not wrong about very many things. Like, ever. "Your appointment is at seven. With Mitch. Okay? You have to go. *Have to* have to. For me. I've already paid for three months of personal-training sessions with this guy and it's nonrefundable."

"Everything is refundable if you annoy the right people for long enough."

"Vivian."

"Fine. I will go. But if I hate him I will get you your money back."

"Deal! I have to jump on another call—get there early so you can fill out intake forms and call me as soon as you get home from your appointment. Make sure you look cute when you go to the gym, okay?! Love you!"

She hangs up before I can ask her what level of cuteness she is prescribing. 7:00 p.m.? Tonight? This means I don't have time to go home to get my workout clothes and shoes before the appointment. Which means I go to the downtown Target during my lunch break. Which means I spend twenty minutes finding parking, which means I have to eat Starbucks food for lunch, on the run. Which means I don't have time to do any Googling of this Mitch person. It means I don't have any time to vent to Marlo about my ex. It means that when I finally call my parents

to discuss Aubrey's upcoming nuptials I am simultaneously driving, putting my hair up in a ponytail, and eating
a grilled-cheese sandwich, which apparently makes me
sound depressed because I don't have a date to the
wedding. Which means I have to put the sandwich down
to get my mom to stop crying and lie to her about how
excited I am to hopefully meet some new people at this
gym I'm going to.

More importantly, it means that when I arrive at the
gym at exactly 7:00 p.m., unshowered and hungry, in my
new workout gear that is an unfortunate shade of neon
lime green due to the limited sizes and styles available at
the small urban Target, I do not look or feel my best when
I walk in and try to remember what looking cute feels like.
Also, they didn't have any sports bras or tank tops with
built-in support in my size. And I refuse to wear the push-
up bra I wore to work under a tank top, so once my jacket
comes off, I will be one layer of ribbed cotton fabric away
from pointing at everyone in front of me without my
fingers, if you know what I mean. If the air-conditioning is
turned up high in there, that is.

And it is.

Of course it is.

It is definitely cool, verging on cold in here.

It's a neighborhood fitness center, at the corner of a
commercial street in North Portland. It's not a strip-mall
fitness center or one of those places that look like former
auto-repair shops where people go to jump on wood boxes
and high-five each other. It isn't exactly a boutique gym
either. It looks like a remodeled studio or warehouse. It is
the perfect size, as far as I'm concerned.

There's a reception area at the entrance, with a clean,

mid-century-modern vibe. Not mid-century modern in Jeremy's interpretation of the style, which he had confused with Patrick Bateman's apartment in *American Psycho*, which was, in fact, eighties modernist. But *you* try explaining that to him. This is the welcoming mid-century modern of clean lines, functionality, and natural materials. Instead of being surrounded by floor-to-ceiling windows so people feel like they're on display, there are skylights and beautiful interior lighting. Bright enough to keep you alert but flattering enough to not make you hate your reflection in all the mirrors. There's even spa water on the reception desk. Cucumber and lemon water. What is this magical place?!

The woman at the reception desk has short blue hair, could be anywhere from thirty to fifty-five years old, and looks like she could lift me up over her head while hiking Mount Hood.

"Hi," I say to her while she's still typing something into an iPad. "I am almost exactly on time for my appointment with Mitch. Vivian Sparks?"

She looks up at me and does not smile at all, but not in an unfriendly way. In a badass way that I respect. "Welcome to Good Form."

"Hi. Thank you so much! This is my first time here. My sister got me a membership? And training sessions. As a gift. Surprise gift! I did not wake up this morning knowing I'd have a training session at a gym today is what I'm saying. Hence the lime green." I unzip my jacket, to give her a glimpse of my neon tank top.

She continues to not smile at me like a badass, and I really want her to like me. "You have to fill out some forms and take a picture for your membership card, but Mitch doesn't like it when people show up late for his sessions. I'll give you this guest pass for tonight, and we'll do the rest of it next time. Show me your photo ID."

I show her my driver's license, even though she didn't say please. "Funny story about what happened when I was at the DMV—"

"Mitch is probably in his office waiting for you," Badass Receptionist tells me without showing any interest at all in my funny DMV story. "Toward the back of the main area." She gestures to some unseen place beyond the partially frosted sliding glass doors. "You'll see a sign with his name on the door. He really doesn't like it when people are late. Have a great session."

"Traffic was terrible and I couldn't find parking!"

"He doesn't like it when people say that."

"Fantastic—thank you so much…!" I wait for her to tell me her name. She doesn't, so I take the guest pass from her and hold it up to the scanner by the doors to the main part of the gym.

I only feel a little like I should be accompanied by Storm Troopers as I march toward Darth Vader's office. This Mitch guy sounds like a peach! I am not going to rush just because he doesn't like it when people are late. I'm the client. If I don't like the vibe, I *will* get my sister that refund.

I stroll past a few elliptical machines and treadmills, a few recumbent stationary bicycles, a lot of weight machines, and various large exercise-equipment thingies that I do not know the names of. I do like how it doesn't smell weird in here. I also like how the music that's coming from the ceiling speakers isn't ear-splittingly loud. Off to the side, there are two more rooms with partially frosted glass doors. In one room I see a yoga class in session and a lot of heads with gray hair; in the other it looks like they're doing some kind of HIIT class that I want no part of.

When I turn my attention toward the back of the main room, spotting a door with a name plate that simply says *Mitch*, I catch sight of the most gorgeous shirtless male specimen I have ever seen in person. A tall man who's standing with his back to me. He's holding a T-shirt in one hand, his fists at his hips, feet planted firmly on the ground as he watches a fit, elderly man bench-press. His brown hair is short in the back, messy on top. He's not swole by any means; he's just in such good shape, it's lovely. Even the back of his neck is in good shape. He looks so fit. As soon as I see him I want to touch him, even from ten feet away. Not necessarily in a sexual way, but in the way that you instinctively want to reach out to touch a marble statue to fully appreciate it.

I feel so drawn to him.

My body is having what I believe they call *a full-body yes* in response to his body.

I want to high-five him for nailing the whole being-in-good-shape thing.

Also, my uterus seems to be doing a TikTok dance.

And yeah, if there's a situation in the future where it would be totally appropriate for me to put my hands on his butt and squeeze those firm yet just-rounded-enough ass cheeks, I would rejoice in that opportunity.

Those cheeks have a kind of friendly, inviting, sturdy slope to them. Like they're calmly saying *Hey, girl. Pretty cool glutes, huh?*

To which I would reply, *Yes, I want to go to there.*

I slow my pace even more so I can stare at his backside for a few seconds longer. I don't get to blatantly objectify men in my daily life, I'm sad to say. He can probably feel the blazing-hot laser focus of my female gaze on the glistening smooth skin of his lower back, just above the waistband of his joggers.

I suddenly realize I should probably take off my jacket —and it has nothing at all to do with an unconscious womanly instinct to display my suddenly hard nipples in a silent mating ritual. I just want that hot guy to turn around and see my boobs while I still have big boobs. Because if that guy goes to this gym, then I will have to return to this gym on a regular basis, and if I work out a lot, I will lose at least one inch of boobage. That's just science. Science made me take my jacket off so he can see my boobs when he turns around.

Maybe it's because I've been hiding in my house for so long all winter, but I have never wanted so badly for a guy to look at me.

To be seen by one person in particular.

Turn around turn around turn around.

He doesn't turn around. But I realize he's staring at my reflection in the mirror along the back wall. Fantastic. He can see my boobs and I can still see his butt. We have the perfect relationship in this moment. Our eyes meet in the reflection. He isn't doing the intense hot guy–stare thing— his eyes are widened. I see what could be a flash of recognition or appreciation. His face comes into focus and looks familiar in a way that confuses me. Is he famous? Is he a model I've seen on Instagram? Should I go up to him and give him my number or get back on the apps and just hope to find him on there? I don't like being this confused. I want to go home.

Suddenly, he frowns and looks away.

Which is probably a good thing.

I realize I am now five minutes late for my appointment with the drill sergeant. I'm going to have to leave it up to fate as to whether or not I get to see that beautiful shirtless man again. I knock on the open door to Mitch's office, peer through the doorway, and find the small room empty.

"You're late," says a voice from behind me.

"Traffic was…" I turn to find the beautiful shirtless man staring at me. Now he has that hot guy–stare thing going on, and I nearly swallow my tongue.

"Vivian…" he says.

I know that voice.

That sexy, deep voice.

"You're looking for me," he tells me matter-of-factly.

"*You're* Mitch?"

He grins and puts that T-shirt on. Slowly. Like a reverse striptease.

I hold my breath. My face feels hot. My mouth is dry. My heart thinks I've started working out already. My uterus is now doing the choreography from the climax of *Flashdance. What a feeling! Let's make this happen!*

He looks me straight in the eyes as he lets go of the bottom of his T-shirt, shrugs, and drags his fingers through his hair. "Yeah. I am. But you might remember me as Fat Brad…"

It's the strangest thing.

He says those words, almost in slow motion, and as I stare into those green eyes, his toned, angular face morphs into the face of a chubby teenage boy. The face of a boy I used to know so well. And I forget where I am. I forget *when* I am.

Brad.

My Brad.

Bradley.

My best friend from high school.

The boy I have missed for so long.

The friendship I've been missing for so, so long.

Here.

Him.

Brad Mitchell.

"It's you?"

He blinks and barely nods as he brushes past me to enter his office. "Come in," he mutters.

What is happening? My brain is caving in. *Aubrey, what have you done?* My sister's words from last night about how I've been trying to fill a void that has nothing to do with Jeremy echoes around my head, and now I know what she meant. I turn on my heel and follow him inside.

"Close the door behind you."

I do. I don't love being told what to do and I guess saying please is not a part of this workplace culture, but I close the door. "Bradley?" I drop my jacket and shoulder bag, take one big step toward him, throw my arms around him, and give him a hug so warm it could melt an ice sculpture in five seconds. "It's so good to see you."

I do not feel his arms around me.

He in fact remains very still, his very strong arms at his side.

This is very, very awkward.

Does he not recognize me?

"Um. It's me. Vivian. Sparky. From high school."

"Uh-huh."

Apparently he *is* a marble statue now.

I slowly pull away, clearing my throat, and pick up my jacket and bag from the floor.

"I go by Mitch here," he says. "The name Brad had… negative connotations for me."

He takes a seat in the desk chair, leans back, his bent legs spread apart, feet flat on the floor. Not at all languid. Open, and yet somehow those wide legs are wordlessly telling me that I could have had what's between them eight years ago, but I blew it. I mean. I didn't *blow* what's between his legs, I blew *the situation*. In my opinion, *he's* the one who blew it.

Regardless—he has assumed a power pose. An aggressively hot one. He gestures toward a bench.

I'm being benched. *No hugs for you.* Fine. I will earn the hug.

"I never called you Fat Brad," I remind him warmly. "You *know* that. But wow. It's so good to see you. You look so…"

"I know. As I was saying. You're late."

"Brad—Mitch. I sent you, like, a hundred emails for a year after we graduated. Did you not read any of them?"

"I did not."

Ah.

Okay.

So he's still mad.

Got it.

Well, two can play at that game. I was mad at him for a long time too. I'm just not as big of a stubborn asshole as he is.

"What's it been," he asks, "seven, eight years?"

"Eight. Since we graduated and you disappeared."

He casually reaches for a clipboard on his desk. "When'd you move to Portland?"

"Two years ago. When did *you* move to Portland?"

He doesn't answer. He hands me the clipboard with some forms and a pen. I happen to notice there aren't any rings on his fingers. And that his hands are larger than I remember. "I'm assuming you didn't fill out the general intake forms when you got here because Gwen knew to send you straight back to me. Since you were late."

"I got here at exactly seven."

He doesn't acknowledge my comment at all. "Please fill out this brief questionnaire. No need to go into detail today, since you were supposed to get here *before* seven. Usually I'd have you fill it out in PDF before you arrived, but I forgot to get your email address from your sister when I talked to her."

"So you talked to Aubrey? Does she know you're you? I'm so confused. Also, I do have the same email address I had in high school. The account I sent you the aforementioned emails from for a year."

And it's as though he didn't even hear me! "Questionnaires will be filled out every week while you have private sessions here. We'll use them to track your progress along with the progress you track in this complimentary Good Form journal." He reaches for a soft cover journal from his desk and presents it to me. There's a Good Form logo on the cover, and under that it says *The 4 F's of Good Form*.

"Thank you."

"Welcome."

"So you *didn't* read my emails wherein I apologized for

hurting you and said a lot of really great things about you and got really vulnerable about my feelings? And therefore you're still mad at me? Is that what's going on here?"

"I'm not mad at you, Vivian. It was eight years ago. Why would I be mad at you?"

"Right. So my sister somehow knew this badass personal trainer named Mitch is my long-lost former best friend—who ghosted me—and she thought she'd surprise me by reuniting us, but it turns out you still bear a grudge. Is that an accurate description of what's happening?"

"I am the badass personal trainer who owns this gym, correct."

"Got it. Cool. Let's proceed, then."

"Fill that out quickly, and then we'll get to the workout. You good?"

"Oh, yes," I say, giving him my most charming smile while also ensuring I have excellent posture, for confidence and boob reasons. "It might take you a while to remember, but I'm kind of amazing."

"We'll see," he says. "We'll see." He crosses his arms—his beautiful, muscular forearms—leans back further in his chair, gripping the armrests, causing a couple of veins to protrude slightly, and waits for me to fill out the forms.

We'll see.

I narrow my eyes at him.

I'm going to make you feel so terrible for missing out on me for eight years, Brad Mitchell.

Good luck trying to resist me now.

CHAPTER 5
BRAD

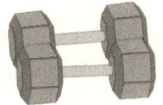

Vivian Elizabeth Sparks.

I see this woman sitting before me, this gorgeous mess of a woman. This woman with a face that's so beautiful I want to punch a wall. This woman with a body that curves and sways and entices, even in that horrible lime-green workout gear. I watched her walk in, saw her reflection in the mirror. I watched her smile and take in the space. *My* space. I saw the men check her out, and I see that she has no idea, absolutely no clue how stunning she is.

And that pisses me off.

Because her sister told me what her ex did to her and I wanted to throat-punch that motherfucker.

But I'm also not going to let on that she's still the most beautiful girl I've ever known. Because I'm a motherfucker too. Because she no longer has the power to bring me to my knees. I have spent the last eight years building up my resistance to Vivian Sparks. Eight years forgetting the way she made me laugh like no one else ever could, before I met her or since I last spoke to her. Eight years forgetting she was the only person at our school that I actually liked. Eight years reading so many books I knew she'd love but never reaching out to her. Eight years watching TV and film adaptations of books we read together and physically stopping myself from emailing her. Eight years becoming strong enough to stare into her big brown eyes and give exactly zero fucks that she broke my heart.

And then she's standing there looking at me like she's so happy to see me. And I did it. I refrained from dropping to my knees. I refrained from wrapping my arms around her and telling her how good it was to see her too. How right it felt to look at her. I refrained from telling her that the instinct to share every single thing I like in this world with her is still there, it never went away, no matter how much I wanted it to. That the emails she sent me went straight to an archived folder and I never even checked to see how many there were in there, but I wondered. I wondered, and the wondering nearly derailed me. But it didn't.

Restraint. That's the kind of strength I care about. That's my fortress.

I anchor my feet to the floor and grip the armrests even harder to physically prevent my consciousness, my entire being, from rearranging itself around her.

But fuck.

She still looks like the hot British actress from *The Mummy*, only she's filled out in all the magnificent ways a woman can fill out when she moves from her teens into her twenties. I can only imagine how gorgeous she's going to be five, ten years from now. Twenty years. But I still see the girl I knew in those eyes, hear it in her voice.

Something is happening. Some kind of emotional time travel. One minute I was in my gym telling Larry to keep his elbows bent at a forty-five degree angle to protect his shoulders and then…and then I saw her and I was seventeen again. As in love as a guy can be with a girl that he refuses to admit to being in love with. Eighteen again, heartbroken and angry. Fourteen again and seeing her for the first time. The shock and awe of a beautiful new girl walking over to me on the way to school, smiling, asking about the book I was holding. Forcing myself not to say out loud the question that was always running through my mind: *Why are you even talking to me?*

You could hang out with anyone at this school and you're choosing to hang out with me—why?

But also, don't ever stop.

She probably wouldn't have.

Thank God I did.

Except where are all the zero fucks I was supposed to give after all these years of forgetting about her? Because it feels like I have nothing but fucks to give her. I definitely want to give Vivian Sparks all my fucks.

God dammit. This was a terrible idea. I can tell by the way she's looking at me that my face and body language and voice are doing exactly what I want them to do. Keeping her at a distance. Holding up the wall between us. But every square inch of the entire surface of my skin, every vein and muscle, every cell in my body, and the energetic frequency of my aching soul is pulsating with desire for this woman. I have never felt this with anyone else. Not even when I wanted to. Not even close.

Which is crazy. Right? I don't know her anymore. I only knew her for a handful of years. This is just an inherent human need to connect with something. It's just my mind telling me I need to reconnect with *her*. Every self-help book I've ever read has taught me that what I really have to do is let myself feel lonely. Move through it. Sit with it. She's a mirror. A lesson. Not the answer.

But fuck.

She stops writing, looks up at me, and hands the clipboard and pen back to me. "All done. *Sir*." She gives me a saucy little smirk. "Do I call you sir in this situation? I've never had a personal trainer before."

Yes. God, yes, I want you to call me sir. I want to push you up against the wall, wrap that ponytail around my fist, make you gasp, and then spank that ass when you call me Bradley instead of sir. "I'm not your drill sergeant. As long as you don't call me Brad or Bradley when we're at the gym, we're good."

She leans forward. "Does that mean we'll be seeing each other outside of the gym, Mitch?"

This familiarity, the way she's talking to me, these spanking thoughts—they won't do. The way she's leaning in and not wearing a bra—that really won't do. "That is not what it means, no."

"And this is your gym? You own it? You started this business?"

"I did."

"That's amazing. I really love what I've seen so far. I mean—the parking situation isn't great, but that's true for ninety percent of Portland. Your parents must be so proud of you."

"They are."

"How are they? I've missed them."

"They're good—thanks." She doesn't need to know

how often they've asked me about her. How anguished my mom was when I made her change her number and promise to cut ties with everyone from the Sparks family after we left Mercer Island.

"Do you make your parents call you Mitch too?"

"No."

"And your wife, or girlfriend? Do you make her call you Mitch?"

I look her straight in the eye and say "I'm unattached, Vivian" as I flip the clipboard around so I can read her answers on the form. "Let's see how you're feeling about things, Ms. Sparks."

Shit. It sounds like I'm flirting with her. Fuck.

I clear my throat and frown at the paper. Her handwriting hasn't changed. I used to always tease her about her girly handwriting, which was dumb, because she was a girl. And she teased me about my excellent penmanship, which was also dumb, because why shouldn't a guy have excellent penmanship? And now I'm just mad because she didn't take the questions on my form seriously. Of course she didn't.

What is your ultimate goal for these personal-training sessions? *To get you and the lady at the front desk to smile at me.*

Why? *Because I'm awesome and it's polite to smile at people who are being awesome to you.*

How much water did you drink today? *Not enough, thanks! How much water did you drink today?*

What are your strengths? *I am determined. Organized. Efficient. A clear communicator. Reliable. Not at all tone deaf. Very good at writing and responding to texts and emails. Forgiving.*

Highly forgivable. Hilarious. Enthusiastic reader. Sensational cat mom. Healthy head of hair. Excellent consumer of pastries.

I tap at the words *cat mom*. I want to ask. I also don't want to know. But I have to know. "How's Hairy Styles?" I hold my breath and brace myself for news of his death.

Vivian's face lights up. "He's still alive! He's great."

I exhale. Thank God. That cat hated me, but I was with her when she adopted him. "Good."

She pouts and makes that girly *awww* sound. I refuse to look at her protruding lower lip. "You remembered."

"Give him my best," I mutter, staring down at the paper. She doesn't need to know that every time I hear a Harry Styles or One Direction song I think about that damn cat. "Weaknesses," I grunt, reading aloud.

What are your weaknesses? Possibly too good at consuming pastries lately. Sometimes excessively hilarious. Overly likable, which can be frustrating for people who don't want to forgive me for being human. Pie. Pie is a weakness. My hair is occasionally a little too soft and shiny. Too punctual, even when traffic is terrible.
How do you rate your body on a scale of 1 to 10? Depends on what I'm doing with my body at the time.
How do you rate your energy level on a scale of 1 to 10? 7.2567
How do you rate your sleep quality on a scale of 1 to 10? I don't.
How many hours did you sleep last night? Not as many as the night before.
How do you rate your stress level on a scale of 1 to 10? Top-tier stress level.

How do you rate your confidence level on a scale of 1 to 10? Yes.

How do you rate your sense of well-being on a scale of 1 to 10? I don't understand this question.

I stare up at her.

She is grinning at me. So smug. This won't do. This dynamic will not do. "How do you rate my answers, sir?"

"1.2748. Do you not want to do this? Because I have a very long waiting list for one-on-one sessions. I did your sister a favor, but if you aren't going to take this seriously—"

"I want to do this, Brad—Mitch. Sir. I'm just not sure what this is."

"This is a personal fitness-training session. That's all it is. That's all it's ever going to be. You're meant to be here so I can help you reach your fitness goals. What are your fitness goals?"

"Well...I do want to be more active and to feel better about...things. But I don't want to lose my very attractive womanly curves."

Thank God. I am silently awarding myself the Best Actor Oscar for my face's performance while she watches me for a reaction. The short film that will be adapted from this interaction will be called *I Hadn't Noticed Your Very Attractive Womanly Curves, Vivian, and I Don't Have the Urge To High-Five You or Yell Out "Fuck Yeah!" At All, but I Can Do My Job and Help You Reach That Goal If That's What You Want.* "Roger that. We can focus on routines that will give you a toned hourglass body type."

"That's a thing? There really are workouts for that?"

"Oh, yeah."

"Great! Let's work on my booty."

Yessssssss. But no. "You got it. There will be minimal cardio."

"Sounds amazing."

"And a lot of strength and resistance training."

"*That* I am less enthusiastic about. Define *a lot*."

"Slightly to a good deal more than you'll feel comfortable with. That's how we get gains. Through systemic progressive overload. We'll build your shoulders and glutes while getting your core tight and strong. Think about creating contrast—wider shoulders, curvier hips, defined waist. It's all about proportions and muscle building. It is very important to combine these workouts with a daily increase in protein. There's an app I can recommend."

The most gorgeous, outrageous smile spreads across her face. "Remember when we went to the Outback Steakhouse in Bellevue and ate *all* the appetizers?"

God dammit. I do remember that. That was a fun day. They were all fun days with Vivian, until that one day.

"The app I'm referring to will track your macronutrients and caloric intake."

"No, thank you. I don't want that."

"Nutritional coaching is an important part of the personal training I offer. A restrictive diet is not required—"

"Good, because I recently got out of a relationship with a man who was very controlling and one of the things I let him control was my diet. I vowed never to allow anyone to control me in such a way again."

Shit.

What a dick.

What a fucking idiot.

"I hear you," I tell her. "I'm sorry if that was a traumatic experience for you."

"He also insisted on jogging a lot, which I did not enjoy."

"Like I said, the cardio will be minimal. Two to three short sessions per week, so we don't interfere with the muscle building. I'm not asking you to limit your caloric intake, Vivian, but sugar isn't good for you. At all. You need protein to build muscle. That's all there is to it."

"Fine. I'll track my macros."

"Great."

"Speaking of keeping track of things and people, are you back on Facebook? I haven't checked in a while."

So she has been checking. I wish that didn't please me so intensely. "I am not. You will weigh yourself first thing in the morning, twice a week only, and keep track of your weight in that journal. Scale weight is not a good indication of your progress at this stage when you're starting to build muscle. You will keep a record of your measurements, and once a week you will take a selfie when you're wearing the same workout clothes each time—preferably tights and a form-fitting tank top or sports bra. Same time of day, same pose, same background—no clutter. Same lighting, same angles. Front, side, and back. Not in the mirror. Use a tripod."

I glance up at her again. She isn't grinning anymore. Good.

"Any questions?"

"What if I don't have a tripod?"

"Then you will find something to prop your phone up with. For the first three weeks you will take pictures of your meals and text them to me before eating them. You will be held accountable for your choices and you will be able to assess how your bad choices have given you an outcome you don't want."

She's frowning at me now. Her nostrils flare. It's fantastic. "Uh-huh. I see what this is."

"*This* is how I am with all of my clients, Vivian."

"Oh yeah? You've really found your calling, huh?"

"My other clients certainly think so." I hand her my business card. "Here's my card. My private number is on the back. Please don't share it with anyone. That's for food diary check-ins only, but I want to see everything you put in your mouth *before* you put it in your mouth."

Shit.

I don't even have to look at Vivian to know what expression is on her face. She smacks her lips together and laughs on an exhale. "Roger *that*, sir."

"This is for the sake of monitoring, not controlling your dietary choices. You will be accountable to me."

"Oh, I get it."

I successfully refrain from telling her she's gonna get it if she keeps up the sass.

"So, do you live around here? I still can't believe you live in Portland. Did you not end up going to Princeton? I can't believe we haven't run into each other at all. Did you know that I live here?"

"Not until your sister told me very recently." Standing, I say, "Let's get to the workout." I go to the door, but before opening it, I continue. "From the brief conversation I had with your sister and from what you just told me about your recent ex-boyfriend, it sounds like you have a lot of motivation to get in shape."

She frowns at me again. "What's that supposed to mean?"

"Well, Aubrey mentioned that he'll be at her wedding, with his new fiancée."

"She told you that?"

"Only because she wanted me to feel sorry for you and make room for you in my schedule."

"Fantastic. So you do feel sorry for me?"

"I'm sorry he deceived you for so long and I'm sorry if he hurt you, but I think you should *reframe* the upcoming situation to your advantage."

"How so?"

"Well, revenge is a great motivator. How do you want him to feel when he sees you again for the first time after he betrayed you and broke your heart?"

She searches my face for clues. Am I serious with this? *Oh yes. Yes, I am.* She shifts her weight from side to side as she places the journal I gave her inside her bag. "I mean. I wouldn't say he broke my heart exactly. We had been growing apart for quite a while and—"

"How do you want him to feel, Vivian?"

She forces a smile. "I wish him and his fiancée well."

"How do you want him to feel?"

"Happy to see me, and I will feel the same way about him because it's healthy and good to forgive people!"

"How do you want him to *feel* when he sees you?"

She sighs. "Proud of me and regretful."

I open the door and gesture for her to leave my office. "Maybe you should just download the Noom app. I will reimburse your sister."

She glares at me. "I want him to jizz in his pants and burst into tears, and I want his fiancée to cover her eyes and run away screaming because she's horrified by how hot I am."

I grin. "Now we're talking. And how will you feel when this happens?"

"Sympathetic."

"That's soft."

"It's beautiful."

"It's not quite an emotion, though, is it? If you have an emotional connection to your goal you're more likely to achieve it."

"Okay. I get that. Right now, I'll say that I will gloat."

"Not really a feeling."

"I'll be gloated. But I will probably feel differently three months from now. I mean, time heals all wounds, right?"

"Not always."

"But it should!" she says, holding up a finger. "I do believe in forgiveness above all else."

"That's adorable. Unfortunately forgiveness is not a strong motivator when it comes to achieving peak fitness levels."

"Says who?"

"Says the one of us who's certified in personal fitness training."

"Well, maybe I'll be the first person in history who gets in shape because she's so forgiving of people's past mistakes."

I lean in and speak directly into her ear, giving her a mere hint of the verbal spanking she deserves. "No, Vivian. You're going to get in shape because *I'm going to whip you into shape*."

CHAPTER 6
VIVIAN

"I'm going to whip you into shape."

The words feel like a quick slap to my ass, or maybe seven of them, in a way that makes all of my nerve endings come alive.

Brad Mitchell always had an attitude that was sexy. To me anyway. Although I didn't really think in terms of sexiness when I was in high school. I thought he was cute. He didn't have swagger by any means. He was sharp-witted. So smart. Total nerd, but confident in a way that was off-putting to some, because he didn't have the looks to pull it off back then. But I always loved his snark. Didn't love how stubborn he was. But the guy could talk.

This, though. This is different. This is hot.

This is something he's cultivated, along with his body.

I am so jealous of every woman he's had sex with and also so proud of him for everything he's accomplished and also absolutely furious with him for being such a stubborn asshole but also sad that he's changed so much.

But also I'm really mad that my knees almost buckled just from the nearness of him.

I hold my breath until he moves away from me.

He gestures for me to follow him across the back of the gym. "In addition to our private sessions," he says, "I encourage you to take brisk walks for twenty minutes, two or three times a week only, and attend our classes twice a week on rest days. Have you ever taken a yoga class?"

"Absolutely not."

"Why not?"

Fear of public queefing. "I don't like carrying around a yoga mat, and I don't want to use one that other people have used" is what I say out loud. "So I do yoga at home. To YouTube videos."

"But you do work on your flexibility?" he asks, without looking at me. He's narrowing his eyes at a guy who's checking me out from the lat pull-down thingy. His jaw is so tense! The other guy notices Brad glaring at him and gives him a barely perceptible *Got it, dude* nod and turns his attention elsewhere.

I enjoyed that tiny interaction very much.

Jeremy never projected that kind of possession or protection of me when we went out. He was too caught up in how we looked together. Brad and I spent most of our time alone together, but when we ventured out in Seattle he always walked on the street side of me and opened doors for me. We never talked about it, but I found it really sweet. Not one guy that I've dated has ever done the street-side alpha-male walk with me, I always noticed.

"Yes," I reply. "I should have added flexibility as one of my strengths. So I've been told."

Brad stops in his tracks and then gives me the side-eye before alpha-male-walking me to a private workout room.

It's very satisfying.

The private room has the same kind of glass door as the others, but more of the door is frosted glass, for more privacy. Once again, I enjoy how not-weird it smells in here. And it doesn't smell like Febreze either, which is a big plus. He adjusts the lighting to make it brighter, but again, I like that it's not the cool white LED lighting you'd expect. I feel alert, but not like I'm at the dentist. There's no music playing, and that is a little awkward.

"You can hang your jacket and shoulder bag up on those hooks," he says, nodding in the direction of the coat rack next to the door. "This will be a slightly shorter session, since you were late, so we'll warm up for five minutes and then I'll have you do three blocks of four sets with ten reps per set so I can assess your form, finish off with stretching. We'll be doing upper, lower body, and core at each session. This will keep your muscle growth balanced and progressing consistently."

"By lower body, you mean my butt?"

"I mean your glutes, yes. We'll be hitting your gluteus medius, minimus, and maximus."

"That sounds fun."

"Not if you do it right."

"What exercises do you do for *your* butt?"

He ignores that very serious question and stares down at my shoes. "Are those the only shoes you have for working out in?"

"No. I didn't have time to go home today, and this was all they had at the downtown Target." I sweep my hand down my torso and then up again, to accentuate my chest area. "Thanks for keeping it so cold in here, by the way."

"Time to warm up," he says. "Arm circles." He does forward arm circles, facing me, five feet away. "You have cross-trainers at home?"

"I have running shoes."

"You'll want shoes with a stiff, sturdy base and a snug fit for strength training. That will help with alignment."

"Wanna go shoe shopping with me?"

"Backward," he says, circling his arms backward and not answering.

I know I don't have to ask him if he remembers all the times I dragged him to the mall to go shoe shopping with me in high school. He was a good sport in the grumpiest way possible.

"High knees," he says. Then he leads me through leg swings, butt kicks, walking lunges. He explains that we aren't getting the heart rate up, we're activating the right muscles to prepare them for movement patterns and to prevent injury.

"Great! Thanks, Brad."

"Mitch."

"I don't want to call you Mitch. You're Brad."

"Mitch is my nickname here. It's who I am here."

"Well, my nickname for you was Bradley. It still is. Your nickname for me was Sparky. I would be fine with you calling me that here."

"I won't."

"Well, I'm not calling you Mitch."

"Then go ahead and call me sir." He strides over to the dumbbell rack. "You ever lift weights at all?"

"Not really."

"Let's try eight pounds to start," he says, handing me two eight-pound dumbbells. "How's that feel?"

It feels kind of heavy, but I say, "Easy-peasy."

"Yeah? You want to try ten pounds? You'll be lifting out to the side, shoulder height. You should use lighter weights for that."

"Bring it. I want the tens."

"You got it." He hands me another pair of weights, which are surely twenty pounds each, but I do a couple of bicep curls with ease.

"Not a problem."

"Great. You can always go lighter."

"Won't have to."

He grabs the dumbbells marked 30 and demonstrates the lateral raises and shows me the proper stance. "You'll do ten of these at this pace." Then he demonstrates lat pull-downs, rear delt flies, and overhead press. "Ten of each. I want to see perfect form. If it's too easy, you'll get heavier weights. If it's too hard to finish the sets, there's no shame in lowering the weight."

"I always finish things off when they're hard." I did not mean for that to sound dirty. "I mean difficult. Even if it's emotionally difficult."

Stone-Faced McGee remains stone-faced as he says, "Okay, let's build shoulder width for that V-taper. Ten reps. Tilt forward a bit more. Less. Good. One... Two..."

I should not have chosen the ten-pound weights for my first session.

However.

I don't give up.

Because when I commit to something, I fully commit.

Even when my arms are on fire.

Even when he's being a stubborn ass.

"Higher," he says, with an annoyingly calm voice. "In line with your shoulders."

I grunt that that is what I'm doing, only I don't say it with words.

"Don't forget to breathe. Your muscles need oxygen."

I suck in an angry breath.

"Inhale on the way down, exhale on the way up."

I growl out an exhale. Not on purpose. Well, maybe a little bit.

"Keep an even pace," he says, watching my movements so closely. "Don't fling your arms to the side."

"I didn't."

"You're creating momentum by flinging your arms instead of using your muscles to lift them up." He walks around behind me and places his hands so gently around my wrists I barely feel his touch. But I feel the heat and mass of his body behind me even though he isn't touching me with it. "Slow it down. Inhale now. Keep your elbows a little bit bent as you use your exhale and your shoulder muscles to lift up and out. Stop when your arms are parallel to the floor."

I do that.

It's harder and I don't like it, but I do it.

"Good," he says, letting go and coming back around to the side of me to watch my form. "Good. This move primarily targets your middle delts. Also the front delts and rotator cuff muscles. We're building out that shoulder line to make your waist appear smaller." He reaches out to touch the side of my shoulder. "You feel this working?"

"Mm-hmm."

"Good. If you feel it here in your traps"—he drags his

fingers down the back of my neck and upper back—
"you're lifting too high. Got it?"

"Got it."

"Good. Your form is good now. Two more reps."

I do not want to love how good it feels to earn his
praise, but it does feel good, so I give him two more reps at
a balanced pace, without flinging my arms out.

"Great," he says. "Now give me ten lat pull-downs.
You want to stick with this weight?"

"Yes."

I stick with the ten-pound weights through the next
thirty reps.

When I'm done, he says, "Good. Did you bring water?"

"My water bottle's empty."

"Go get it and fill it up at that water cooler," he says as
he puts my weights away and then carries a bench over to
the center of the room.

Once again, I do not love that he's telling me what to
do and not saying please, but I also don't hate it.

I fill my water bottle with plain water from the cooler
near the door. I am already parched. "So, tell me about the
four F's."

"We can talk about them after you've started using the
journal."

"Is one of them for *frank* discussions?"

"No. Let's move on to the lower body."

"Buy a girl dinner first, will you?" I joke.

He doesn't laugh. He doesn't even smile. He sits on the
ground, back against the side of the bench, arms spread
out to the side, then slides up so his upper back is flat
against the top of the bench and says, "Starting with hip
thrusts. We won't add extra weight today, we will work on

proper form. Bottom of the scapulas against the edge of the bench. Feet planted firmly on the floor, toes pointed out. A little more than hip-width apart. Chin tucked, looking forward, drive through your heels to activate the glutes, squeeze your glutes hard at the top." He points to the sides of his butt as he squeezes and thrusts upward. "Exhale on the way up. Control the descent. Drop all the way back down."

He lowers his butt to the ground and then stands up without the use of his hands. Core strength only. Then he goes back to the rack to grab a pair of weights marked 12. He demonstrates a Romanian deadlift, followed by Bulgarian split squats, and then a weighted sumo squat. "Any questions?"

"Did you delete the emails I sent you?"

He blinks. "No," he says, as if that would be horrendous of him and he's not a monster.

"So you saw them, you just didn't read them?"

"Take a seat on the bench and then slide down until your back is flat against it with your feet flat on the floor."

I put my water bottle down and sit on the floor in front of the bench, spreading my arms out wide so my headlights are pointing directly at him. He almost does a really good job of not glancing at them. "So you just haven't read them *yet*."

"You need to stay focused, Vivian. Mind to muscle. Think about your glutes."

"I think you should read my emails before my next session with you."

"I'm not going to do that."

"Why not?"

"Because you're my client and I need to stay focused too."

"On my glutes?"

"In a minute, yes. I want your feet about two more inches apart. Flat on the ground." He reaches around to feel my back. "Bottom of your scapulas against the edge. Do you know what your scapulas are?"

I lift myself up an inch. "Do you remember what manners are, sir?"

"Weight in the heels, drive your hips up and squeeze your glutes."

I do that, locking my eyes with his as I thrust and lower, angrily but perfectly every time.

"Good," he says. He holds his hand out to help me up off the floor after my tenth rep.

I take his hand, still locking eyes with him, trying to control my breaths. My heart is beating as hard as it does after a run but not as fast, and I like it. "Thank you."

"You're welcome."

"Can you put on some music in here?"

"Sure. All you had to do was ask." He crosses over to a panel on the back wall.

"You still listen to Pearl Jam?"

His body tenses up a bit. As if he can't believe I remember what kind of music he used to listen to when we were best friends.

I do my gruff Eddie Vedder imitation, muffling my voice into my fist like it's a microphone. "*Even tempohhhh. Thoughts on muscles, drive through the heels! Ohhhhh, her form is perfect, though. But he frowns at her anywayyyyyy.*"

His face almost breaks into a smile. And then it doesn't.

"Sometimes. Pick up those twelve-pound weights for the deadlifts...please."

Well, now. I believe that's what we call progress. "I shall. Thank you."

"I'm putting on an upbeat pop music playlist with one hundred thirty to one hundred fifty beats per minute. I'm sure you'll find a number of your favorite terrible songs on there."

"Ooooh, them's fightin' words."

I wait for him to lovingly make fun of my taste in music. Which is something he used to do, even as he let me listen to whatever I wanted to listen to when he was driving. I didn't even like Top 40 music as much as I liked Fleetwood Mac and Stevie Nicks back then; I just liked to annoy him. But he doesn't make fun of me. He just tells me to hinge from my hips and keep my arms straight.

Finally we're onto the core workouts, and I'm thinking about faking an illness like I used to for gym class occasionally. I do not think he'd be as sympathetic as Mrs. Brodzki was when I told her my ovaries felt vulnerable and were asking for some TLC. So my ovaries and I take one for the team.

"You know what," he says, "I don't normally recommend sit-ups as part of this type of workout, but let's get you in touch with your core before we do the other exercises."

"Awww, that's fine. I've stayed in touch with my core. I'm very good at keeping in touch with people and cores."

He gets a mat from the side of the room and places it on the floor in front of me. Then he gestures for me to get down on the mat. "Down you get."

"Ya don't usually make your clients do sit-ups, huh?"

"Not if the goal is an hourglass shape. But it sounds like you've mostly been doing cardio for a while, so I want to make sure you feel connected to your abs."

"Ah. Well, it *has* been a while since I've done sit-ups. Why don't you demonstrate proper form for me?" I arch an eyebrow at him.

"Sure, no problem." He gets down on the mat. "Lower back flat against the mat," he says. "Feet flat on the floor. Legs bent at ninety degrees. Hands behind the head, elbows bent. Engage your core first, then slowly curl up." While he's at the top of his sit-up, he removes one hand from behind his head, to pull up his shirt. "See that? My core is engaged."

I do see that.

I see his abs. His beautiful, toned, engaged six-pack. And I can't look away.

"And then you'll control the descent, because that's where the real work happens," he says, his abs still exposed, still engaged.

"Can I see that nine more times?"

The corners of his lips tip up and he doesn't even flinch. He gives me nine more perfect sit-ups. I am mesmerized by his abs. But I also can't help but notice the area just south of them.

Yup. Brad Mitchell grew up good.

And he's watching me stare at his sweatpants bulge.

"Ten. Got it?"

"Got it."

"Good." Again he stands up without the use of his hands. Sadly, his shirt goes back down as he goes up. "Your turn. Let's start with ten."

I lower myself to the mat and assume the same position. I don't mean to groan, but I do. I bend my legs to ninety degrees, frowning up at him.

Maintaining eye contact, he lowers himself to a kneeling position and places his hands firmly on top of my feet.

I don't mean to gasp, but I do.

I have no idea why the weight of his hands on my feet is sexy, but it is. "To ensure your feet stay anchored to the ground," he explains. "This will make it easier for you to lift yourself all the way up."

"Thanks," I squeak.

"Sure thing." He moves my feet a couple of inches farther apart, still locking eyes with me.

I gulp. My mouth is dry. I should have had more water.

"Keep your lower back flat against the mat," he says. "Hands behind your ears. Engage your core. Inhale, exhale on the way up."

I suck in a breath and fling my torso at him.

"Slow and controlled!"

I roll my eyes at him.

"Vertebra by vertebra."

"Right." I lower myself down, with control.

"Engage your core," he snaps.

"It's engaged!"

"I can literally see that it isn't."

I scrunch up my face and my core, growling as I glare at the ceiling.

"Keep your chin slightly tucked. You don't want to strain your neck."

No, I want to strangle your *annoyingly sexy, handsome, somehow muscly-but-not-too-thick neck.*

"Vertebra by vertebra," he says. "Controlled movement. Keep your eyes up. Eyes on me."

I narrow my eyes at him.

He's enjoying this.

"Give me six more," he says.

I give him six more, and then I collapse. "I hated that!"

"I don't think you've activated your core, Vivian."

"Oh, it's activated. It's on fire."

"I want you to give me ten more, perfect form."

"No."

He arches an eyebrow at me.

He always did have great eyebrows. I used to be jealous of his eyebrows. Now I want to shave them off while he sleeps, I am so mad at him.

"Yes," he says calmly. "You want your ex's fiancée to scream in horror when she sees you, don't you?"

She'll scream in horror because I'll arrive with your severed head on a stick.

"I mean, if you can't do it," he continues, "you can't do it."

"I can do it!" I give him ten more sit-ups. Perfect, furious form.

He grins at me, anchoring my feet.

He is basically kneeling between my legs and my face is melting and I am so mad at myself for eating that pie last night and that makes me even madder at him.

"Ten!" he says. "You did it." He stands up and holds his hand out to me again.

I take it, and he pulls me up and he's so strong and my knees go weak and I don't stop moving toward him. If I didn't have such big boobs, my mouth would be on his neck right now. That stupid, muscly, sexy, handsome neck.

His Adam's apple is gorgeous. Does he do Adam's apple exercises or something? How is the bony lump in his throat in such good shape? Anyway my boobs are smooshed up against his hard chest.

"Oops," I mutter. He doesn't let go of my hand. He stares down at me, still grinning. It's an evil grin. An *I just might make you do twenty more sit-ups for that, young lady* kind of grin. I continue to press my lovable boobs up against his hard, stubborn, unforgiving chest.

"You good?" he asks.

"Yup. You?"

"I'm really good. You ready for the real core workout?"

"Yup."

"You in touch with your core now?"

"Deeply."

He takes a step back and slowly releases my hand.

I do not fall over.

Yay me.

Next he has me doing dead bugs, planks and side planks, and something called Pallof Presses with a resistance band. I don't hate it. He has me so focused on my form that I can feel the strength of my core. I am so aware of his fingers on my waist and his attention to my body and my breaths that I don't want to drop to the ground screaming and crying and cursing my abdominal muscles for being such wimpy assholes. I am so mad at him for being so hot and obstinate that I want to be better than he expects me to be at every single thing.

By my third Pallof Press, I tell him, "I think *you're* a stronger motivation for me than seeing Jeremy at the wedding."

"Three," he says, counting. "Yeah? Keep facing forward. How so?"

"Because you're such a stubborn, unforgiving asshole. But I've been mad at you too, you know."

"Great. Everybody wins."

"I'll be the winner. I will win."

"Okay. Give me five more. Keep your shoulders down."

I keep my shoulders down and give him five more, and then he tells me to drink some water, which I was going to do anyway, and then he leads me through cooldown stretches. We don't talk at all, I just follow along with him. Sassily. The truth is I feel good. It feels like I did something good for my body, and I did better than I thought I would, and I have never had a personal trainer before but Brad seems to be good at this. I want to be proud of him for it, but I also want him to apologize for ghosting me. And I want him to feel really bad about making me feel bad about accidentally making him feel bad. And I want him to take his shirt off again, and that makes me really, really angry.

"Okay," he says when we're done cooling down.

"I'll drink some water!" I announce before he gets the chance to tell me what to do.

"Good job," he says in a tone that is not at all condescending. "How do you feel?"

"Good."

"Great."

"Yup."

"So, I'll see you on Wednesday. Be sure to come in earlier so Gwen can set you up with your membership card."

"Okie doke." I put my jacket on and catch him glancing down at my boob area, and that pleases me to no end.

"Where did you park?" he asks, as if he's expecting me to tell him I parked on top of his car or something.

"Down the street."

He rolls his eyes and grumbles. "How far down?"

"I parked a few blocks away."

"Of course you did." He frowns and drags his fingers through his hair, the way he used to when I'd ask him to help me with my AP Calculus homework. He opens the door and looks around the gym. It's a little busier than it was when I got here, with the after-work crowd, I guess. Not seeing the heads with gray hair like I did earlier. The vibe is a little more how I imagine things at other gyms. More bros and babes.

Brad is grimly scanning the bros who are casually eyeing me as we walk toward the entrance and says, "I'll walk you to your car."

"Oh. Are you leaving now too?"

"No."

"Oh. You need to grab a jacket?" When we hung out in high school, I always had to remind him to put on a jacket, and he'd mutter that he had an extra layer of fat to keep him warm.

"Nah. My muscles keep me warm now."

"How sweet of them."

"Nah. It's badass of them."

The glass doors slide open, and Brad gestures for me to exit first.

Checkin' out my glutes, probably.

I sway my hips a little. A little for him, a lot for me. I notice him noticing.

"Be right back, Gwen," he says to the blue-haired lady behind the desk.

"See you next time, Gwen!" I call out.

She nods at me without smiling.

And I still respect it.

Brad holds the front door open for me.

"Thanks," I say. And then I walk, slowly, in the direction of my car.

And he still does it. He's still walking on the street side of me as we walk down the sidewalk. It's dark out and it just rained a little bit and it will probably start sprinkling again soon. The wet street reflects the streetlights. It's pretty quiet. For the first time since I moved to Portland, it feels romantic.

There's so much I want to say to Brad. I have so many questions. I have so many answers. But I guess I have three months' worth of sessions, so I can pace myself.

"Mitch!" Three spry elderly ladies in leggings and puffer coats call out to him at the same time from half a block away.

"Ladies…" he says, grinning.

Grinning.

I can see his left dimple.

Nice to know it's still there.

"We had tacos and margaritas down the street!" The one in the purple coat shouts. I detect a New York accent. "One of these days we'll get you to join us, motherfucker!" I don't think I've ever heard someone use that word in such an affectionate yet also loud way before.

"Use your *quieter* outside voice, Dolores," the redhead in the black coat says. "You're scaring Mitch's girlfriend."

He waits an entire deep inhale before saying, "Not my girlfriend, Cindy."

"Oh, why not though?! She's absolutely gorgeous!"

I like Cindy a lot. I detect a bit of a southern accent, Texan perhaps. I like all of them already. They are probably around seventy, and they're making me reconsider my energy level on a scale of one to ten. Compared to them I'm a four at best. These ladies are #Goals.

"Cindy thinks everyone's in love like she and Larry are," says Dolores.

"This is a new client. Vivian. Vivian, this is Cindy, Dolores, and Mabel. Longtime members of Good Form."

"Very nice to meet you, ladies."

"Well, it is so nice to meet you, our beautiful new friend Vivian!" Cindy says. "Now, are you a Leo or an Aries, hun? You look to me like an Aries."

"I am an Aries, actually. Nobody's ever told me that before."

"Hallelujah—thank you, Universe!" she says gleefully, holding her hands up to the heavens. "I love it! Honey, we've known Mitch for years and he has never walked anyone to their car before."

"Now, you don't know that, Cindy," Brad says, but he has none of us convinced.

I love you for saying all that, Cindy.

"Oh, Mitch," Mabel says, rubbing his bare arms. "You should be wearing a jacket."

"That's what I was saying."

"Ohhh, his skin is still warm, though. Feel that!" she says to me, and to her friends.

Brad stands there and lets us feel how warm his skin is.

And I can't help but notice that he's flexing. "Okay, ladies. Vivian needs to get home."

"Oh hey, I hit a deadlift PR today!" Cindy yells, her arms raised again. I have a feeling she gets excited and raises her arms in the air a lot. "Ninety-five pounds, baby!"

"Nice!" He high-fives her. "Was Larry watching?"

"Oh, was he ever!"

There's a little more chatter about Larry and Cindy, and then the ladies walk off and we continue on toward my car.

"Well, they're fun!" I say. "You train them too?"

"I worked with Cindy for a couple of months a couple of years ago, yeah."

I wait for more information, but that's all I get.

"So, none of these people from the gym know your legal name?"

"Some of them do. But they call me Mitch because I ask them to and most people aren't sassy little turds."

"I know. That's *my* thing."

"It certainly is," he says under his breath.

"So just Mitch? Like Adele?"

"Like Mitch."

"Like Prince."

"Like Arnold," he says with a Schwarzenegger accent.

"Gotcha." We're quiet until I reach my car, but there's one thing I just have to know. "Have you been watching *You* on Netflix?"

He blows air out of his nose and looks down at the ground. I can tell he's trying so hard not to smile, not to turn this into a conversation. We read *You* together for our two-person book club when we were seventeen, before it was a show. We both liked it so much, felt so cool to be reading it, thought it was like a fucked-up new adult *Catcher in the Rye*, and Brad would read sections aloud to creep me out. It wasn't necessarily my favorite book that we read for Asshole Book Club, but it was my favorite memory of Asshole Book Club. The show started the year after we graduated high school. Penn Badgley sounded so much like Brad, I actually thought it was him doing the voiceover for most of the pilot episode.

"Sure," he says. "Everyone watches that show."

I wait for him to mutter something Joe Goldberg-like: *You have questionable taste in music and prom dates, Sparks, but You always did have good taste in books and TV shows.*

Alas, he does not.

We reach my car, and I say, "Well, this is me."

"Yes," he says. "This is You…" Is that a nod to the voiceover or not? With that delivery I can't tell.

I still can't believe it's him. I can't believe we're together again. I really can't believe he's being such a stubborn asshole.

I want to hug him again. And smack him. At the same time. But I don't.

"Well. I'm still really happy to see you again, Bradley." And here come the tears. Shit. "Even though you're a stubborn turd for not reading my emails. And honestly, just cold and rude, but whatever. And I'm not just happy to see you because of how you look. I've missed you. I really, really missed you. Even when I was mad at you. I missed you so much. Even when I didn't think about you, I've always been missing you." I sniffle and wipe my eyes and nose. "And it's not just you that I missed, it was us. Us hanging out together. How I was when I was with you.

How it felt to have a best friend who gets you... But I don't know. Maybe it was just nostalgia for being young. Maybe we would have grown apart after we graduated anyway."

He exhales, like I just punched him in the gut or something. Although I doubt me punching him in those abs would cause him to flinch at all. "Okay," he says. He pats me on the shoulder. So awkward. "Well, I'm happy to hear that your cat is still alive and kicking. Although I continue to believe you named him after the worst member of One Direction."

And there we have it. One of our old jokey arguments. Or argumentative jokes. He's still in there. My Bradley's still in there. Beneath the stubborn, cold demeanor and the warm muscles.

"Drive safe, drink a lot of water with electrolytes tonight, and text me your meal before you eat it."

"Yes, sir."

CHAPTER 7
BRAD

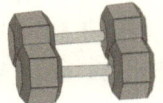

I don't like this feeling I have in my chest.

This is not delayed-onset muscle soreness related to hypertrophy of the pectoralis major and minor.

This is not an inflammatory response caused by microscopic tears in the muscle fibers.

This is originating from the muscle that is no longer supposed to respond to Vivian Sparks, and there is no recovery strategy I can employ aside from not thinking about her—or *only* thinking about how much caring about her hurts.

But fuck.

She still wears that thin gold chain necklace that's so dainty you only notice it when the light hits it. I wonder if it's the same one she wore in high school or if she got another one. I wonder if she wears it in the shower. I wonder if she's taking a shower right now...

Nope.

Not thinking about that.

Thinking about my goals.

Thinking about what fires me up.

I can't believe she kept calling me Brad. That's not who I am at the gym. I don't show up at her work calling her Sparky and telling everyone about our two-person book club and how we'd hang out on a big rock and a log in the cove by my house and once she fell asleep on my shoulder while we were reading *The Martian* and I couldn't breathe because I didn't want to wake her up and because I thought maybe I was the one who was dreaming.

Such a turd.

Vivian, of all people, should understand why I don't identify with the name Brad in my new life here. In my new body here. Vivian, of all people, because she's the one who went to prom with the dickhead who dominated the Brads at school from kindergarten through senior year. The shitbag who bestowed the moniker of Fat Brad upon me when we were eight. The fuckwit who carved the words *Fat Brad* into my locker on the first day of school every year that I had a locker. The douche-ass-dickwad who shoved me into a ditch when he saw me out running junior year because I was trying to get in shape. *There's only one Hot Brad at this school, fattie.*

Brad Turner.

Such a dick.

She should understand. Yes, I incorporated my origin story into my brand as a personal trainer even though I call myself Mitch here. No, I don't talk about the Fat Brad piece of it. Yes, that's my fire. My motivation. Ever since I moved to Portland nearly eight years ago.

But fuck.

It may be true that I didn't tell her everything about how he treated me because I was so ashamed.

I mean, why would I tell the only girl who wanted to hang out with me that the most popular guy at our school treated me like shit because we had the same name?

Why would I waste our precious time together talking about *him*?

She knew he got all his asshat friends to call me Fat Brad all through school—that should have been enough.

Fuck.

Now I'm thinking about it.

All of it.

I wonder if she still dresses a little bit hippie-dippie and likes to walk around barefoot. I wonder if she still listens to Fleetwood Mac and picks wildflowers and places them behind her ear. I wonder if she still likes to read, and if she does I wonder if she still thinks of me when she reads a book she likes because I never stopped thinking of her.

That's not true.

I stopped myself from thinking about her when I realized I was thinking about her.

I can still do that.

This was a bad idea. I shouldn't have taken her on as a client. I'll give her to Gwen.

Except if Gwen's her trainer and she's still going to my gym and I see her, there isn't as much of an excuse for me to *not* hang out with her. If I hang out with her I will definitely fuck her.

Fuck.

I go to my bedroom, open the top-right drawer in my dresser, and reach toward the back of it. There it is. My old phone. And the charger.

The best thing to do right now would be to face this

head-on. To revisit that last conversation. Not to reopen the wound—that scarred over years ago. To remember and to know and to have clarity. Wondering leads to obsession, and clarity is the end of wondering.

I plug that old phone in. The screen doesn't light up, but it will. It's been eight years since I used this phone.

I'll do ten minutes of burpees—forty seconds on, twenty seconds off—until the battery gets enough juice.

I'll film it for an IG reel. This is work. This is staying focused on me and the business I'm building.

If she happens to find my Instagram account and see it, well, she'll know I'm busy living my life and not thinking about that ponytail or the heat in her eyes when I pulled her up off the floor or the scent of her shampoo—the same shampoo she used in high school. This I know. Because that time she went to Orcas Island with her family for a week in the summer between junior and senior year, I missed her so much I went to the drugstore and sniffed every bottle of shampoo I could open. And I bought that bottle of shampoo with shea butter, and I absolutely punished my aching heart and cock at the same time while smelling it when my parents were out. I tried to convince myself that I wasn't in love with her all the way up until the second I saw her again when she returned and hugged me and I buried my face in her thick, dark hair and inhaled and I realized—*Shit. I'm in love with her.*

And the last thing I needed to do was tell her and ruin my friendship with the only person at my school that I really liked. The only one who really liked me. So I threw away that bottle of shampoo and I forced myself to picture the actress from *The Mummy* when I jerked it instead.

Not a hardship.

But I still loved Vivian.

I loved her so fucking much it hurt more than that time a client dropped a twenty-pound weight on my foot. Landed right on my metatarsals, but it was only from a few feet up. Every time I looked at her it felt like I was slowly dying from not telling her how I felt. Like every cell in my body was giving up on me for being so lame. Like I knew without a doubt that I would never have her the way I wanted her, and that was so much worse.

But it was also fine.

Until it wasn't.

My ten-minute timer goes off. I check the video, do a quick edit to speed it up, and post it to my Instagram before checking my old phone. It's alive. The past has come back to life in the palm of my hand. The phone that connected me to Vivian for nearly four years is ready to give me the clarity I need so I can get back to being the guy who can live without the girl. Any girl. But mostly the girl who is now the woman who wants me to work on her booty.

And there it is. The texts between me and Vivian. From eight years ago, going back three and a half years, maybe. But I need to see the final texts, from those last few weeks of high school.

I scroll up, up, up. To the night before the day that will live in infamy. She made me read *Twilight* for ABC. Our two-person book club was called Asshole Book Club, and the first rule of Asshole Book Club was you couldn't just say *It was great—I loved it!* you had to be an asshole even if you really did love the book. I came up with that rule. Vivian came up with the second rule, which was that we had to read whatever book the other person chose and even if we hated it we had to say three things we liked about it.

And then we started coming up with so many ridiculous rules we couldn't remember any of them.

The one rule we never came up with was how to handle being a guy and a girl who were best friends.

Especially when it was coming to the end of high school and I was planning to go to Princeton in a few months.

CHAPTER 8

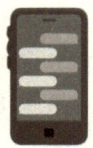

May 16, 2017 at 8:35 p.m.

VIVIAN

I don't know who needs to hear this, but you need to finish reading Twilight so we can talk about it.

BRAD

I don't know who needs to hear this, but I don't need to finish reading this book in order to tell you how much I hate it. The writing is terrible.

VIVIAN

It's really not, though.

BRAD

No, it isn't. The writing is better than expected. But the story is stupid.

VIVIAN

Compared to what?! War and Peace?

BRAD

Literally every book that isn't Twilight is better than this book. I will never forgive you for making me read this.

VIVIAN

I told you I would get you back for making me read Dune. 😅

Are you just being an asshole because this is Asshole Book Club or do you really hate it? I need to know.

But also, I really do want you to like it because it was my first favorite book that wasn't a children's book. I could totally relate to Bella because I had to start at a new school in the middle of the year. I still like it and I think deep down you do too.

BRAD

I don't know who needs to hear this, but I am not a twelve-year-old girl.

Also, you started school here two months into freshman year. That's not the same as transferring to a new school in a different state well into senior year when everyone else at that school grew up together.

VIVIAN

I don't know who needs to hear this, but it shows a real strength of character that you've committed to reading this for our little book club even though you aren't a twelve-year-old girl. 😊 You're such an agreeable grumpy old man. I just can't believe how long it's taking you to read it.

BRAD

First of all, I usually have to wait for you to catch up when we read books together. Secondly, I finished reading it this afternoon.

VIVIAN

You did? Why didn't you tell me?!

BRAD

Because I also had to finish my final project for Independent Study. And because there was so much talk about prom in that book, and prom tickets go on sale tomorrow. It kind of felt like you were trying to tell me something...

VIVIAN

I definitely wasn't...

I mean, I really wasn't. But we should talk about it tomorrow morning. Unless you want to talk about it now? I can come over real quick.

BRAD

No, don't. I have to do something.

VIVIAN

Okay, then. I look forward to discussing this further on our walk to school in the morning. And there's also another thing I need to talk to you about.

BRAD

Okay. There's something I need to talk to you about tomorrow too. And not just about how much you owe me for making me read this book and the fact that you're making me read this now. This could very well be the last book I ever read for ABC. And it's Twilight. The fuck?

VIVIAN

I mean. We can still do long-distance book club. It's not like we're going to completely lose touch just because you're not going to UW.

Just because you're going to Princeton to be with the fancy brainiac matriculators.

Right?

Not loving the silence.

Okay, you need to say something exceptionally nice to me immediately before I spiral.

BRAD

Okay. You were nothing like Bella Swan when you started school here. You weren't totally pale and you didn't quiver at all.

VIVIAN

...that it?

BRAD

No. I have always liked that you aren't too pretty.

VIVIAN

BRAD

I mean you're really pretty. Beautiful, even.
Just not in an annoying over the top way.

VIVIAN

BRAD

I mean like the hot girl in The Mummy.

VIVIAN

OMG I do look like her, don't I?!

BRAD

Calm down, Sparky.

But yes. That was what I thought the first
time I saw you. And you're kind. And
smart. And funny. You are literally the only
person in school that I actually like. As a
person, I mean.

...you need to say something nice to me
now, before I spiral.

VIVIAN

Thank you. Those were the nicest things
you have ever said to me. Go to your front
door immediately. ;)

BRAD

Not again.

VIVIAN

Immediately!

BRAD

You left a Twinkie and a banana on my
porch?

VIVIAN

IDK what you're busy doing, but I know you're forgetting to eat.

BRAD

And so you brought me two phallic snack foods?

VIVIAN

What can I say, it's the shape I automatically reach for nowadays.

BRAD

Chokes on golden sponge cake

You can't say that kind of thing to guys, Vivian. Someone will get the wrong idea.

VIVIAN

Calm down, Bradley. I was just being quippy with you.

BRAD

I was actually craving a Twinkie, though, you devious witch. Thank you.

VIVIAN

See you in the morning?

BRAD

You definitely will.

May 17, 2017 at 7:43 a.m.

VIVIAN

Where did you go?!

I didn't know he was going to show up like that, I promise!

Are you okay?

I have to get to class. I'll find you at lunch.

May 17, 2017 at 3:30 p.m.

VIVIAN

Seriously, where did you disappear to? You aren't really mad about this, are you? It's just prom. He asked me yesterday afternoon and I was going to tell you this morning.

Bradley. Are we okay? It was so sweet what you did. 🥺

You do know that I was always Team Jacob, though, right? 😬

Too soon. I'm sorry.

I am honestly so sorry.

VIVIAN

Please call me back.

May 17, 2017 at 7:35 p.m.

VIVIAN

Seriously, dude? I know you're at home. Open the door.

Bradley. It's just prom. He asked me before you did and he did it in front of like a hundred people. I didn't know what to say.

BRAD

Pretty sure you would have said no if you didn't want to go with him.

VIVIAN

You're right. I'm sorry.

BRAD

To be clear, I don't care that you don't want to go with me. It is just prom. I just can't believe you're going with him of all people.

VIVIAN

I'll tell him I won't go with him.

BRAD

Damage is done.

VIVIAN

Well, I think YOU'RE the one who's being an asshole for not talking to me about this.

May 18, 2017 at 12:05 p.m.

VIVIAN

Okay, Stacy B. just explained to me that Brad Turner had pushed you into a ditch once and some other stuff ever since kindergarten.

I'm so sorry. I knew he gave you that nickname, but I had no idea he was that big of a dick to you. You never told me.

BRAD

Why would I tell you about something that humiliating?

VIVIAN

Because I'm your friend.

BRAD

You just don't get it, do you?

VIVIAN

I'm going to tell him I won't go out with him.

May 18, 2017 at 8:15 p.m.

VIVIAN

Okay, I had a long talk with my sister and she made some very good points. It's not a great idea for me to back out on prom with Brad Turner, so I should go with him. But I promise I won't enjoy it. Can we please talk about this before school tomorrow?

BRAD

No. I have to turn in my Independent Study project and I'll be working on it in the morning. Not everyone cares more about their social life than anything else.

May 19 at 7:37 p.m.

VIVIAN

I'm outside your house. I can see that your parents aren't home. Can we talk?

Okay, now I'm starting to feel like a stalker, but I get that you don't want to talk to me face-to-face because I'm so unbearably charming and you want to stay mad at me...

VIVIAN

So that's it? You're going to stay mad at me forever and pretend we were never friends because of this one thing?

Fine. I can be stubborn too.

BRAD

It's not this one thing, Vivian. This is the only thing. I've been waiting for you to catch up, but I'm tired of waiting.

VIVIAN

I'm so sorry I hurt you, but I think you're being irrational and this is really unfair.

BRAD

Yeah. It is unfair. Just let me go.

CHAPTER 9
BRAD

Okay, now that I'm reading through the texts, I can see that it definitely read like she was sending mixed messages and also that I never really told her how I felt about her.

But I always hung out with her. I helped her with her AP Calculus, and I hated AP Calculus. I read whatever book she asked me to. I listened to whatever music she wanted to listen to most of the time, and I only complained about it when it was genuinely terrible. I read the entirety of *Twilight* for her. No guy would do that for a girl unless he was in love with her.

We were going to hang out at my place for senior prom like we did whenever there was a school event, but then she asked me to read *Twilight* and it was right before tickets went on sale for prom and Edward took Bella to prom, and I was like, *Yeah, this is how I've felt about her all along and she must know it. It's like I've been fighting my insane attraction to the scent of her blood or whatever and this is her way of telling me she doesn't want me to resist her anymore, she wants to become a nerd like me and she wants us to go to prom. Together.*

So I spent hours trying to figure out how to get my hair to stand up like Robert Pattinson's. I sprayed silver sparkles all over my face, and I didn't have time to get amber-colored contact lenses but I fucking looked up how to get them—that's how much it mattered to me. I frowned all the time, but I practiced looking broody. I practiced a slow-motion swoony walk. And then I went to meet up with her on the way to school, like always, with sparkles on my face and mousse in my hair.

She was waiting for me on the corner like always, looking kind of nervous. I handed her a red apple instead of a rose, and I said to her, "I want to take you to the prom, because I don't want you to miss anything." Which was kind of a quote from *Twilight*. And I asked her if she'd go to prom with me and she looked up at me with tears in her eyes. I thought she was going to say yes, that this was exactly what she was hoping for. Except she said softly, "Oh shit, Bradley…" And then the other Brad, my fucking nemesis, was walking down the sidewalk toward us with his dickhead friends and they were all laughing and he was like, "The fuck is this, Sparkle Fatty? She's going to prom with *me*."

I looked at her, and she just whispered, "I'm sorry."

Other Brad grabbed her hand and pulled her off toward school, she dropped the red apple, and I took the long way to class. I laid low at school for the rest of the day and managed to evade Vivian, Brad Turner, and all of his dickhead friends.

It wasn't just about prom.

It was never just about prom.

I was planning to go to UW instead of Princeton so we could be together.

She didn't know it, but I would have done that if it was what she wanted.

I didn't go to any of the senior events except the graduation ceremony. I wanted to skip the ceremony, but my parents strongly discouraged it. Which is to say that my mom cried and my dad said, *Now look what you've done.* So I went to the ceremony, didn't make eye contact with anyone, and left as soon as it was over.

I never went to Princeton because I decided to get into fitness and wanted to start my new life, my new body as soon as possible.

Extreme reaction?

Obviously.

But I didn't need a college degree anymore, and I didn't want to be found.

For the rest of my life, I promised myself, I'd only do what I needed to do to be the person I want to be, and I would build a career helping others to become the person they want to be.

It was never only *her* that I was mad at, but it's not like I'm going to tell her that while I'm training her. If she wants to use her anger toward me for being angry at her, then great. But I didn't blame her for the way other people treated me or for not being a dick to the person who was a dick to me. I just never wanted to feel like that again, and I sure as hell never want to feel worse. I cut her off for the same reason I cut out junk food. Empowerment. So I could take control of my life.

How lucky was I? I was only eighteen when I learned how devastating it is to have your soul crushed by the one person you allowed yourself to imagine was made for you. I will never make that mistake again. Not with anyone else, and I sure as hell won't let it happen again with her.

And okay, yeah, now it has finally occurred to me that the resentment I have held on to I held on to because it kept me tied to her.

Maybe it's the resentment I feel attracted to, not Vivian.

Nope, I am definitely, one hundred percent completely attracted to Vivian, and I'm going to choke that attraction to death in the shower now.

I don't want to want her. And now that I've seen her again I don't want anyone else to have her. This was a terrible, horrible mistake. I'll be hitting another personal record tonight. And I will not be filming it for IG. I'll be thinking about that ponytail and the exposed creamy, soft skin of her waist and upper hips and the way she glared at me when I made her do those sit-ups. I'll be thinking about the outline of her hard nipples and how I know it had very little to do with the temperature of the room and everything to do with the way she was squeezing her thighs together whenever she wasn't moving. I will imagine what it feels like to bury my face between her tits and what she tastes like between her legs and how she'd comb her fingers through my hair so lovingly and then grab me so hard because she doesn't hold back and I like it. I will imagine her on her knees and begging me to forgive her, and I will imagine her breathlessly screaming about how she'll never forgive me for ruining her for all other men while I take her from behind and spank that plump, round ass that will only get rounder the longer I work with her. And by the next time I see her, I will have gotten every possible filthy thought out of my system.

Filthy thoughts are tiny fractures.

My fortress will remain intact.

But fuck.

Her birthday's coming up later this month. I should get her something. As a client.

My phone buzzes with a text notification from an unknown sender, and I know as soon as I see the photo of the massive salad that it's from Vivian. The dopamine rush I get from this is…not ideal. But it's just a dopamine hit. I can get that from setting a goal of cleaning the bathroom in fifteen minutes while listening to the Red Hot Chili Peppers and then achieving that goal. Doesn't mean anything more that.

I add her number to my contacts before inspecting the image. She must have ordered takeout. Piled on top of some lettuce is a ton of shredded cheddar cheese, blue cheese crumbles, gigantic croutons, and balls of fried chicken. It looks delicious, but she cannot continue to eat like that if she's training with me.

VIVIAN

Please note that I did not add ranch dressing.

Or a Danish.

Or ice cream.

Or pizza. I was really craving pizza.

I have almost an entire pint left of sea salt and caramel from Salt and Straw. I would rather do two extra hours of cardio this week than give up this ice cream.

That is my favorite flavor of ice cream from Salt and Straw. I only allow myself two scoops a year, and I will add licking it off every inch of her body to the fantasy menu tonight. And that will go toward my two scoops for the year.

ME

> You would have to run twelve miles to burn those calories. But suit yourself.

> Enjoy that salad. In the future, here's what I'd encourage you to include in your salads: Your base should be 30 grams of protein. Options: Baked or grilled chicken, turkey breast, or baked salmon. Lean cuts of grassfed steak. Get a food scale. Add organic romaine lettuce or organic raw kale massaged in olive oil, to make the kale easier to digest. Tomatoes or organic bell peppers, as long as you aren't allergic to nightshade vegetables. A quarter to half of an avocado, depending on your caloric intake and output for the day. Pistachio nuts, pumpkin or sunflower seeds, no more than two tablespoons. Olive oil and lemon juice for dressing. Consider nutritional yeast flakes as a cheese substitute.

VIVIAN

> ☹ You used to be a lot more fun to text with.

> Please tell me the yeast flakes are a joke.

ME

> I never joke about nutritional yeast flakes.

VIVIAN

> I'm not eating that. What about croutons?

ME

No croutons.

VIVIAN

What about gluten free croutons?

ME

Gluten free does not = fat free. There aren't enough nutrients to justify adding them to an otherwise healthy salad.

Do you really want to argue with me about croutons?

VIVIAN

Kind of.

What about tacos?

ME

What about them?

VIVIAN

They're essentially protein-based salads in a crunchy tortilla shell.

ME

You can eat all the tacos you want, minus the crunchy tortilla shells.

VIVIAN

☺ You let Dolores and Cindy and Mabel eat tacos and drink margaritas.

ME

I advised Cindy not to while I was training her, but she stays on track most of the time and she doesn't add sour cream to anything.

VIVIAN

I don't know who needs to hear this, but you're no fun and I'm not seeing any of the good F's listed here in this Good Form journal. This journal makes me sad.

ME

The fire can be anything that motivates you. Including the good F words.

VIVIAN

Feelings and fucking?

ME

The first rule of 4F's Club is we don't talk about feelings. Good night.

Enjoy your salad. Drink plenty of water, add electrolytes if you have them, and stretch before bed and when you get up tomorrow.

VIVIAN

Good night, Coach.

ME

Don't call me Coach.

VIVIAN

Fine. Enjoy bossing me around, Mitch. I apologize for making it so hard for you to stay mad at me. It is literally impossible for me to be less charming. 🙄

I'm not going to respond to that.

VIVIAN

I just want you to know that I forgive you
for not responding to my text about how
charming I am, and thank you for letting
me have the last word because I know
how hard that is for you too. Nighty night!

Not falling for that.
But fuck.

ME

I highly recommend not eating an entire
pint of ice cream, but that's just advice.
Good night.

CHAPTER 10
VIVIAN

Why am I so attracted to men who love discipline and hate sugar?

It wasn't all that hard to live without the croissants and the Danishes before. I can live without them again. But I'll be damned if I'm going to give up tacos and artisanal ice cream and pie.

My phone vibrates in my pocket again. I left my sister a message on my way home from the gym. The message was: *Aubrey, what the fuck?* She has been texting and calling and FaceTiming me for the past hour. I've finished my dinner and taken a shower and tried to talk some sense into my throbbing clitoris and vulva, but they are determined to convince Brad Mitchell that he has unfinished business with them. I've snuggled with Hairy Styles and done the dishes, and now I'm ready to find out what the hell Aubrey has been up to.

I settle into my armchair, cross-legged, even though my legs are already feeling kind of tight, and then I accept her FaceTime call. She looks very impatient. And judging by the way she's swaying back and forth, I'd say she's on her stationary bicycle. "Oh my God, finally! Tell me everything."

"Hi, how are you?" I ask, playing it cool.

"How was it?"

"Good! I slayed."

"Wait, what? What about Brad?"

"Yeah, that was a surprise."

"Don't mess with me—tell me!"

"*You* tell me! How did you know? How long have you known? Why couldn't you give me some warning—oh my God, I was wearing neon Target gym clothes, Aubrey! Neon! How did you find him?"

"Oh, pffft. You know." She waves her hand dismissively and starts pedaling faster. "I low-key hired a private investigator."

"What?"

"It's not a big deal."

"You hired a detective?"

"It's seriously not that big of a deal. People do it all the time."

"People Google people all the time. I'm pretty sure they don't hire PIs all the time. Oh my God, you're so intense. When did you do this?"

"After the second time I came to visit you, after Jeremy left and you…began your love affair with yourself. You were so depressed, Vivi, and I hadn't seen you like that since Brad ghosted you. I just didn't think you cared that much about Jeremy, so I figured it was more about Brad. And I've just always felt so guilty about insisting you should go to prom with Hot Brad. It was not my finest big-sister moment."

"Well. First of all, Brad Mitchell is the Hot Brad now."

"Oh, I know."

"And I still don't think he'd forgive me for going to prom with Other Brad just because you insisted."

"Wait, he's still mad at you?"

"Big time."

"So he wasn't nice to you?"

"Enh. He was not warm. He was kind of a dick sometimes, actually. But he was professional."

"What an asshole. He gave me no indication that he's still mad at you—I'm so sorry. I will get him to give me a refund. You don't have to keep going."

"No! I'll work on him."

"Oh, *really*?"

"I mean, he's actually a good trainer, I think. But he seems to have built his new life around his anger. You should see this journal he gives his clients. It's like he's weaponized his backstory."

"Mmmm."

"And by *backstory* I am not only referring to his butt."

"Well. I am a soon-to-be happily married lady, however I did notice his excellent gluteal situation in various Instagram posts that I only looked at because I was tracking him down for you."

"So thorough. Anyway, I don't think it's just me he's mad at."

"It better not be. I'm serious—if you don't like the way he's treating you, we end this. Right?"

"Of course. Yes. I just want to prove to him that I'm awesome and he shouldn't be mad at me, and if I happen to get hotter and hotter while working out with him, then where's the damage? Right? And if me getting hotter causes him to suffer, then that would be amazing and I still get to take the high road."

She stops pedaling and guzzles from her enormous water bottle and then says, "Okay. I like this for you. I really am a genius for making this happen even if he's being an asshat."

"Thank you for doing this. Really. This was top-shelf big-sistering."

"I really hope he realizes how awesome you are."

"He never read all those emails I sent him. Can you believe it?"

Aubrey looks aghast. "Did he delete them?"

"No! He said he didn't."

"So they're just sitting there in a folder unread?" She smirks. "I bet he's reading them tonight."

"I don't think so. He's really stubborn."

"Well, he will… Oh!" Her eyes widen. "Vivi!"

"What?!"

"If Brad never read your emails he probably thinks you had sex with Brad Turner!"

"Oh, shit. You're right." Poor Bradley. All this time, he probably just assumed I boned his nemesis just because I went to prom with him. "Oh no. No wonder! Oh, the poor guy! Should I text him and tell him right now?"

Aubrey smacks her lips together. "Um. Probably not the kind of thing you text your new personal trainer. What were you gonna say? *BTW, I didn't bone Other Brad. Have a good night!*"

I mean, honestly, that is exactly what I would text him, and I hate that she knows that. "No, more like, *FYI, in case you have been operating under the assumption that I had sex with Brad Turner just because I attended prom with him—I did not. See you on Wednesday."*

She wrinkles her nose. "This is probably a face-to-face conversation."

"Yeah. You're right. I should go to the gym tomorrow after work."

"Or. Make him wait. Since he was such a jerk to you."

"Oh, well, I like that even more. Thank you."

"Vivi, can I just say—do you see yourself? You're glowing. Not in a sex way. You're just so much more, you know, alive than I've seen you in months. Years, even."

"Yeah. Yeah, I feel that. I mean, regardless of what a dickhead he was being, it was...significant...seeing him again. Finding out he's here. Just being with him. He walked me to my car after the session and—"

"Wait a minute, hold up." She picks up her phone, dismounts, and starts stretching. I should really join her in stretching, but I don't. "He walked you to your car? Did you ask him to?"

"No, he offered."

"Interesting."

"Right?"

"Very significant. And adorable. Continue."

"I mean, it's not that significant for him. For the old him anyway. That's just the kind of thing he'd always do. When we hung out he always insisted on driving or walking me home even though it was only a few blocks. He was still being a stubborn turd, but it felt...I don't know. Even though I was walking down the sidewalk at night with a hot guy who was being kind of a jerk to me, it was the first time I've felt that thing here, you know? That I never had with Jeremy. It felt kind of romantic. I feel hopeful. Maybe I'll be open to dating again soon. Even if it's not with Brad."

"Okay. Okay, I like it." She holds her index finger up. "But if you don't like the way he treats you, you do not have to stand for that."

"What are you gonna do? Low-key hire a hitman?"

"I mean. I'd send him a strongly worded email first."

I smile at that. She writes really good strongly worded emails. "I think it'll be okay. I think it's good for me to be around him, even if he is mad at me. He reminds me of who I was before I got so into dating apps and then tried so hard to prove that I could be in a relationship with a sociopath."

"Yeah," she says, glancing around to see if her fiancé is within earshot. "I mean. Jeremy isn't actually a sociopath, but—"

"Okay, I'm not at the point where I'm willing to hear anyone say he's not a terrible person yet."

"Got it. Yes. I support you returning to you. This is exactly what I wanted for you, Vivi. Not that I thought there was anything wrong with the dating-app phase."

"Um. You literally said you've known fruit flies who have longer lifespans than my relationships."

"I only meant that you deserved better. But that was very clever of me."

I am clearly still on an endorphin high from the workout and seeing Brad, because I can only laugh at that. "It was funny because it was true."

"Yeah. I can see you getting that spark back already, and I'm glad." She rubs her lips together and gets this elfin look in her eyes that makes me uncomfortable.

"But?"

"But you still have to bring a date to my wedding, so if it doesn't work out with Brad, then maybe you can meet someone else at the gym."

I sigh. "Okay." *I wonder if Dolores is single...* "But enough about me. How many items did you check off of your wedding-planning to-do list today?"

Aubrey tells me about all nine things she checked off of her to-do list today, including securing the hotel and event space and minister, and my mind only wanders to Brad's butt in those joggers five times. And then she does that thing. She clears her throat and her eyes get watery. "I just love him so much, Vivi."

"Aww, I know."

"And I know it probably looks like I'm obsessed with the wedding and the ring and the *I'm getting married!* of it all, but that's not the thing that makes me so happy."

"Tell me."

She clears her throat and then coughs a little and finally says, "It's the little things. Just living with him. We're so comfortable around each other. He wanders around naked all the time, and not in a sexy way. We have conversations where I'm brushing my teeth and he's clipping his toenails. He farts in bed and we laugh, and it's just so cozy."

My brain just caved in. "Please tell me you fart around him too."

"No, I don't fart—that's gross." She bursts out laughing. "I do, Vivi! He is literally the only person I fart around besides you, and I know that doesn't sound romantic but it's really and truly lovely, and I want that for you. I want you to have someone you can be that cozy with. And if that somehow sounds condescending, then I give up, because it's the most loving big-sisterly thing I can say to you right now." She clears her throat and sniffles. "If you make me cry, I'm hanging up."

I instantly burst into tears because it is honestly the sweetest thing she's ever said to me. I'm not done enjoying living by myself yet, but if I ever live with a man again, I want it to be someone who cuts his toenails in front of me, but not in a gross way. Aubrey makes a squawking sound, tells me she loves me, and hangs up.

What a day.

Now I can't wait to see Brad again so I can clear things up and hopefully start over.

CHAPTER 11
BRAD

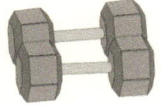

"**S**weet little birdy told me you were spotted walkin' a peach of a girl to her car the other night," says Larry, the seventy-year-old millionaire from Tennessee who's been divorced four times. "You gotta lock that down, bruh."

I guess my thoughts drifted. Larry likes to count out loud when he's doing reps, and his form has gotten really good by now, so I don't have to pay as close attention as I do with newer clients like Vivian. Clients like Vivian who text me full-body selfies in a plunge sports bra and leggings from four different angles at 6:00 a.m., forcing me to take a second shower.

Yes, I told her to take selfies to track her progress, but I did not tell her to do cheesecake pinup poses and send them to me right before I have to go to work. That was a dick move. And I hope she does it again soon.

"Huh?"

"Yeah. You got the Pussy Face."

"I do not have the Pussy Face."

"Pussy on the brain," he says. He's on the lat pull-down machine, and I might have to add more weight because he is not struggling at all. "I know what's on your mind because it's all over your face."

"Why don't you try slowing down your reps," I tell him. "Five seconds on the way down, squeeze those shoulder blades together at the bottom of the rep like you're squeezing a little stress ball between them… Good. Slowly back up. Feel the difference?"

"Fuck yeah, I do. And you still have the Pussy Face."

"It's complicated, and Cindy had the wrong idea. Vivian and I were friends in high school, and now she's a client. End of story."

"Sounds like you're the one with the wrong idea, bruh. Am I saying *bruh* right?" Larry looks like a sixty-year-old hippie who has reluctantly gone through a makeover or seven, in order to please the women in his life and various board members. His whole vibe screams *I give exactly the right amount of fucks, but at the end of the day I am who I am and you can fuck off if you don't want it.* I can coach him on how to build muscle and train without getting injured, but we both know which of us is the real mentor here.

"There's no right way to say it," I grumble. I have never been able to relate to my own generation. Aside from that one person who is of my generation who I will not be relating to, except as a client.

He does his fifteenth rep, and I grab the bar to let it up slowly. He gulps down water and then says, "Well. One thing I do know is Cindy always has the right idea. She said Scorpio men like to keep things close to the vest. I get it. But if you ever need to talk about feelings for a lady—

I'm the guy who's been married four times and doesn't understand women at all."

"So...*don't* talk to you about feelings for a lady?"

"Don't talk to me unless you want to be inspired by my deep capacity to love and my astonishing inability to learn from past mistakes. Cindy says that's the eternal optimism of my Sagittarian nature. She likes that I keep tossing my heart back into the ring. And I like that she likes it."

God, he's just fueled by joy right now, and for the first time in a decade, I think I'm feeling envy instead of pity for someone who is clearly in love. "Are you into astrology too, Larry?"

"Fuck no. But I am into Cindy. So I dug up my birth certificate and let her do my chart. Turns out we're a good match."

"Well, *I* could have told her that just from watching you guys together."

"I tell you what, though. You telling her that wouldn't have given her the confidence to do the things she did to me." He whistles. "Now I *have* to marry her," he says, grinning.

As much as I admire Larry and Cindy and feel a sense of pride that they're as healthy and confident as they are now, I really don't want to think about them doing things to each other. My watch starts beeping, and I'm reminded that Vivian will be walking in for her session at any moment. Which is not the only reason I feel the need to remove my shirt right now, but if it happens to elicit the reaction I'm hoping for, then that will please me a great deal.

And not a second later, the sliding doors open and

Vivian enters. "Thanks, Gwenny!" she calls out as she leaves reception.

"Please don't call me that," I hear Gwen yell back.

She's wearing her hair down, flipping it over one shoulder and strutting, almost in slow motion. A Doja Cat song is playing from the ceiling speakers, and I watch her nod her head, roll her shoulders and hips as she sings along, so casually. God, her posture is beautiful. Always has been. She has the grace of a dancer, but there's still something awkward and charming about the way she moves through the world when she knows people are looking. And they're always looking. All the men in here are looking now. She's confident, but she doesn't take herself too seriously. That's one of the things I loved about her in high school, and I know nobody else appreciated it about her.

She scans the gym, just like I saw her doing the other day. Except today she clearly planned ahead. She's wearing a skintight black workout jacket and leggings that, shall we say, accentuate her curves in a very flattering way. And by that I mean she looks incredible and I can't wait to see her from behind and she is the devil. I unintentionally release a guttural sound at the exact moment the song changes.

Loud enough that Larry hears and chuckles.

I clear my throat.

"Lemme guess," Larry says. "That's the Aries high school friend."

"The Aries new client," I correct him as I adjust my stance. Feet flat on the floor, arms crossed, like a bouncer. No one can knock me over.

"Uh-huh."

I do the hot-guy squint thing I used to practice in the mirror when I first moved to Portland. It comes naturally, usually, but I have to remind myself to do it right now.

And finally.

Vivian sees me.

She gives me a once-over.

Her lips part.

She bites her lower lip.

And trips, just the slightest bit, bumping into Cindy.

She recovers quickly, laughs, as Cindy and Mabel grab her arms to steady her. I can see her blushing from here. She glares at me and then turns her attention to the ladies, who surround her.

It's awesome.

"She's just another client now," I reiterate to Larry as I put my shirt back on.

Larry gets up from the bench and stretches. "Suit yourself, man. But what you resist persists. That's a fact."

"I hear you," I say. "Thanks."

And then a blonde gym member comes over to talk to me. I keep my eye on Vivian. She's giving Cindy, Mabel, and Dolores her full attention most of the time but keeps glancing over at me and the blonde. I watch as Cindy enters her number into her phone. This…could become a problem.

I answer the blonde's question as succinctly as I can, and she walks off. When Vivian looks over again, I hold my watch up and tap at it, signaling that it's time for her session. She nods, tries to wrap things up with the ladies by giving all three of them hugs. Mabel and Dolores go off to their yoga class, but Cindy comes over to join me and Larry.

"I got here early today, Coach. I swear," Vivian says.

"Don't call me Coach."

Larry and Cindy have their arms wrapped around each other, facing us, like they're posing for a prom photo. "Oh, y'all have got to join us for dinner and drinks after your session tonight," Cindy says to me. "Vivian said she'll come if you do."

"Aww, we wouldn't want to impose." Shit. I made us a *we*. "You and Larry are still in your limerence phase. You need to enjoy more time alone together."

"Mitch does make a good point," Vivian says, without missing a beat. She places her hand on my bicep, so breezily, like we're a couple. I flex, not because I want her to feel my muscles, because I want her to know how uncomfortable I am. "*We* wouldn't want to be the third and fourth wheels on your date. You two lovebirds have a wonderful dinner." She holds her hand out to Larry. "You must be Larry. I'm Vivian. I just heard so many wonderful things about you fifteen seconds ago!"

"And Mitch was just telling me everything I need to know about you," he says to Vivian and Cindy, very meaningfully.

"Let me guess—by refusin' to talk about her, right?!" Cindy says.

"You know it."

"Great talk," I mutter. "Time for Vivian's session."

Cindy reaches out to squeeze my cheeks. "My sweet, scared little Scorpio baby. It'll be okay."

I refuse to look at Vivian but I can feel her studying me, and I have lost control of this situation, and I hate it. "Okay, thanks. Great workout, Larry. Have a great night."

I walk off toward the private room, slowing my pace when I realize Vivian is hugging them goodbye.

She catches up with me and says, "So, what did Blondie want?"

Aww, she's jealous. We're back on track. "She just had a question."

"Oh yeah? Was the question *Hi, can you look at my butt and tell me if it's perky enough?*"

"That may have been the subtext."

"Did you get the progress pics I sent you?"

"I did." I need to change the subject immediately. "You didn't check in with your meals after breakfast today."

"You're right," she says, feigning innocence. "I forgot."

I hold the door to the private room open for her, ushering her inside. Just as I thought. She's wearing those new kind of leggings that are cinched in at the back to make the booty look more rounded and perky. It is definitely perky enough. She is hot and evil, and I'll be damned if I'm going to let her get to me today. "Did you forget, or did you not want me to know what you ate for lunch?"

She exhales loudly. "Fine. My friend Marlo really wanted me to check out a new fish-and-chips food truck near our office, and I have no regrets because it was delicious." She hangs up her bag, places her water bottle on the floor near the coat rack, for no reason I can see other than to bend over and stick her beautiful round ass out. Then she unzips her tight little jacket, still facing away from me, and shrugs it off. She gingerly hangs that up and then turns toward me, revealing a black sports bra that lifts and pushes her tits together, and I want to stick my face in there.

Fuck.

Well played, Sparky. Well played.

"I also had a grande caramel macchiato after lunch because I had back-to-back meetings and I deserved a caffeinated treat."

"That's, like, two hundred fifty calories and over thirty grams of sugar."

She places her hands on her sexy hips, flares her nostrils, and says, "No. Regrets."

"Okay. Sounds like you want to do some HIIT today." I stroll over to the center of the room.

In the mirrors I can see her grab her water bottle and follow me. "I absolutely don't want that. Bradley, I have something important to tell you."

"Mitch. More important than the seven thousand calories you consumed at lunch?" When I turn to look at her, the expression on her face is so earnest I'm actually nervous. "What?"

She reaches out and places her hand on my shoulder. "I just want to tell you, assuming you still haven't read the emails I sent you…"

I shake my head.

She rolls her eyes. "Okay, well, if you *had* read the first email I sent you, you would have found this out eight years ago, but I want you to know that I didn't have sex with Brad Turner." She pauses, waiting for me to react.

I don't have a reaction for her. My brain cells aren't ready to hold this information yet. "Say more."

"In case you assumed that I had sex with the other Brad, just because I went to prom with him, I want you to know that I didn't. At all. I didn't even make out with him. I didn't even have fun with him at prom. At all."

My throat makes a sound.

Her hand is still on my shoulder.

Some small part of my brain is accepting this as a relief.

My heart beats out a little *fuck yeah!* fist pump, and then it goes back to its regular rhythm.

Am I glad to hear this?

Yes.

I am glad. I did assume that, but I also didn't allow myself to picture it. The fire is an all-consuming fire. This changes nothing.

She's searching my face. I think she was expecting me to drop to my knees and forgive her for everything. Take her into my arms and thank her for not fucking Brad Turner even though she still went to prom with him. Suddenly morph back into her doughy BFF who'd do anything for her.

"That it?" I ask.

I watch the optimism drain from her pretty face as she realizes that I'm not going to squeal with delight and hug her. "Yes. That's it." She lets her hand drop from my shoulder.

"Okay. We'll warm up first. Starting with general movement. Give me thirty seconds of arm circles."

She laughs to herself, shaking her head. "Wow. Back to our regularly scheduled dickishness, huh?"

"That's right."

Vivian sighs and crouches down to place her water bottle on the floor, giving me an excellent view of her sensational cleavage, along with the desire to put my fist through the wall.

I do forward arm circles. "Come on, let's go."

She faces me, glaring, and immediately starts circling her arms forward.

After fifteen seconds I tell her to reverse the circles.

And then: "Give me thirty seconds of jumping jacks."

She gives me thirty seconds of jumping jacks, locking eyes with me, and I have to work so hard at not staring at her boobs that I cross over to the equipment storage cubes and pull out a pair of boxing gloves and focus mitts, taking my sweet time because I don't want to go back over there. "Now jog lightly in place," I call out, glancing at her reflection in the mirror.

She jogs over to me. "Like this?" she asks, very seriously, as I turn to watch her bounce with perfect posture, like a she-demon.

"Like that," I grit out. I can't decide if I like it better when she wears her hair up or down. I liked seeing her bare neck when she had her hair in a ponytail and I liked thinking about grabbing that ponytail. But today her thick, dark hair is being tossed around the way it would if she were riding me and I can smell that shampoo and she's smirking at me because she knows exactly what I'm thinking right now, and I'm not going to let her win this session. "Okay, that's enough," I blurt out as I carry the boxing equipment back to the center of the room.

I demonstrate some shadow-boxing warm-ups, get her practicing jabs and crosses without putting any power into it. I can see by her breathing rate and slightly flushed skin that she's ready for the HIIT. Keeping the boxing mitts under my arm, I hold out the gloves to her. "Put these on," I tell her. "We're going to do ten minutes of pad work."

"Is this my punishment for enjoying my lunch?" she asks in a sexy tone that makes me regret all my life choices.

"Or you could think of it as your reward for having a personal trainer who'll keep you on track even though you broke our agreement in favor of immediate gratification." I step back, strap the training pads onto my hands, and hold them up. These are designed to absorb the punch impact safely, but I'm going to keep them moving as a target.

"Oh, thanks!" she says, sarcastically. "I will!" She pulls on the boxing gloves, punches them together, and shifts from one foot to the other, sneering and posing like a boxer. "Bring it."

She's fucking adorable, and it has zero effect on me.

I take a step closer to her, about three feet away from her. "We're going to do thirty seconds of punching with ten seconds of rest. This is a full-body workout. I want your feet shoulder-width apart. Left foot slightly forward. Good." I keep my voice calm and authoritative, and I see her thighs tensing up, she wants to clench her legs together. She likes it. "Bend your knees slightly—you're too stiff."

"That's what she said," she quips, bending her knees a little too much.

"Don't bend them that much. Put your weight on the balls of your feet, not your heels."

"I am."

"I can literally see that you're not."

She rolls her eyes and makes an adjustment. "There's no music."

"I'll turn on the music if you make it through the HIIT. I need you to focus." Positioning my mitts at shoulder height, I say, "Remember the jab, cross, and hooks we did during the warm-ups?"

"Yessss," she hisses. So annoyed with me already.

"I'm going to call out combinations, and you're going to do them. You're going to punch these focus mitts. I will determine the pace and the combinations. You keep your eyes on these mitts, not me, not your gloves. Are you ready?"

"Beyond ready," she says, glaring at the mitts.

I call out combinations, starting out simple, and she punches the mitts like she's afraid to break a nail. "I said *punch* the mitts, not delicately tap them. It's not going to hurt your hands—come on. Jab."

She sighs an exasperated sigh but puts more force behind the next jab.

"Good. Jab, jab, right hook. Come on, harder. Okay, active recovery for ten."

She jogs in place.

"Don't jog—shake out the arms and shoulders. Keep it loose."

She huffs as she shakes out her shoulders and I accidentally stare at her cleavage, and I will not make that mistake again.

"Keep breathing," I say, as I realize I was holding my breath. "We go again for thirty. I want to see a jab, jab, cross. Hands up to protect your face." She starts jabbing at the mitts. "Elbows in—don't flare them out like that."

She frowns as she makes the adjustment, putting more power behind the next punch.

"Good. Again. Jab, jab, cross. Keep your core tight." She glares at me. "Eyes on the mitts."

She growls. Actually growls at me. "Oh my God, so bossy—why couldn't you channel your fire rage into becoming a massage therapist or a hair stylist?!"

"Drop your elbow," I tell her during the active recovery. I lean in to gently touch her left elbow, guiding it into position. "Keep it tight to your ribs. That's your defense."

Once she's got the hang of it, I start stepping to the side, forcing her to pivot and follow me. I move around her, making her turn to keep facing me, calling out combinations. Like a choreographed dance, I step back so she has to step forward; I angle the mitts higher, lower, to the sides. Her focus is incredible. She reads my movement intuitively, following me, and fuck, it's so hot. Her coordination is fantastic. I can control the tempo and direction, create a flowing, rhythmic sequence for thirty seconds, and then for ten seconds, we're both breathing heavily, just staring at each other. It's like a physical chess match—I test her, she rises to meet me. She's glowing with perspiration. By the end of the tenth round, it feels primal and intense.

After ten seconds of heavy breathing, I lower the mitts and say, "Okay, let's—"

And she punches my right pec. Hard. "Shit! Sorry!"

I cough, from the surprise of it more than the impact. "Nope. No problem."

"You didn't tell me to stop!"

"Yup. We're stopping."

"Oh, are you okay?" She pulls her right glove off, such concern in her voice. "I'm so sorry." She places her hand flat on my pec. "I didn't hit you that hard, did I?"

Not physically, no.

I stare right into her eyes and say, "I didn't feel a thing. Grab a mat. I'll put on some music."

She removes her hand from my pec and says, "Can you remove this glove for me?"

I remove the mitts, hold them under one arm again, and pull off her glove.

"Thank you. I'll take those if you want." She reaches for the mitts.

"Thanks. Good work."

"Thank you. It was fun. Let's do it again sometime."

I put on a playlist, and the first song is "Keep Driving" by Harry Styles.

"Aww, my boy!"

"Can't believe you still like his stuff." We used to argue about this all the time.

She grins. "I mean, you have to admit his songs are incredibly catchy."

"They're literally just lists of things that he likes. Or lists of feelings. Or lists of things he does."

"Yeah. And?" she says, like *what's the problem?*

"And if that's songwriting then anyone can write songs. 'Hey, what's going on today, Mitch?'" I start singing a list of things like a skinny pop star while she rehydrates. *"Vanillaaaa protein smoothie, black coffee too… Hiking, hydrate, egg whites, recoveryyy day…"* She frowns at me and it's glorious, so I just keep singing. *"Epsom salt bath and a podcast too, rehydrate more and then take a nap, infrared sauna and then meal prep, rehydrate some more and then do yoga."*

"I'm just going to remind you of what you once said when I spoofed the Red Hot Chili Peppers album you were obsessed with one summer: Effective parody depends on the distinct characteristics and familiarity of an artist's work."

"Yeah, but the Chili Peppers are cool." This is just friendly banter. No different from what goes on between Larry and me. "Get on your hands and knees."

"Oooh, yes, chef!" She lowers herself to the mat, sitting on her knees. "Question. Did you tell Gwen about our high school situation? I don't want to be dramatic, but she's literally the only person in the entire world who hasn't liked me as soon as they met me."

"I haven't told anyone about our high school situation. She doesn't *not* like anyone. She just doesn't care if anyone likes her or not."

"Wow." She covers her heart, dramatically. "That's a thing?"

She knows it's a thing. It used to be Vivian's thing before she started wanting douchebags to like her right before we graduated. But I don't bring that up, because I'm on the clock, in the here and now. I'm a pro. "I said get on your hands and knees."

She does, and I like it, and we do half an hour of lower-body workouts that have her alternately complaining and trying to hide her fatigue. "What's the deal with the demographic of the members here?" she asks while doing goblet squats. "And before you answer, just know that I am very supportive of it. If I'd known so many senior citizens work out in gyms I probably would have started going to gyms a long time ago."

"I got my Senior Fitness certification last year," I explain. "The plan is to open up a separate location that's exclusively for seniors. Eventually develop it into a franchise. Larry wants to invest."

"Wow. I love that—I really do. And that's so smart because it's a growing market."

"I know."

"That is so impressive, Coach."

"Don't call me Coach."

"Okay, my sweet, scared little Scorpio baby."

I frown at her and bring her a heavier dumbbell

because it shouldn't be this easy for her to have a conversation.

When we're done with the monster-walk squats, I say, "Good. Cool down. Get back on the mat."

She does, dropping to the floor dramatically, spreads her legs apart, groaning as she reaches for her right foot, then her left foot, then she reaches out in front of herself, looking up at me innocently.

It's a fine sight to behold, but that's not what I had in mind.

I stroll over, get down on my knees in front of her and say, "Lie back."

She does. Without hesitation.

"We'll do assisted stretching. I'm going to help you get a deeper stretch than you can on your own."

"'Kay," she says, her voice more high-pitched than she wanted it to be, I'm sure.

I circle my hands around her ankles, kneel between her legs, and pull them closer together on either side of me. Then I bend her left leg, placing her foot flat on the floor, and gently lift her right leg toward her chest as I slowly stand, holding her right ankle, letting my hand slide down to her calf. She gasps, holds her breath, then exhales. "You feel a good stretch in your hamstring?"

"That depends on where my hamstring is."

I drag my fingertips up the back of her thigh, very slowly, totally inappropriately. "Feel that?"

"Yes," she whispers.

"Good. Keep your leg straight. More?"

She nods.

I grip harder as I guide her leg a little higher. "Breathe into it."

"Uh-huh."

"I'm not going to push too far too fast. Let me know when you want more."

"More," she says.

I let her heel rest against my chest as I hold her ankle with one hand, her knee with the other, and lean in a little more.

Her calf is aligned with my torso.

She really wasn't kidding.

She is flexible.

She crosses her forearms over her eyes, and I feel her trembling.

"Breathe into it," I say softly.

She does, and I feel her relax into the stretch.

Then she uncovers her eyes, brushes her hair out of her face with her fingers, and stares right at me. "Deeper," she says.

One more inch and I hold her leg in place, holding her gaze. She's holding her breath again. "Breathe."

She sucks in a breath.

I repeat the same assisted stretch on her other leg, slowly lower her leg and kneel before her again. "Now we'll open up the hip flexors," I explain. "You'll love this one. Stay on your back."

She does. She's breathing a little heavier than she should be at this point, but I'm not worried about that. Except she stretches her arms up over her head, her hair fanned out around her flushed face. She smirks at me, and I might not be as in control of this situation as I thought I was.

I extend her leg to the mat and place her foot flat against my chest so that leg is bent. I am very professionally positioned between her legs, supporting her thigh with both hands. I lean toward her. "Just relax and feel the stretch in the front of your hip and your glute. You feel that?"

"Yes."

"Take a deep inhale."

She breathes in.

"When you exhale I go deeper."

She watches me as she exhales and I press in closer.

"Good?" I ask.

"Very," she replies. "Have dinner with me tonight."

"No."

"As friends."

I arch an eyebrow.

"As former friends."

"No."

"As trainer and client."

The truth is I can handle my feelings about Vivian in the past. Handling my attraction to her now, in the flesh, is something else entirely. I had to get out of some sticky situations that first year I'd started out as a personal trainer. Working with clients in their homes. Since opening my own gym, I usually only agree to training straight men, happily married couples, and baby boomers. Anyone else gets assigned to Gwen or Curtis. And I've had to become more judicious when it comes to taking on married couples and female baby boomers, because there are a lot of flirts out there. Bottom line—I've never dated a client or a member of my gym.

And I'm not going to start with Vivian.

"No, thank you," I say.

She presses her foot against my chest, and I dig the tips of my thumbs into the flesh of her thighs.

She gasps and then groans.

I lean in a little more. If anyone were to see us on the floor here, this would look perfectly legit. I'm helping her target her IT band and her piriformis. I guide her foot toward my right shoulder, and she sighs. I'm getting deep into her glutes without even touching them.

And that's just how it has to be.

CHAPTER 12
VIVIAN

I t's Saturday and I'm kind of blue, so I'm treating myself to a visit to Powell's City of Books.

I can't eat my feelings anymore, so I'm going to buy my feelings a lot of books and then stay home with them for the rest of the weekend.

Yesterday I received a letter, in the mail, from Jeremy. I had recognized his handwriting before I saw the return address—his office in Seattle. It was such a thin envelope, I'd thought maybe he'd sent me an old receipt that he'd found or something, but it was just a handwritten note on his company's letterhead. It said:

> Dear Vivian,
> I know that you have heard about my engagement by now.
> I didn't call you because I didn't know what to say.
> But you know now, so...

See you at Aubrey and Eric's wedding.
I hope you're doing very well, Vivian.
Tell Hairy Styles I miss him.
—J

I told Hairy Styles that his former housemate misses him but that he is still a stupid idiot lying cheating asshole who hasn't apologized for anything and isn't coming back. And then I told him that it has nothing to do with him, because the stupid idiot lying cheating asshole still loves him even though he isn't here. Then I burned the note and the envelope in the kitchen sink while listening to nineties angry girl music.

Meanwhile, my third training session with Brad came and went, with about as much sexual tension as a dentist appointment. My dentist is not hot. I have no idea what changed between the second and third session, aside from my asking Brad to go to dinner with me. And I still can't believe it made absolutely no difference to him that I didn't sleep with Other Brad. But yesterday we only talked about the exercises. There was no eye-boning, no banter, no joking around at all. He never commented on my objectively hot baseline selfies for tracking how much hotter I'll be getting over the next three months.

He was wearing an ultra-tight black tank top and gray sweatpants that were deceptively plain and simple because they hung from his hips and hugged his ass and crotch in a way that complicated everything.

He didn't hold out his hand to help me up from the mat at all, not once. He didn't even touch me with a finger to make any adjustments to my form. He very much did not assist me with my stretches.

When I sent him pics of my food, ever since Wednesday night, he just replied with thumbs-ups or emojis, which is universally acknowledged to mean *I have no feelings for you, so please find someone else to have sex with.*

By Friday afternoon I was trying really hard to get any kind of reaction from him at all. I would have been thrilled to get a thumbs-*down* emoji for a change. I sent him a photo of a leather shoe and told him the cow was grass fed and raised without antibiotics or growth hormones.

No response.

Nada.

I sent a photo of a live squirrel outside my house. It was standing on its hind legs, clasping its little hands and staring at the camera. Super cute.

Nothing.

I felt so guilty about joking about eating it that I went back outside to leave a little bowl of unsalted peanuts for the poor guy (the squirrel, not Brad).

I would have left out a bowl of peanut butter–flavored protein powder for Brad.

I don't even know what was more infuriating—his cold demeanor, his hot body, or the fact that my vibrator died and I didn't have any spare batteries in my house.

This morning I took a picture of a weird, crooked, uncircumcised penis that I found on the internet. No response. No thumb of any kind.

But it's fine, it's all fine.

He is cold and it's nothing more than a personal trainer–client relationship between us now and I can live with that.

I have closure.

Ish.

I can move on.

I will re-download an app or two in the next couple of days, but first I need to buy a paperback or ten for my new bookshelves. And I mean, if I can't meet an interesting guy in the largest independent bookstore in the world, then where in this Godforsaken world can I meet one? I walk in and inhale deeply. It smells like books and coffee and hope.

I'm here to get a John Green book. Nonfiction. Not the new one that everyone's talking about now, the one that came out a few years ago, *The Anthropocene Reviewed*. I was too busy screwing around in Seattle when it was released, and then I was too busy being told by Jeremy that going digital is better for the Earth.

This is a four-story building on an entire city block. The rooms are color coded, the floors are cement, the bookcases are unfinished wood, the ceilings are exposed, and I can't believe I don't come here more often. It was the reason I was most excited to move to Portland with Jeremy, but he refused to come here with me, which shouldn't have surprised me since he didn't believe in owning books that are made of paper. So this is only the third time I've been here, and I remember being melancholy the first two times I came here as well. Not because of Jeremy. I'm realizing now that it was because I wished I could be here with Bradley, but at the time my brain wasn't letting me consciously think about him.

Now I'm melancholy because I can't stop consciously thinking about him and how much I hate that he won't let me bite his butt cheek just one time.

Sighing, I look up at the overhead sign near the entrance to figure out where I'll find my John Green book. It's nonfiction, but it wasn't on the new nonfiction or best-selling nonfiction shelves. There's no nonfiction section listed on the guide, nor is there a section for essays. There also does not appear to be a section for books of essays that are expanded from podcast episodes wherein a human reviews human things.

I decide to browse. Browsing is my best option anyway. It is, after all, the only way to truly experience a bookstore. Even one that's sixty-eight thousand square feet. Especially when I hate asking clerks for information because that would require talking to another human being and I'd rather talk to a book.

So I browse.

I wander.

I glance at various men's behinds and feel sad because they don't give me even half a percent of the jolt I get when I look at Brad's behind. I bet their brains wouldn't stimulate me anywhere near as much either. If I asked them what they thought of a book they'd probably just say something dumb like, *It's really good*. Boo. Give me something to work with.

I wander and browse some more, picking up a copy of *East of Eden*. Then I grab a copy of *A Little Life*, because the guy on the cover looks as sad as I feel about never getting a chance to touch Brad's butt. I see a couple who are holding hands. They're around my age, adorable, and clearly very much in love. I take a right and go down another aisle so I don't have to look at that shit. No, thank you.

And then I go by another aisle and I stop in my tracks

and walk backward and then hide behind a bookcase, because two aisles down I spy the outline of a behind that thrills me one hundred percent as much as Brad's behind does. Because it is Brad's behind. And one of his beautiful, veiny hands is holding a copy of...*The Anthropocene Reviewed* by John Green.

It's a sign.

It's a sign!

It's a sign that he will be mine.

Suddenly my heart is beating as fast as it did when Brad was leaning on my leg—which sounds very weird when you say it out loud, but it felt amazing.

He shifts around, looks up at another shelf, and I hide around the corner. I should probably just walk right by him and pretend I didn't see him. That would be a baller move. Instead I whip out my phone and take a selfie pretending to eat the two books I'm holding in my other hand, my mouth open wide. I wish I'd grabbed a funnier book, like *The Grapes of Wrath*, or *Green Eggs and Ham*. But I look hot in this picture, so it will have to do.

I text it to Brad and then peek around the corner. He pulls his phone out of his pocket right away and opens the text. I am inwardly cackle-laughing, so I cover my mouth. I watch as he uses his thumb to press the phone screen once, flick the app away, and then slide the phone back into his pocket.

I know even before I see the message that he merely gave it a thumbs-up response.

I could kill him right now.

But I don't.

I decide to be direct, or at least direct-adjacent, so I text him to tell him that I'm at Powell's Books right now and if he has the day off, we should meet up.

I watch and wait for him to look at his phone again. He does. He looks around. I hide again. My phone dings, and I read the message telling me that he has an appointment later.

That's it. Just that he has an appointment later. *Later* could mean ten or twenty-four hours or a week from now. I poke my head around the corner again, and he's gone. He left that copy of the John Green book on a shelf and bolted.

Welp.

That's a sign.

CHAPTER 13
BRAD

I don't know why I bolted, but I bolted.

I knew she was there.

I'd spent fifteen minutes following her around Powell's, casually strolling behind her, stealthily weaving in and out of aisles.

She looked so forlorn and lost. And tight. I could tell by the way she was walking that she hadn't stretched enough last night or this morning, as usual, and it was killing me not to reprimand her for it. And she looked hot. In her skinny jeans and long flowy cardigan over a flowy blouse, a little feminine undergarment-top thing peeking out beneath it. With layers of necklaces and bracelets. The bracelets were jingling.

It reminded me of the opening of the first episode of *You*. In my mind I was muttering, *Well, hello there, You. What are you doing here all alone on a Saturday? Looking all pretty but not too pretty in an obnoxious way, with your jangling bracelets that draw attention but not too much attention. What books are you looking for? You'd better not be here hoping to meet a guy. I do not like that you've taken off your long sweater. I like that I can see your ass in those jeans—love it, even—feel a sense of pride. Not of ownership. I helped grow those glutes. I see those gains. But I do not like the way that guy with the Kurt Vonnegut book is checking out your ass. Fuck you, you poser. You didn't tell her to squat. She didn't get on her hands and knees for you and curse at you while you made her do donkey kicks.*

That ass is mine.

It's mine.

And so I decided to stop and let her find me.

And then she found me and I decided to bolt.

It was too perfect. I was there to buy her that John Green book for her birthday—a gift for a client, no different from me giving Larry a copy of one of my favorite books. It drove me nuts that I didn't know if she'd read it or not; I just know she'd love it. And she was there? What the fuck? What were the chances? What were the chances of me *not* kissing her if I wandered around a bookstore talking about books with her? It would change everything, and I'd finally found a way to create some distance from her in my mind. *Mind over matter* wasn't working, so I had to maintain that distance. Emotional and physical, whenever possible. That's just how it has to be. And now I'll have to order the book online—not because I need to give her a birthday present, because she's a new client and I just know she'll like it.

I pull into the street-level garage of my condo. My two-bedroom unit came with two parking spaces. It was a brand-new building when I bought it, and I'd gotten a great price and mortgage rate from a couple of clients. At the time, I was feeling like I should invest in a space that had room for another person. I didn't have another person in mind and I certainly hadn't met anyone here that I'd felt even remotely serious about. I just knew that one day I'd want to be in a relationship and I wanted to create space for that woman. Literally. I just haven't created space for one figuratively yet. Every time I pull into the garage it's a reminder that I am totally single. Most days I'm happy about it. Today, not so much.

As I pull into my space, I notice something small and dark in the corner, by my other parking spot. When I park, I can see that it's a black cat. A little one. Crouched low, and I can tell by its big, alert eyes and tense body that it's ready to bolt. It's really small, but not tiny. Black, fluffy fur and trembling. Around the size Hairy Styles was when Vivian adopted him. Turning off the engine, I open the car door slowly and don't shut it all the way, keeping my eyes on the kitten.

There's no one else in the small garage. There are only four units in this building. All the other tenants' cars are parked on the other side of the garage, so there isn't really a space that this cat can run to hide in.

"Hey, buddy," I say quietly, but my voice echoes off the concrete and metal. I probably sound loud and menacing to the poor thing. It doesn't look unhealthy, it just looks scared. "Hey, do you belong to someone?" I take a few steps closer. It's so tense and its fur is so puffed up, but it's so cute. "Is your mom around?"

I get about three feet away and hold my hand out, but it hisses and spits, pressing itself back into the corner and swatting its little paw at me. I jerk my hand back, because I was not expecting that response. "Okay. Okay. Not touching you. It's cool. Are you hungry?" I don't know what to feed it, though. I should maybe get it some water before I knock on my neighbors' doors and ask if it belongs to them.

"Okay, I'm gonna back away slowly and bring you something to drink, because it's important to stay hydrated. All right? If you aren't here when I get back, then I'll assume you went somewhere else and you're fine. Deal?" It hisses at me again, very vampire-like. "Right on. Deal."

When I return with a bowl of filtered water, the cat is right where I left it. "Okay, buddy," I say, softly. "Not going to touch you. Just leaving this bowl of water right here." I put it down on the ground, about four feet away from it. "I'm gonna go see if anyone else knows about you, but I'll be back to check on you, okay?" It hisses again.

I don't look back as I walk away. I knock on my neighbors' doors and find that none of them know anything about the kitten and none of them have seen any other kittens around either. When I return to the garage, the kitten's still in the same corner. I check the water level in the bowl I left, and it does look like it drank some of it. That makes me feel strangely excellent. "Okay. Good for you, buddy. We did something good for your body." It hisses at me, and I don't even reach for it.

I don't actually have an appointment later today, aside from the standing appointment I have with myself to not have sex with Vivian Sparks, so I guess this is what I'm doing. Figuring out what to do with a feral kitten. Which is not ideal. I don't love how this thing just showed up out of the blue, and I can't change my life to accommodate it. But I have a couple of hours to spare on my weekend off, I suppose.

But fuck.

I literally can't think of one person to ask for help with this aside from Vivian Sparks.

And it's not because I'm always thinking about Vivian Sparks.

It's because she's the only cat person I know right now.

I step away from the kitten, still facing it, and pull out my phone. I don't think it likes the sound of my voice, so I'll text first.

ME

Hi. Are you still at Powell's?

I have an angry kitty emergency.

That's not a euphemism. There's a feral kitten in my garage and it doesn't want me to pick it up. There aren't any other cats around. No one here will claim it. I don't know what to do.

I wasn't sure who else to ask for help, but you're probably busy. Never mind.

VIVIAN

Oh no, please. A big, strong man who's afraid of a tiny kitten? This requires no explanation. Of course you need my help.

ME

I am not afraid of the kitten. I do not want to scare the kitten with my big, strong man-ness.

VIVIAN

I'm going to need a little more information before I proceed to save you from this tiny animal. Can I call you?

I call her, watching the kitten, who hasn't taken its big eyes off of me since I walked back in here.

She answers on the first ring. "Hi. How old do you think this kitten is?"

"I have no idea how to answer that. It's not a baby. It looks pretty healthy. It's just scared, but it also isn't going anywhere."

"Awww. Sounds like it wants to be rescued."

I sigh. "Should I call an animal shelter or something? Is that a thing?"

"I mean. What I would do first is take it to a vet, probably the nearest animal hospital to make sure it doesn't have a microchip, and then we go from there."

"Okay. And how would I do that?"

"You'll wait for me to show up with a cat kennel that I purchase on my way there. I'd bring Hairy's, but his smell would probably make the kitten nervous. Do you have time for this? You said you have an appointment."

"Yeah, that's not for a while. I'll take it to an animal hospital. Do *you* have time for this?"

"I do. Text me your address. Also, get a towel to wrap it up in. I'm in line to pay for some books, and then I'll stop by a pet store and come over."

"A towel. Got it. Thank you." I feel really bad about lying to her earlier, but I guess this is my punishment.

Half an hour later, I'm standing outside the door to the parking garage. I don't want anyone driving in or out. I can't let Vivian park in my extra spot because it would probably scare the kitten. I see her driving up in a Toyota and direct her to park right in front of me. As luck would have it, there's a space nearby. I'm holding two towels—a hand towel and a bath towel, because I have no idea what they're going to be used for. Vivian parks and climbs out of her car, carrying a small pet kennel and smiling. Now I feel really guilty for lying to her and bolting.

"Hi," she says quietly as she approaches me. "Where is it?"

"Inside. Thanks for coming." I guide her by the small of her back and then, realizing what I'm doing, yank my hand away as fast as I did when the kitten hissed at me. I open the garage door for her, letting her in first, shutting the door as quietly as possible. Then I point toward the opposite corner of the garage and lead her to it.

"Awww, what a sweetheart," she says.

And the cat doesn't hiss at her.

"Yeah, this kitty's old enough to be weaned, I'd say. Oh, I see you got it some water. That's sweet."

"It's not sweet; it was the logical thing to do."

"Okay, tough guy. Give me that bath towel. I'll put it inside the kennel." She places the plastic kennel down on the ground and opens the front of it. "You're going to use that hand towel to pick up the kitten, and then I'll help you wrap it up so it feels safe."

"Got it," I say, even though I have no idea what she's talking about. I hold the towel out in front of me like a lion tamer, slowly stepping toward the kitten. It gets tenser and tenser as I approach, hissing and spitting and swiping at the air, backing itself into the corner even though it can't get any closer to the wall. It's so fucking small, but my nervous system seems to believe that it could kill me.

"Okay," Vivian says. "New plan. I'll pick it up, wearing these gloves that I had in my car. You hold the towel out for me."

"Good idea."

And then she steps slowly toward the tiny creature, wearing leather gloves, cooing and lovingly telling it not to worry. She does, in fact, seem totally trustworthy and not at all capable of breaking hearts and ruining lives. The kitten hisses, but in a much quieter way than it was hissing at me, allows her to pick it up, even though it struggles. Vivian carries it over to me and the hand towel, holding it close to her breast, tells me to wrap the towel around the kitten. There is literally no way anyone could wrap the towel around the kitten without touching her breast, so that's on her, and she smirks at me like she enjoyed it.

Then she somehow manages to wrap up the kitten with the towel, like a burrito, its paws tucked into the hand towel, unable to swat or wriggle around. Subdued. Still alert. Occasionally hissing just on principle. But resigned, for the moment anyway.

I personally wouldn't give up so easily, but I am very impressed with how she handled this.

CHAPTER 14
VIVIAN

I t is strangely comforting to watch this man wrestle with his emotions about accepting responsibility for a feral kitten, to the same degree I've seen him struggle with his feelings for me. But if I'm being honest, I'm just a little bit jealous of this little girl because Brad has decided to take her home with him. It was cute, but it hurt. Like being stabbed in the heart with a Hello Kitty knife.

The vet tech at the animal hospital confirmed that there's no microchip, that it's a girl, around seven weeks old—old enough to eat solid food and to be properly socialized. When she told him that black cats are less likely to be adopted from shelters, Brad frowned and huffed but immediately declared that he would look after her until he can figure out what to do with her. He had asked me if I could take her, but my landlord has a one-pet limit. The vet tech said he could put up a sign on their bulletin board in the waiting area, that there was a good chance someone would adopt her. But he just shook his head and said he'd figure something out, as he picked up the kennel and I followed him out of the exam room.

He said almost nothing as he drove to the pet supply store I directed him to. Anything he did say was grumbled while staring straight ahead. He had resolved to look after this kitten until some vague point in the future when he seemed to envision himself suddenly relinquishing her to another home, but he very much resented that he felt this responsibility. He also seemed really confused by how any female mammal could find him so off-putting, and that warmed my heart. Almost as much as I enjoyed watching him startle every single time she hissed at him.

When we drove back to his parking garage, he turned off the engine of his compact SUV and grumbled, "Can you come in and help me get her acclimated?"

"It would be my pleasure," I replied.

The vet tech had given us some tips as well as a pamphlet on how to socialize a feral cat. I was, honestly, flattered and surprised that Brad had reached out to me for help, and I really do love this for him. Being a cat daddy. It makes my heart and ovaries ache, but the former best friend in me knew he would be amazing at it and that this little kitten has no idea how lucky she is.

And I have been dying to see where he lives. His condo is only a five-minute drive from my house. How have we never run into each other before?

He opens the car door for me and takes the kennel from me, holding his free hand out to help me out of the passenger seat. He's still frowning and being a grumpy grumpster grumpyface, but his hand is warm and I give it a little squeeze as a silent thank-you. He holds the door to the lobby open for me and then leads the way. I'm still a little hurt that he didn't want to hang out with me at Powell's, but this is as good a way as any to spend time with him outside of the gym.

As soon as he opens the door to his condo and I walk in, my eyes get watery.

Not from allergies.

Because the first thing I see when I enter his open living room area is a wall of bookshelves. Floor to ceiling. The entire width of the room. With built-in spotlights under the shelves. And so many books.

"Should I let her out of the kennel?" he asks.

I sniffle and try to swallow a sob. "No!" I squeak out.

He puts the litter box filled with cat food and supplies on the ground, cradles the kennel in his arms, and turns around to find my face wet with tears. He is genuinely perplexed at the sight of me. "What happened?"

"Nothing!" I hiccup, waving at his bookshelves. "That!"

"My books?"

"I ju—I jus—I can't believe you read all those books without me! Don't look at me. I'm hideous." I wipe my face with both hands.

When my vision returns, I see that Brad is laughing. At me. For real.

I slap his arm. "Asshole."

"I mean. I haven't read *all* of them yet."

"Shut up. It makes me sad. But I'm over it."

"Clearly. There's Kleenex in the guest bathroom if you need it."

"Don't let her out of the kennel yet. We'll put some food in the kennel and then get her set up in her own room, okay? Probably the guest bathroom." I check out the guest bathroom down the hall, and it is indeed the perfect size for a tiny kitten to live in while she adjusts to being in a home. And I also burst into tears again because it's so clean and the soap and hand towels are neatly laid out and there's a framed black-and-white photo of the dock by his family's old house when they lived down the street from us on Mercer Island. As teenagers, we spent so many hours sailing and sometimes just reading on the deck of their boat while it was docked. For someone who doesn't seem to want to remember that time of his life, I'm surprised to see this displayed in his home.

After pulling myself together and setting up the litter box, litter-disposal set, and a bowl of water in the bathroom, I join Brad in his kitchen. I manage to refrain from crying at the sight of the clean counters and the rows of labeled storage bins with various powders and smoothie ingredients. It looks a lot like Jeremy's old kitchen in Seattle, aside from all of the journals and paperbacks lying around.

He's adding filtered water to a small bowl of wet kitten food. "Does that look okay?" he asks without looking at me.

"Yeah."

"Do you want to put it in the kennel for her?"

"Oh, no. I think you should do it."

He frowns at me, picks up the bowl, and I follow him back into the living room. "Should we put the kennel in the bathroom first?"

"Yeah, let's do that." I pick up the kennel and take it to the guest bathroom, placing it on the floor, against the wall opposite the door. The kitten makes loud little mewing sounds. A little anxious, but not distressed.

I get down on my knees to talk to her. "Hey, girl. You're going to be living in this little room for a while, okay? You're very safe here. You can stay in this kennel as much as you want, but we're going to leave this cage door open and you can just roam around and get to know the place. That big, nice man, Brad, is going to take care of you, but he's going to stay on the other side of that door most of the time. Okay?"

I get up, and when I turn around, Brad has that look on his face, like he was staring at my butt. I hold his gaze for as long as he'll let me, and then he shifts his body sideways in the doorway, allowing me to pass by him. "I'll close the door behind you, and you can open the kennel and put the food in there."

"You want me to stay in there with her?"

"I mean, you can come out once you've put the food in the kennel. Just don't let her out."

"Roger that."

I close the door behind him and press my ear up to the door. I hear him clearing his throat. I hear her little mews. And then I hear the latch to the cage door open and he says, "Hey, girl," and then there's so much hissing.

I jump back from the door when it opens, and he exits the bathroom, closing the door behind himself so fast.

"Sounds like that went well."

"Yup." He catches his breath. "Now what?"

"Do you want me to go?" I ask.

"No."

"Okay. Well, she needs to get used to the sound of your voice. So why don't we just hang out by the door and talk?"

He crosses his arms in front of his chest. "About what?"

"Well… Any ideas for a name?"

"For whom?"

"The kitten."

"Oh. No." He frowns again. "I don't know if it's my place to name her. Why did you name your cat Hairy Styles again?"

"Because he's skinny and he's got swagger." I step over to the bathroom door and press my ear against it. I gasp. "I can hear her eating," I whisper.

"Really?" He presses his ear up against the door, next to me, facing me. He smiles. "Wow, she's so hungry," he says softly.

"Yeah." I touch his arm. "It's a nice thing you've done."

He shrugs. "Thanks for helping me."

"Welcome." We keep leaning against the door, facing each other. I stare into his intense, green eyes. "For what it's worth, I think you'd make a great cat daddy. I mean, who better to transform a feral feline than a personal trainer? You have all the skills necessary to motivate her to want to live with you and give her clear guidelines for how to be a good, healthy indoor kitty cat."

He sighs and touches the door with one hand. "I don't know. I'm not home very often. It wouldn't be fair to her."

"Well. Let her decide. Once she's ready to come out and explore your place—after you've cat-proofed it. See if she likes it. I mean, it seems like she chose you. It would be rude to just let someone else take her when she just showed up for you like that."

He frowns again.

I change the subject. "So, how were you able to afford your own gym at such a young age anyway?"

He shifts around, leaning his back against the door, so we aren't facing each other, but he's still so close I can smell his fabric softener. He still uses the same kind his mom used to use. "My grandmother passed away when I was twenty and left me quite a bit of money."

"Oh no. Grandma Mitchell?"

"No, my mom's mom. You never met her."

"Right. The wealthy one. I'm sorry to hear that."

"Yeah, I had only met her a couple of times when I was a kid, but she was my pen pal for a while, and I guess I made a good impression on her. Anyway, I invested it. I made some really good investments, lived below my means for a few years while I saved more. I used some of the money for a down payment on this place, put some of the money into the gym, and the rest was funded by a small-business loan from a banker who was one of my first clients when I was working as a trainer at another gym. He liked my business plan, and he knew I had a high client-retention rate, knew I was disciplined." He shrugs. "It all worked out."

"I'm glad for you."

"Thanks."

"Be right back." I go to the front door, where I left my bag, and pull out the copy of *The Anthropocene Reviewed* that I got for him. Handing it to him, I say, "You left this on the shelf when you bolted. Believe it or not, I went to Powell's to get this for you."

He lowers his head, covers his face with the book. "I'm an asshole."

"Yeah. You are."

"I'm sorry. I actually did see you there."

"What?!"

"I just…it's not a good idea for us to hang out, Sparks."

"Sparky."

Brad stares down at the book. "Sparky… Believe it or not, I went there to get this for your birthday."

"What? Say that again."

He smiles, shaking his head. "I went there to get this for your birthday. As a client gift. I was going to order it online."

I give his bicep a playful shove. And then I place my hand on his arm. Playfully. Feeling his muscles. "Well," I say, trying to circle both hands around his bicep as he flexes, "I got a copy for myself too. I was thinking we could start up ABC again. As friends."

"I don't think that's a good idea."

"Okay. We'll start it up as enemies, then. I get first pick, and this is it." I tap the hardcover book in his hand. "You can read it to your kitty through the door. Then talk about it with me. At the gym."

After an eternity, he says, "Fine."

I keep hearing my phone buzzing in my bag and go to retrieve it. There are a bunch of texts from an unknown number, and it turns out it's Cindy. Inviting me out for drinks with the gals. "Hey, it's Cindy," I tell him. "She's inviting me out with the girls. Tonight. She says to tell you they're going to be my wingladies." I look over to find his jaw clenched so tight I'm worried he might crack it.

"Yeah?"

"Unless you'd like to hang out with me tonight," I say.

"Can't."

"How about tomorrow?"

"Can't. You should definitely go out with Cindy and the girls."

"Okay. Well. Aubrey has challenged me to find a date to take to her wedding in June, so if I don't meet someone tonight, then the only place I'm likely to meet someone, aside from the apps, is your gym."

His nostrils flare. "I don't think there's anyone there that you'd like."

"I happen to already know there's someone there that I like." I pick up my bag and open the front door to leave, before I start crying again. "But he's kind of a stubborn dick, so I guess I have to go wash my hair and get ready to go out."

"Hey," he says, grabbing my hand.

I spin around to look at him. "What?"

He stares down at my mouth, grunts, and says, "Don't drink too much. Text me pictures of everything before you put it in that sassy mouth of yours."

I cock an eyebrow. "Everything?"

His jaw tightens again. "Drink vodka if you can."

"Maybe. Don't forget to talk to her through the door. Read her a book. Oh, and put a rolled-up pair of dirty socks in the bathroom with the kitten."

His brow wrinkles. "What?!"

"So she can get used to your scent."

"Oh. Okay."

I get onto my tiptoes and inhale near his neck. "You smell fucking amazing, Bradley," I whisper, plant a kiss on his neck, and then run away.

Take *that*, Mitch!

CHAPTER 15
VIVIAN

"Ugh! You know how they say that the brain is the largest sexual organ?!" I shout into Cindy's ear, probably louder than I need to in order to be heard over the karaoke singer's rousing rendition of "Part of Your World." "I mean, I don't know who 'they' is, but first of all, they have clearly never seen the bulge in Brad's—I mean Mitch's—sweatpants."

I snort laugh. She giggles and holds up her hand for a high-five.

"I wanna be where the bulge is in his sweatpants. That's my 'I Want' song." I crack myself up, but I don't think Cindy gets my reference. "Secondly," I continue, "Mitch's brain is the biggest cockblocker I have ever met!"

I punctuate that declaration by taking another big sip of my strawberry daiquiri, which is kind of the opposite of vodka, but it's sooooo delicious. I earned this because I did five back-to-back YouTube workouts with the word *booty* in the title this morning and then I did two arm workouts, even though it was supposed to be a rest day, but I feel fine. Still, I accidentally, totally on purpose, did not send Brad a photo of this gorgeous bowl of alcoholic liquid sugar.

And I hope he finds out and punishes me for it.

"Oh, honey. I feel your sweet pain. And all your hormones."

"I'm not usually like this with guys—I swear! I've never experienced this kind of lust tornado before! I don't usually proposition people! And I definitely wasn't like this with him in high school. I think I'm experiencing my Dirty Thirties four years ahead of schedule."

She squeezes my arm, tosses her head back, and laughs so joyfully. Cindy was a business consultant who retired early and now flips houses for fun and money. She sees all human relationships through an astrological lens, and she's the only person I've ever met who makes astrology sound logical and a hundred percent accurate. "Oh, sweetie. Wait till you experience your Sexy Sixties."

"And your Oversexed Seventies!" Dolores adds, winking as she holds up her mai tai to clink glasses with me across the table. Dolores, it turns out, is a renowned tattoo artist, former classic car–restoration specialist in New York, and a pretty good yodeler to boot. She's wearing a short-sleeve top tonight, and her remarkably toned arms are covered with beautiful ink designs.

"Here's hopin'," Cindy says, crossing her fingers.

"Or," adds Mabel, "look forward to not having to shave or share your bed or bank account with some asshole ever again!" Mabel had some toxic ex-boyfriends during her time in Big Tech, bless her beautiful heart.

I raise my glass to Mabel. "Been there for the past few months, Mabel, and it's glorious."

We're in a dimly lit red booth at a magnificently kitschy, divey tiki lounge. I always wanted to check this place out when I'd drive by, and it turns out my new best friends have been regulars here for years. They may be twice or thrice as old as the average customer, but they're ten times as cool and all they want to talk about is how dumb Mitch is for not wanting to date me, so I love them a lot. Also, the lighting and decor and just plain fun nature of this place makes me horny, and that makes me wish Brad was here, and that makes me sad.

"Listen," Cindy says, angling herself to face me. "He's a Scorpio. Now that I've met you and heard what he was running from, I see his pain so clearly. This is what Scorpios do when they're hurt. Instead of processing the pain, they transform themselves. They shed their exoskeleton like a scorpion and totally change their appearance and persona. That's what he did when he became Mitch. He tried to kill off the part of himself that loved you. And he did love you, Vivian—I know it. And he will love you again. You have to be patient and you have to be strong. You need to be brave and humble enough to reach beneath his hard shell to where he was hurt and show him you're safe. And you'd better get your lady bits ready for a pounding because once he gives it to you, it will be intense."

"Gosh." I suddenly feel my face getting warm at the thought of my former best friend Bradley giving my lady bits an intense pounding. And then I think of my current personal trainer Mitch doing it, and the rest of me gets all warm and tingly. "I feel like he'd make me wait forever just to punish me."

I told them about Fat Brad and Hot Brad and prom

and the *Twilight* situation. I'm pretty sure he won't hate me for sharing this story with them, since I have seen his website and he does discuss his origin story, minus the details.

"He's built quite a fortress around his big, beautiful, jacked-up heart muscle, but you're the fire that's going to melt his armor, you fearless Aries queen, you."

"Meanwhile he's melting everyone else's panties with those buns of his," Mabel says into her beer.

"You wanna know what I think?" Dolores hollers at me.

"I honestly want to know what you think about every-thing, Dolores."

"I love Mitch to death and I wanna see him happy, but I think he's being a little twat and he'd better snatch you up before someone else does. You could be strong and wait around, sure, but in my experience—and I had a shit ton of experience before and after my ex-husband—with a man you got two options. You can fuck or you can fight. You could also do both. In fact, I recommend it. But life's too short to fight with a man you aren't fucking. All there is to say about it. He wants to fight about *not* fucking you? Pah! Move on. You're a beautiful delicious snack. Let someone else unwrap you and put you in his mouth if Mitch ain't gonna."

Mic drop.

"Marry me, Dolores."

"One more of these mai tais and I might."

"What do you think, Mabel?"

She squints at me from across the table. "You really want to know?"

"I do."

"I think you owe that boy a pretty great BJ considering he read *Twilight* for you, whether he'll date you or not."

Cindy and Dolores both shrug and nod in agreement.

"Hey, you get no argument from me."

I check my phone to see if I've gotten any texts from anyone I know who has recently brought home a feral kitten.

Alas, I have not.

I sort of hope it's because he's too busy cowering in a corner, afraid to reach for his phone, because that tiny animal might hiss at him.

Cindy pats my arm. "Hey, girl. Larry's taking me out on his yacht tomorrow, and we would love it if you'd join us," she says. "If you don't have any other plans."

"Wow, I haven't been on a boat since I moved down here. Are you sure? I mean, you *are* still in your limerence phase."

She rolls her eyes, and it makes me want to kiss her entire face. "We are so beyond the limerence phase. I think he was really talking about the two of you."

"I don't think he ever talks about the two of us," I say, sighing.

Now someone's singing "Total Eclipse of the Heart," and I feel it in my soul. Glancing around the bar, the view from the end of this booth is fairly bleak. I see one, maybe two prospects, if I were forced to choose someone to be my wedding date. If I had to choose between going home with a guy who's currently in this bar or going home to my bed and my cat, let me open my Uber app right now, because I love these ladies, but I would rather get a good night's sleep than make out with anyone other than Brad. But I gotta keep myself busy.

"I'd love to join you for some boating—thank you. Should I bring anything?"

"Just your beautiful smile and a sweater." She winks.

I could swear she mumbles "and those BJ lips," but the karaoke singer is belting out the chorus and I need Brad now tonight and I need him more than ever.

Mabel and Dolores scoot out of their side of the booth, arguing about what song to do.

Cindy pats my arm again, leans in while staring over toward the bar, and says, "Listen. Never play games with a Scorpio. Let me do it for you."

"Huh?!"

She waves someone over and says to me, "I'm not sayin' you oughta go home with that fella who's been ogling you for ten minutes straight. But I am sayin' I will winglady the bejesus out of you if you let me do that too."

I glance over to see one of the two guys who were sort of maybe prospects approaching our booth.

"Say yes and I'm off to the races," she stage-whispers into my ear.

"Yes?"

CHAPTER 16
BRAD

"I mean, yes, it was very kind of her to help me out—help *us* out—even though I've been kind of a dick to her."

I've been sitting on the floor here for half an hour. Shifting positions, I lean the back of my head against the door to the guest bathroom, accidentally knocking it. "Shit. Sorry," I say to the kitten. She could be asleep in there for all I know. Or crouching next to the inside of the door, waiting for me to open it so she can run away or slit my throat or both.

"I mean, yes, Vivian Sparks is a kind person in general. She was never not kind to me—that wasn't the problem. I'm not going to get into what the problem was, or is. It's complicated. Or maybe it's incredibly simple. But I'm not going to bore you with it. Unless you want to hear about it?"

Nothing.

No response.

For all I know, Vivian was messing with me when she

said I should talk to the cat through the door. I read her the introduction and first chapter from the John Green book earlier. I played her an entire *Huberman Lab* episode about creatine while I ate dinner. I started a journal to track her behavior, likes, dislikes, what she ate. She seems to like almost everything except me. I get it. The girl's probably been living on the streets, and she's got the fortress thing down. Right now it's my job to provide her with fuel. Her fire has just been to survive, ever since she was born. And my other job is to ensure that I don't fracture her spirit. I can do that.

She ate everything I gave her today, licked the bowls clean. I was thinking about texting Vivian to ask if I should feed her some more, but I don't want to overdo it. With Vivian, I mean. I'm not going to text her after she kissed me.

I can't believe she kissed me.

"Can you believe she kissed me?" I say to the door. "And then ran off like that? I take back what I said just now—she's not always kind to me. That was a dick move. It was a hot move, but it was a dick move. Sorry—I probably shouldn't say *dick* to you. But she shouldn't have done that. She knew what that would do to me. People don't just go around kissing each other, okay? That's not a thing if you aren't dating. Clients definitely can't go around kissing their personal trainers, in or out of the gym. Just because we used to be friends, just because I used to have feelings for her, that doesn't give her the right to just kiss my neck. If anything, that's exactly why she *shouldn't* kiss my neck."

Fuck, that was hot, though.

Why hasn't she checked in with me since she left? I

don't believe for a second that she hasn't consumed any food or drinks tonight. Why hasn't she asked about the kitten, even? Is she that busy partying with the sassy seniors? I pull my phone out of my pocket to make sure the ringer's on. It is. But there are text notifications from Vivian and I didn't hear them come in. It's eleven thirty.

"This should be fun," I mutter.

I open the text app to find a photo. Of Vivian singing into a microphone with some guy who looks like every other guy in Portland. And she looks like she's having fun. That does not make me happy.

VIVIAN

Hiya, hun. It's Cindy here with Vivian's phone. As you can see, our girl is busy entertaining us all with a very spirited duet of Summer Nights. Y'all should join us here at the tiki lounge. ;) Looks like this gal's gearing up to put a large portion of unsanctioned meat in her mouth. 🖤

Also, y'all should know that she enjoyed a very large serving of strawberry daiquiri and one third of the loaded nachos we ordered for the table. This is Cindy again. 🖤

"Shit."

This is none of my business.

This literally has nothing to do with my business.

Except that four of my clients are out together and the one who's dating a future investor in my business is insinuating that I should pick Vivian up and save her from that terrible piece of singing meat.

So I will do the professional thing and drive to a tiki lounge to retrieve a client at around midnight. It's a rescue mission. I won't even talk to her.

After brushing my teeth and changing into a pair of jeans, putting a minimal amount of product in my hair, and also using a little cologne—because I am not human garbage—I return to the door of the guest bathroom to let the cat know I'm leaving. "Hi. I'm going out for a little while, to pick up a client. To prevent her from putting someone else in her mouth. To make sure she doesn't put *anyone* in her mouth, I mean. I am not abandoning you. I will return. Do you need anything?"

I take a deep breath and slowly open the door. The lights are off in there and I just hear a lot of hissing from inside the kennel, so I immediately shut the door.

"Great. See you later."

I do not drink much anymore, and the only time I came to this bar before tonight was for Dolores's birthday party last year. It was a rager, and I left early because I couldn't keep up. But I have to say, as soon as I walk in here, I am reminded of just how much fun I haven't been having. I enjoyed about three weeks' worth of debauchery when I first moved to Portland, and then I got straight to work, staying focused on my goals. There's no room for partying in your twenties when your ambition is to be an invincible top-tier personal trainer who owns more than one profitable gym before turning thirty.

But damn, this place is fun.

And loud.

And what the fuck does that guy think he's doing putting his hand on Vivian's shoulder when she clearly isn't into him?

I walk right up behind her, touch the small of her back, and say into her ear, while looking at the guy, "You ready to go, Vivian?"

The guy unhands her, but it takes Vivian a few seconds longer to react. When she does, it's like she has no idea that the guy is still standing there or that there is anyone else here besides me. She slowly turns around, slow-blinks, nearly loses her balance. When I steady her by grabbing her hips, she places her hands on my chest and then slides them up to my face, strokes the stubble on my cheeks as she stares at the beanie on my head.

Her lips are glossy and full and parted, and I hate the idea of them being on or around any other guy. I hate that idea so much it scares me. Even more than it scares me how badly I want them on and around various parts of me.

"Fuck me, you look hot in a beanie," she finally says, and she sounds angry about it.

"Yup. Let's get you home."

She narrows her eyes at me. "Whose home?"

"Your home. I'm going to drive you home, and you're going to go to bed. By yourself."

She frowns at me, places one fist on her cocked hip, and pokes me in the sternum with her index finger, like an old-fashioned cartoon bad guy. "No, *you* are!"

"Yes. I am also going to go to bed by myself in my own home after I drop you off."

Her face lights up and she wraps her arms around my neck. "After you get me off?!"

I remove her hands from my neck. "*Drop.* I'm going to drop you off at your house—let's go!"

"Stop bossing me around, Coach! How's the kitten?!"

"Fine."

"Good! Hang out here with me!"

"No! Come on!"

That guy who's still standing behind her says, "So are we still hanging out, or what?"

Vivian waves him away without even turning around. Suddenly her other hand is under my shirt, flat against my abs. "I'm gonna reach under your hard shell and touch that sad little underbelly that hurts— Holy shit, your abs are amazing!"

I remove her hand from under my shirt. "Don't touch the abs."

"Boooo!"

"Mitch! You're here! Time to go, hun!" I turn to find Cindy, who's holding up Vivian's jacket. "We had such a good time with you, doll, but Mitch has to take you home now. Your phone and wallet are in your jacket."

"Ugh! Fine!" Cindy helps Vivian put on her denim jacket while telling her something that I guess I'm not supposed to hear. Meanwhile I get a better look at her outfit.

Miniskirt and black tights and boots and a red top that hugs her curves so tight I can't think straight.

The fuck was she thinking, coming to a bar dressed like that?

As soon as Vivian manages to get her hands through the sleeves of her jacket, I grab one of her hands and pull her to the door, saluting Cindy and Mabel and Dolores.

"Good night! I love all of you!" Vivian calls out, her other hand raised. "Had me a bla-aast!"

I don't slow down until we're out the door and on the sidewalk. Then I let go of her hand, expecting her to latch on tighter. Surprisingly, she lets her arm drop and then skips ahead while singing *"Doobie dow doobie doo doobie doobie doobie dow!"*

"Hey, get back here."

"Why?" She spins around and sings. "You wanna get friendly holdin' my haaaaand?!"

"I don't want you to fall on your face. My car's parked around the corner."

"Because you like my face so much?" She crosses her eyes and sticks her tongue out to the side—which is something I taught her to do one summer.

"Because you're drunk."

"I'm really not. I'm just tipsy."

"You can't stand or walk straight."

She stops in her tracks. "I am standing straight right now. Look at me." She does indeed stand straight. Until she starts swaying. "Whoa. I don't like that."

"Come on. Let's get you home."

"Ohhhh, yes!" She stomps past me, wagging her finger. "Let's be a grumpy grumperson and order me around!"

I catch up to her and walk on the street side. "Try walking like a normal person."

"Like zis, you mean, monsieur?" She sways her hips and swings her arms from side to side.

She starts to cross the street, but I grab her arm and

pull her back to the sidewalk. "This way." I pull her to the left.

She blows raspberries at me. "Wait, why are you here, even?"

"Cindy told me to come pick you up."

"Ohhhhhhhhh! And you came because you were jealous!" She leans into me, wrapping her arms around me. "Poor widdle Bwadwee."

"I wasn't." I remove her arms from around me and open the passenger door to my SUV. "Get in."

"That's what *she* said!"

"Vivian, I don't have time for this."

"Oh!" She holds up her hands in front of her chest. "What are you gonna do, ghost me again?!"

"Get in the car."

She reaches for my beanie.

"Do not touch the beanie. Get in the car, Vivian."

"If I don't get in the car, will you spank me?!" She turns, bends forward, resting her elbows on the passenger seat. "I think you should because I've been a very bad girl."

Jesus.

"Boop!" She reaches back to flip her skirt up. She's wearing black tights, but I can see the curve of her ass and the white of her panties and the smooth bare skin of her upper thighs. *What the fuck—those are thigh-high tights?!*

That's a thing? She went to a bar to meet other guys with nothing between her ass and this miniskirt but panties? Oh, hell no.

The only reason my sanity is still hanging by one thread is that she doesn't look back at me over her shoulder while she's sticking her ass up at me. It's almost like she knows it would put me over the edge. And I bet she's not as bold as she thinks she is either.

"Get. In. The. Car."

"Uggghhhh. Fine!" She gets in the car.

I shut the door. By the time I get around to the driver's seat, she's pulling off her jacket. Now I'm going to have to see the outline of her hot body in that hot red shirt out of the corner of my eye when I'm driving. She is a driving hazard. She's an everything hazard. "Put your seat belt on."

"I'm going to! I had to take my jacket off first. Geez!" She makes a big show of clicking the seat belt in.

I hand her the small bottle of water that was in the cupholder. "Drink this."

She bursts out laughing. "You brought me water?!"

"You need to start rehydrating immediately."

"Oh, sir, yes sir, yes, captain, oh my captain!" She salutes me and then tries to open the bottle but can't even twist the cap off. "Ow."

"Are you kidding me?" I twist it off for her.

"My arm's sore."

"You didn't stretch today, did you?" I start the engine.

"No. I worked out this morning."

God, that pisses me off. "Rest days are not optional, Vivian. That's why we train three days a week. More isn't better—smarter is better. Trust the process."

"You didn't tell me that."

"There's no way I didn't tell you that." Shit. I probably forgot to tell her that because she scrambles my brain, and that is exactly why I can't be around her.

I open up the GPS app on my phone. I already programmed in her address, which is in my client database, before I left. I don't talk again until I stop at the next street light. "Rest days are when the body actually builds the muscle we're working for. When you do strength training you're creating microscopic tears in the muscle fibers. It's the repair process that's going to make the muscle fibers grow back stronger. That only happens during recovery."

She takes a sip of water. "That's what we need to do," she says, looking straight ahead.

"What?"

"The muscle fibers of our friendship were torn, and now we need to take a rest from all the tension between us so we can grow our relationship back stronger." She's speaking so thoughtfully now, she doesn't even sound tipsy. She gulps down more water, puts the cap back on the bottle, places the bottle in the cupholder, and clasps her hands in her lap, like a good little girl.

She doesn't say a thing for two blocks.

Maybe she got everything out of her system.

When I stop at a red light, she exhales and says, "I cannot believe you're being such a dick about what happened eight years ago."

And here we go.

"I'm not being a dick about what happened eight years ago."

"You still haven't read the emails I sent you!"

"What difference does it make?"

"If you read them it might change everything."

Exactly.

I have nothing to say to that.

"You are such a scaredy-cat," she says, matter-of-factly.

"I'm not."

"You are. You're a scaredy-cat who's scared of baby cats and the woman who knows you better than anyone. Which is me, by the way. You're being a stubborn ass, and it's boring."

"Oh, is it?" I guess those nachos she ate were a little spicy.

"Yeah. Did you read the book I gave you yet?"

"I mean, it's only been a few hours, but yeah, I read a couple of chapters."

"And? What's your asshole review?"

"The kitten was not impressed by John Green's prose."

She snorts. "I haven't read any of it yet."

"Well, I'm not going to wait for you to catch up."

"Well, I'm not going to wait for you to catch up either," she says, languidly turning her head in my direction.

I turn onto her street and pull up outside her house. Put on the parking brake. Close the app. Leave my phone on the dashboard mount. I don't unlock the doors. Her house is cute. I like it for her. She's left the porch light on. I wonder if she thought she was going to bring some random guy home tonight or if she has it on a timer. "You're home," I say.

"I know." She looks straight ahead when she sighs and then says, "Look, I don't believe in playing games. I really don't." She sounds so rational I almost believe she's sober. "Cindy told me not to play games with you…" She looks over at me again. "But I think you want me to."

Uh-oh.

"The thing is, Bradley, I feel good. I spent three months feeling bad. Years, maybe, even. And I feel good again. I feel good in my body and I feel good because I'm with you. Even though you're being a stubborn ass, I'd rather be with you than with someone who isn't being a stubborn ass. I wasn't sure if I could ever find my way back to myself—the part of myself I lost after you left. But I feel that spark again, and it's because of you, even when you're being a dickhead."

"I'm glad you feel good, but I can't date you, Vivian. I don't date my training clients. It's gym policy."

"Jim who? Let me talk to him." She smirks, but there's sadness in her eyes, and I can't look at her.

"It's a strict gym policy that I expect my employees to adhere to and that I myself have been adhering to."

"Easy fix. You're fired." She unbuckles the seat belt, maneuvers the seat back a few inches, and turns her body to face me.

"Your sister hired me."

"Then I quit."

"I still won't date you."

"So what you're saying is you want me to date other guys?"

"I am definitely not saying that."

"But you don't want to date me?"

"I don't *want* to date you…" I say.

She blinks at that. Bites her lip. She sits up straighter—in that tight, red top—leans in across the center console, and rests her hand on my right thigh. "Do you want to fuck me, Brad? Because I think fucking me could be all four of the F's you need to become the best Mitch you can be."

Fuck me.

"Do not make fun of the F's."

"I'm not; I'm very fucking serious about all of the F's. We have a lot of tension between us, Coach."

"Don't call me that," I manage to grit out.

"And instead of having that tension we could be fighting and fucking our way through our issues. Doesn't that sound fun?"

Fucking hell.

She squeezes my thigh. Her hand is about one inch away from the throbbing part of me that's trying to unzip my pants from the inside and bury itself so deep in her that neither of us will be able to walk straight for days. "You can do every single thing you ever thought about doing to me in high school."

I inhale a heavy, frustrated breath, and it betrays me by leaving my body as a groan.

She places her right hand on the left side of my face and strokes my cheekbone with her thumb. "Did you imagine us together in your old car like this? Parked by the beach at night. In the rain. Like this?" She caresses my lower lip so gently with the pad of her thumb. Then cups the sides of my head and leans in farther to whisper into my ear. "I did. When you weren't talking to me. When you asked me to prom you gave me permission to think about you like this, and I liked it."

She takes my earlobe between her teeth and tugs. Then she licks and sucks and twirls. "I would have done this to you." She presses her lips against my cheek. Tenderly. "I wanted to, Brad. I wanted to kiss you—I did."

I am so hard. Just this. God dammit, just this is so much. It's too much.

"I'm gonna go," I mutter. I think I said it out loud, but she's ignoring me. "I have to get back to the cat."

She releases my seat belt and slides her hand up my chest, over my shirt, her fingers stretched out. I lock eyes with her. She stares at my mouth, licks her lips, and it's so fucking hot. Her hand begins to slide down my abs. Slowly, not slowly enough. I grab her wrist. "Get out of the car."

"I know you want me," she says, very matter-of-fact.

"Irrelevant."

"Relevant and significant. And I am trying to convey to you as clearly as possible that even though I just got out of a relationship with a man who had control issues, you have my consent to do whatever you want to do *with* me, whatever you want to do *to* me. Whatever you want me to do, just tell me and I might want to do it. If you feel like I need to be mildly punished, for instance…"

"Jesus. Vivian."

"I am open to it. I trust you."

"You can't go around saying stuff like that to guys."

"I don't. You're the only person I've ever said it to. You're the only guy I've ever really trusted."

Fuck. Me. This is what I've spent my whole adult life training for.

I realize I'm squeezing her wrist too tightly. Way too tight. And she's taking it. I loosen my grip on her. I also realize that my other hand is squeezing her left thigh. "You are such a fucking menace."

She grins and pushes my hand up her thigh, under her skirt.

Jesus, I can feel the damp heat radiating from the most dangerous place in the world—between her legs.

I can feel the bare skin of her upper thigh.

She sucks in her breath, and I realize I'm squeezing and kneading the soft flesh.

I stop doing that.

"You're a fucking coward," she whispers.

I am tense as a coiled snake that's about to attack. "Not falling for it."

She leans in, an inch from my face, lips parted. "Oh, yes you are."

One inch. One inch separates my mouth from hers. One inch and eight years. And I can smell that strawberry daiquiri she drank, and I want to taste it on her tongue. But I won't.

Because she swipes my phone, pulls the beanie off my head, grabs her jacket, and unlocks the passenger door.

"Vivian."

I turn off the engine.

"Come and get me, Coach!" She hops out and runs up the path to her front porch. Doesn't even close the car door.

Fuck.

She leaves the front door open.

By the time I walk through the front door, carefully closing it behind me, she's sitting in the middle of an over-stuffed sofa in the small living room. Knees together, feet spread apart on the floor. There are, like, three hundred peach-colored glowing Himalayan salt lamps in here. It's cozy and feminine, and I really like the vibe.

I see a little black-and-white blur dash out of the room. I guess that's Hairy Styles, and I guess he still doesn't like me, and I really don't care right now, because Vivian Sparks is daring me to fuck her and I'm not going to. But I am going to make her suffer in the absolute best way possible for both of us, and she's going to be so, so sorry she decided to play this game with me.

I stand before her.

She stares up at me. Her hands are behind her back. She's probably hiding my phone and my beanie. She bends her right leg. I can tell she's feeling stiff, but she lifts her leg and places the sole of her boot against my chest. She watches me as she presses the heel into my rectus abdominis. Not too hard, but hard enough. "Take my boots off."

I grip the bottom of her thigh with both hands and slide my right hand down past her knee. Her boot is leather, and it hugs her calf pretty tight. I trace along the top of it with the tip of my index finger, around to the zipper. I unzip it slowly, all the way down, pulling it off her foot. She rests the sole of her foot against my abs again, stares up at me, her lips parted, and lets that foot slide down, down, down, so slowly, until I catch her heel and pull it away just before it reaches my crotch. I am so glad I changed out of sweatpants and into jeans, or there would have been a significant protrusion for her to rest her foot on.

Pressing herself down and back into the sofa cushions, she bends her left leg into her chest. Her upper thighs are exposed, but she's squeezing them together, wriggling around a little. There must be so much tension between those legs, and I am going to make it so much worse.

CHAPTER 17
VIVIAN

It's hard to believe that only one week ago, I was on this sofa with Hairy Styles on a Saturday night, in the pajamas I'd been wearing since the night before, eating old-fashioned donut holes and potato chips while watching *Practical Magic* on my iPad. I enjoyed that a lot. But this is maybe just a little bit more fun.

Brad slowly pushes up the sleeves of his Henley, exposing his forearm candy, smirking as he watches me stare at those veins. Evil. He's just evil. Then he grabs the ankle of my bent leg with one hand and unzips the boot with the other, real fast this time, yanking it off my foot, tossing it away. Every muscle in my body is sore from working out, but it's my clitoral muscle that is suffering the most. Is it a muscle? I don't know. It's an angry, horny bitch right now, and if I don't start humping Brad's leg immediately it will somehow make its way to the vibrator in my bedside drawer all by itself.

"Take your shirt off," I say in my most commanding voice.

"No."

"Fine." I shrug, super nonchalant. "I'll take off mine, then." This was my plan anyway—force him to deal with my amazing tits. And I would definitely pull this shirt off over my head right now if my stupid sore arms would let me.

"No," he says, way too calmly. "You won't."

He's rubbing my heel with the palm of his hand, digging his fist into the arch of my foot, kneading the flesh of the ball of my foot.

"Shit," I whisper. That feels amazing. *Why does it feel like you're stroking between my legs, damn you?*

"You're sore all over, aren't you," he says. It isn't really a question.

"Not really." I almost believe myself.

"Liar." He massages my entire foot with both hands, and my stomach dips. "You can't fool me. Your legs are stiff."

"Wanna bet?" I probably wouldn't be able to walk right now, but I will wrap my legs around his neck to win a bet if I have to.

"No," he says. "I don't." He massages my ankle. Circling, tracing figure eights around the outside of my ankle bone.

What?

Jesus. The flutters in my belly. I didn't know ankle massages were a thing or that ankles were an erogenous zone, but my ankle is stimulated and responding to his rhythmic touch and my hips are doing figure eights, rocking to that same rhythm.

"Brad... Shit." *So good.*

"You shouldn't have worn high heels after working out

all week for the first time ever and not stretching enough, Vivian." His hands slide down my leg. "That was not a good decision."

I gasp when he digs his knuckles into my calf muscle. "But I looked hot in them."

"True."

"I look hot out of them too," I manage to say before whimpering and clenching my core and rubbing my thighs together. Rocking. This is pure agony. My pelvis is desperate to find something to bump and grind against. *God, the tension—fuck you, Bradley—don't stop.*

"You do, Vivian. You look really hot tonight."

"Brad…" I can't decide if I love hating this or hate loving this, but I know I hate not kissing him. I am gripping the edge of the sofa cushions, but my back arches in an attempt to raise myself to him. I have to kiss him. I need him to kiss me. My eyelids are so heavy, but I can see his tight jaw. My vision is blurry, but I can see him staring at my breasts. I am offering them to him because it's easier than lifting my head all the way to his face. I know he wants me. I know he wants this as much as I do, but he's being a fucking asshole.

"You didn't stretch or give yourself a rest day like you were supposed to," he says—as if that's really what's on his mind right now—and his voice is deep, but I can hear the struggle to control his desire and it's giving me life. "You worked out too much—"

"Again," I interject, "you did not properly convey the importance of the muscle-recovery phase."

I can sense every muscle in his body and his entire soul tensing up, and it's delicious. "And then," he continues, as if he didn't hear me, "you wore high-heeled boots out to a bar. Where…you drank a large strawberry daiquiri and ate loaded nachos? And you didn't text me first."

Cindy, you genius Judas.

"Yeah, that's right. And I loved them."

I don't know how he does it, but he grabs both my ankles and swings me around so I'm face down on the sofa with my legs straight out behind me. I lost track of his phone and the beanie a while ago—they're probably somewhere in the cracks between the cushions. As for my own cracks, well, they are swollen and soaking wet and dying for anything of his to come between them.

"There's strength in resistance, Vivian. You *know* what happens when you do something you regret. Why do you keep doing things you know neither of us will like? All you had to do was be accountable to me."

Oh. God. I can't tell if this is a game or not and he might not know either, but I'm going with it.

"I don't regret a single thing about today. I feel great."

"You sure about that?" he asks from somewhere behind me. "Because if you're tight anywhere, I will give you a massage."

"I did a lot of booty work," I declare without hesitation.

"Booty work, you said?"

I turn my head to say very clearly, "Yeah, there's a lot of inflammation in my glutes."

He grunts. I feel the weight of him on my lower legs. He's straddling me. One of his legs is bent alongside mine, one foot on the floor, I guess.

"Whoop!" I shout out when he flips up my skirt. There's a sudden rush of cool air on the backs of my thighs that's surprising and satisfying.

"Fuck. Vivian." He groans. But he doesn't touch me.

"God dammit, Brad."

His hands are on my hips now, over the skirt, pressing his thumbs into the small of my back, and it feels so good. He massages my hips. "You sure this is what you want?"

Oh, Jesus. "Brad. Mitch. Bradley. Hottest Brad of All Time. Once again—I consent. I consent to this."

And hallelujah, his big, warm hands stretch across my butt cheeks and he squeezes. He squeezes so hard. "This is a fucking great ass, Sparks." He cups both cheeks gently, lifting them up and letting them drop and jiggle into the palms of his hands. I should be embarrassed—a little, maybe—but I can tell by his grunts that he likes what I've got going on back there, so I feel great about it.

He strokes up the sides of my hips, under the skirt, softly slides his hands, one following the other, across my waist from hip to hip. He lightly caresses the entire surface of my badonkadonk. Over my cotton panties. Grazes the skin of the backs of my thighs with his fingertips. With the backs of his fingers. Down and up. Around the sides. To the inner thighs. I'm trembling, and I can barely feel the pressure of his touch anymore. It's so mean.

"Brad."

"Vivian." He grips one side of my panties and rips them apart at the seams—thank God. He yanks them off of me, tossing them away. "Hold on to the arm of the sofa."

I do that. I reach up and grip it tight. Suddenly he's on the floor, on his knees beside me, aligned with my waist. He unzips the back of my skirt, and I wriggle around to help him pull it down my legs, and off it goes. I turn my head, trying to see him.

"Close your eyes," he demands.

"I want to see you."

"Kind of impossible for you to see me while I work on your glutes."

I huff and squirm around. "You need to work *a lot* harder," I say before burying my face into the sofa cushion. "So bossy." I feel a rush of cool air again, and he's gone. "Brad."

He's back by my side. "Lift your head a little," he says, softly this time.

I lift my head and feel soft material slide over my eyes. I can smell my own perfume. I know what this is. It's the long, skinny velvet scarf I ordered from Etsy last month because it had the words *Stevie Nicks* in the item description. One of those purchases I never would have made when I was living with Jeremy.

Brad makes sure the edge of the scarf sits at the bridge of my nose so I can breathe. He ties it at the base of my skull, over my hair, just one knot, not too tight. I can't see, and the fabric feels so good on my face when I move my head from side to side.

"That okay?"

"Yes."

"This is what you want?"

"Yes. I mean. I wanted you to fuck me, but this is fine for now."

I hear him breathe out a laugh, but the tiny laugh doesn't affect his tone. "You gonna relax?"

"Maybe."

I get a quick slap on my left butt cheek and an electric charge all the way up my spine for that, and then his hands slide over my waist, toward my right hip. Sliding back and forth across my waist again, and then he kneads the flesh and muscle, pinching and rolling, at my hips, my waist. The palms of his hands graze the top of my bottom, gliding across my skin, even though there's no oil or lotion. There's a little friction, in a way that feels so good, in a way that I need. But he does not give me the butt massage I was hoping for, and it's making me furious and it feels amazing. He rubs deeper and deeper, above my ass, and if my desire and senses weren't awakened before, they are wide awake and screaming for him now.

I am not relaxed. My breaths are heavy and ragged, my heart is racing. My lower body is still squirming because of all the pressure and slick arousal between my legs.

I get this flash of a realization that this is *Bradley*, my nerdy best friend from high school, who's doing this to me, and it's so strange, but it also is relaxing. Finally. I melt into the overstuffed sofa cushions, sighing on an exhale. I melt into the sensation of being touched by this man who means so much to me, even though he means to punish me, and I can't tell if he's going to do it by not letting me come or by making me come so hard that I black out.

I really hope it's the latter.

I think?

Finally his hands are finding their way back to my butt. Measured strokes up the back of my thigh to my booty, circling, lightly pinching, fanning outward and then kneading the mound of flesh with both hands. Methodically. With determination. He keeps grunting, almost in response, like he's having a silent conversation with himself, but there's still so much restraint.

It is so frustrating, and I can't tell if I like it or not, and I hate that.

I take a deep breath and try to wait for him to do whatever he's planning on doing, but...

Nope.

Can't.

"You actually think you're doing this as part of my personal training, don't you?"

"You are a foolish new client who needs extra guidance and care."

He presses down on both butt cheeks with the full weight of his upper body, and it feels so good, I cry out. "Oh, God! Yes! Don't stop!"

He stops.

He goes back to circling and kneading the other cheek.

That feels good too, but I really hate him right now.

"So, you do this for all your new clients?"

"No, I don't. Would you like me to stop doing this for you?"

"No. Aren't you going to ask how the pressure is?"

"How's the pressure, Vivian?"

"The pressure between my legs is fucking unbearable, Mitch! Could you put your knee up in there at least?"

"Trust the process, Vivian."

"The Good Form process? Am I your fuel, your fire, your fortress, or a fracture?"

"Right now you're a fucking pain in the ass."

Slap.

Slap.

Freeze.

Quiver.

The stinging sensation is the divine shock to the system that I needed, but it's not enough.

He caresses both cheeks, soothing them. "You okay?"

"Yeah."

"Tell me to stop and I'll stop."

"I don't want you to stop." I remove the scarf from my face and rest on my elbows, clenching my fists. "I want you to go. You have the green light. Why are you keeping us both on the edge when you can have me any way you want me here and now?!"

He slowly stands. "You literally said I could punish you."

"I was hoping your big, hard cock would get involved at some point!"

"God, you've got a filthy mouth, Vivian."

"Don't you want to know what I can do with it?"

"Jesus."

I press myself up to a sitting position, and now I'm face-to-face with the absolutely enormous bulge in his jeans. "Oh my God, Brad, that must be so painful." I reach for it, mostly out of concern.

He swipes my hand away and takes a step back. "Don't."

"Bradley."

I start to stand up, but he holds his hand up so power-fully, I sit right back down on the sofa, very still.

Yes. Sir.

He's staring at my nether region, and I am just now realizing that I'm naked from my waist to just above the knees.

Naked, with my arousal dripping down the inside of my thigh.

Frowning, he appears to be thinking things through. He grunts again, licks his lips, flicks at the stubble on his jaw, and says, "Fuck it."

Brad lowers himself to his knees, very carefully. Pushes my knees apart, very slowly. Hooks my legs over his shoulders, decisively. Reaches under me to squeeze my ass with one hand, uses the thumb of his other hand to expose my clit, and then says, "You asked for it, Sparky."

He proceeds to give me what I asked for.

With his beautiful mouth and his warm, skillful tongue.

The friction of his stubble against the skin of my inner thighs is heavenly, and I hope it scrapes me bad enough to leave me raw and pink.

He licks and swirls and flicks and sucks and fucks me with his tongue.

He says nothing with words, but his moan tells me I taste so good.

The way he pants and grunts as his tongue savors and taunts and pleasures me, I'm hearing that I'm so hot and wet and perfect.

But Brad Mitchell is exactly as determined and methodical as he was when he was massaging my ass, and I don't even care because it only takes me about thirty seconds to come.

I orgasm all over his face for somewhere between a minute and a year.

Trembling and humming and then undulating and screaming. I hit high notes that I usually only hit singing ABBA songs when it's raining. And he never stops squeezing my ass or fucking me with his tongue.

He doesn't give me a hand to buck against or a moment to catch my breath when the orgasm subsides. Because he doesn't let the orgasm subside. He grabs onto my hips and pulls me into him as he sucks hard on my clit and then punishes me in the best, meanest way possible. He sits up taller, wrapping his arms around my waist, and tongue-fucks me from a whole new angle. This man is really giving my lady business the business. Relentlessly. It's too much, but not really. I come again. This time convulsing, calling out his name the way I would if he'd burst through the door and pointed a gun at me.

Brad is breathing as hard as I am. This time he just holds me by my waist and lets me flop around until I am limp like a ragdoll.

He lowers me back down to the sofa, tries to catch his breath. I lick my lips and open my mouth to say that it's my turn, but before I can form the words, he rolls back onto the rug, pulling me down with him. I'm on my hands and knees, and he slides down between my legs, on his back, the way a mechanic rolls under a car to work on the undercarriage, forcing me to mount his face and ride his tongue.

I curse and I curse at him, try to pull away at first, and then some part of my blissed-out brain reminds me that he could disappear at any minute. My blissed-out body finally remembers how it feels to be me. So I arch my back and roll my hips and comb my fingers through my long, wild hair like a fucking goddess. I curse at Brad some more until he silences me by sucking on my clit again, and he might never stop. I'm bucking my hips. It's the most terrible, horrible, incredible thing I've ever felt. It's antagonistic and so generous, abrupt and endless. He spanks me just once. A punctuation. A short, sharp, shock. This orgasm is a jolt, and then it keeps passing through me like an angry, sexy ghost.

And then I just kind of sink down to the floor.

Brad is no longer between my legs or under me at all.

I float into oblivion, drift in and out of consciousness, or maybe I'm dreaming and then I wake up again. Who knows how much time has passed. A throw blanket is covering my lower body. Brad is standing over me, holding a glass of water, looking like he totally didn't just devastate me and give me a lower-body workout in the best, craziest way imaginable.

Bradley.

My Bradley.

All grown up and he should have to carry a license for that tongue of his because it is an assault weapon.

I am too tired to feel the jealous rage in my body, but I will wake up at four thirty in the morning, aching all over but mostly in my brain, wondering how many women he's done that to. I don't want to know. It makes me sad and furious and weirdly proud, but mostly ragey.

He's wearing his beanie and probably has his phone in his back pocket. No sign of that third arm he was hiding in his jeans earlier. He crouches down and guides me to sit up so I can replenish my fluids. I think my undercarriage may be damaged, but she has no complaints. I take the glass of water and gulp it all down.

He stays there, crouching by me, until I finish. He holds his hand out, offering to take the glass from me, so I give it to him. He gets up and disappears to the kitchen. I hear water running and splashing. He's washing the glass for me, and I bet he doesn't just leave it in the sink either—he'll place it on the drying rack. It's considerate of him, but it has nothing to do with feelings. He isn't doing it because he cares about me—that's just how he is.

When he walks back out, he stops a few feet away from me.

"Well. I think I've learned my lesson, Coach."

"Don't call me Coach. That will never happen again. It shouldn't have happened. No one can know that it happened—"

"Yeah, yeah, yeah. I get it, Mitch. You're off the hook."

He nods. "I'm going to go. I need to get back to the kitten." He gestures at the blanket he placed over my naked hoohah. "It didn't feel right to go to the bedroom to find something for you to wear, so…"

"Yeah, this is fine. Thank you."

"I can help you up."

"I think I'll just stay on the floor for a while."

He clears his throat. "Your legs probably feel weak right now, but they'll get stiff again, so you should walk around."

"Well. I guess that's another lesson I'll have to learn by making yet another mistake."

He nods and looks at the front door, then back to me. "Are you okay?"

"Sure. Thanks for the ride."

He frowns at that. "I'll see you at the gym on Monday. Right?"

I give him a thumbs-up. Like an emoji-diss, but with my actual thumb. I hope it feels as cold to him as the lack of kissing did to me.

He takes a few steps toward the front door, then says, "I saw Hairy Styles while you were passed out. He looks good."

I nod. Give him another thumbs-up.

"You should drink more water before bed," he advises.

I lazily watch his butt as he walks away, and then he goes out the front door. Before he closes it all the way, he says, "Do not forget to lock this."

Thumbs-up.

And he's gone.

I hope he doesn't text me that he had a nice time tomorrow, so I can be mad at him for something other than being way too good at oral sex. And for not reading my emails. And for being so hot. And for not kissing me or touching my boobs. And for not letting me love him the way I want to. And for not being madly in love with me the way he could have been if he'd just waited for me to catch up eight years ago.

CHAPTER 18
BRAD

Fitness Journal—Sunday, March 9

Today's Intention: *1. Keep all parts of my body away from all parts of her. 2. Do not text her. Not even about the kitten. Do not say, write, or think her name. 3. Decide on a name for the kitten. 4. Definitely do not read the emails.*

THE 4 F'S OF GOOD FORM

FUEL: *6:00 a.m.—Fucking Daylight Savings Time. This morning I lost an hour, last night I lost my mind.*
Four scrambled eggs, half cup cottage cheese, steamed broccoli. Black coffee. Gave a spoonful of scrambled eggs to the cat and she went nuts for it. First Googled whether or not it's safe for cats to eat, instead of texting she who shall not be named. Should have done that when I found the kitten yesterday.
Going to meal prep for the week before leaving for the marina so I don't have to make any decisions about food. Even though the only thing I want to eat for the rest of my life is her—nope!

FIRE: *I will channel all my energy into business development tasks for the gym expansion this week, starting with today's meeting with Larry. I will not find a market analysis of Portland's aging population filed away inside her vulva.*
Her tight, warm, impossibly wet, inviting — nope.

FORTRESS: *Blasted through a bullshit "short on time workout" of burpees, squat jumps, and mountain climbers for an Instagram paid sponsorship with a new brand of electrolytes this morning. That's it. That's most of my exercise for the day.*
I need to rebuild my mental fortress of solitude. Being on a boat with Larry all day will give me the distance and emotional reset I need.

FRACTURES: *7:00 a.m. — Didn't want to eat breakfast because I could still taste her on my tongue this morning and smell her on my fingers. Will visualize scrubbing her from my mind while I shower today so Larry doesn't comment on my "Pussy Face" and force me to talk about how my unexplored Scorpio tendencies led me to punish her by making her come on my face.*
"What you resist persists." I can't stop thinking about this. Is that the whole "let's just get it out of our systems" logic that has worked for exactly no one never times in the entire history of humans? Or will I finally be free of her if we fuck while fighting? Or fight while fucking?
Nope.
Not going to think about it today.

7:30 a.m. — Fuck. She sent a photo of her breakfast. She made a happy face out of two sunny-side-up eggs, three strips of turkey bacon, and half an avocado. With cottage cheese for hair. It made me laugh, so I gave it a Ha Ha response. I should have just given it a thumbs-up.

But I can't fucking believe how happy I was to get a text from her. This is bad. I am so grateful to Larry for convincing me to go cruising with him today or I would be driving straight back to her house right now.

CHAPTER 19
VIVIAN

Fitness Journal—Sunday, March 9

Today's Intention: *1. Do not text or call him unless he texts or calls first to tell me what an amazing time he had between my legs last night. Or if he needs help with the feral kitten. 2. Drink more water, because apparently brain cells dehydrate due to moisture loss through the lower lady parts. 3. Shit. I have to text him my breakfast. And I can't not make a happy face out of my breakfast because I'm fun and adorable and if he can't handle how fun and adorable I am, well that is literally his problem, because I can't not be fun and adorable.*

FUEL: *Two eggs, three pieces of turkey bacon, half an avocado, half a cup of low fat cottage cheese, and the unbridled pleasure of receiving a Ha Ha reaction from my personal clitoral trainer. I won breakfast!*

FIRE: *I still don't completely understand what this is all about,* *but I'll just say that I feel hot and I look hot and I am hot and therefore I am the fire.*

FORTRESS: *My butt looks amazing and I can literally feel the torn muscle fibers repairing themselves into even hotter butt muscles. My amazing butt is my fortress. It allows me to sit comfortably—when it isn't super sore, that is—and it allows me to walk with the jaunty juiciness of my youth. I have no idea what this F is F-ing about and I'm not going to text my F-ing trainer to ask him. Even though I really want him to massage my jaunty fortress again.*

FRACTURES: *His hands and mouth and tongue have ruined me for all other hands and mouths and tongues. I am torn between wanting to melt his armor, wanting to strangle him for being such a stubborn assmonkey, and wanting to cautiously, quietly, patiently wait for him to realize that I'm here. I'm here for him but I don't want to scare him off because I don't want to lose him again. But I also don't want to lose myself to yet another guy who isn't capable of loving me the way I want to be loved. I don't really even know if this Mitch person is capable in the way that Bradley was. And even though I may have been the trigger for his transformation, I need to make sure I don't stick around out of guilt if we can't have the kind of relationship I want for us.*

I don't want anyone else's hands or mouth or tongue on me, but I won't let Mitch break my heart the way Bradley did. Only Brad and I can heal it.

Jesus, this is weird.

CHAPTER 20
BRAD

Larry's response to my tagline idea for the senior fitness brand is less than wildly enthusiastic. Partly because he's checking the fuel level, here in the helm of his yacht, partly because he keeps checking out Cindy's backside as she strolls around on the main dock. She's alternately checking her phone and scanning the marina. It's a beautiful day. Partly cloudy, light winds. That could change later in the day, but it hardly matters. This isn't a sailboat.

The *Nautical Smile*—which is seriously one of the cheesiest boat names I've ever known—is a forty-five-foot motor yacht, and it's moored in slip three, a premium slip at the nicest marina around Portland. With direct access to the Willamette River, it's perfect for lazy Sunday cruises along the protected waters of the Multnomah Channel, even in March.

I've been out on this boat with Larry before. He lets me operate it. Since I had plenty of experience handling my dad's motorboat and our family sailboat back at Mercer

Island, he even added me to his insurance policy as an approved operator. I fucking love this vessel, and it inspires me to succeed in a way that's very different from my initial motivations for getting into the fitness business. I can tell that was Larry's intention. To inspire me to make "own-a-yacht kind of money."

But I don't seem to be inspiring him with my business plan this morning. "Apps can't spot you," I repeat. "Because fitness apps are so popular now, but it's imperative for seniors to have human trainers nearby, spotting them and ensuring their form is—"

"Yeah, I got it," he says as he tests the navigation lights. "I like it, bruh. You didn't actually think I invited you out here so we could talk business on a Sunday, did you? On my boat?"

I slowly lower my backpack to the seating area behind me so he can't tell my laptop is in there. "Well, we talk business all the time, so I figured—"

"Gwen told me you haven't taken a weekend off in months."

"I didn't go into the gym at all yesterday. And I brought a book to read, so…"

"Atta boy. You feel comfortable with her system?" he asks, gesturing at the instrument panel.

"Uh. Yeah. You want me to start her up?"

He checks his watch. "I'm gonna go ahead and start her up now. I already checked the oil and fuel levels before you got here. Turned on the fuel valves, checked the battery. You got to know this system pretty well last time —it's all the same."

"Yeah. You want me to take the helm?" Larry did not mention I would be piloting the boat today, but if we aren't going to be talking business, then this is exactly what I need to do if I want to keep my mind off Vivian.

"For sure. Why don't we do a walkaround, check the exterior while she's warming up?"

"You got it."

"A little walk and talk. You can take your backpack with the laptop and put it in the main salon if ya want," he says with a wink.

"Can't fool you, huh?"

"Have to get up pretty early to fool a fool, bruh."

I stow my backpack in the main salon and then help Larry with final prep. As we're loosening the dock lines, he says, "So, I hear you gave your Aries friend a ride home last night. She sounds like a real firecracker."

"You heard correctly" is all I'm planning to say about that. I turn my head away from him, staring out at the horizon, so he can't see my Pussy Face.

"I already saw your Pussy Face, kid. You don't have to look away."

Fucking know-it-all Larry.

"She really knocks you on yer ass, doesn't she?"

"You could say that."

"It's rare to meet a woman like that—a woman who knocks you on yer ass, y'know?"

"You aren't the most convincing person to spout this theory, Larry."

"They didn't all knock me on my ass. One of them I married specifically because she didn't. That was after the first one who did."

"And the third was an ass knocker?"

"You can say that again. Fourth was a church mouse. Number five could be the death of me, but I made the decision. I don't want to live the rest of my life without her."

I look over at Cindy, who's still pacing around on the main dock, staring at her phone. But I see a smile spread across her face. I know she heard him. I wonder if they're talking about marriage already.

"Lemme ask you something," he says as he checks that the anchor is properly stowed. "That little cat you rescued. If someone showed up and said, *Hey, that's my kitten. I want her back.* Would you give her back? Don't think about it, just answer."

"No. I'm keeping her—she's mine." I am startled to hear myself answer so quickly, but I've known it was true ever since we were at the animal hospital. "She doesn't know it yet. But she's mine."

"And how would you feel if another man wanted Vivian? You think you'd be cool with that? Every day, for the rest of your life? Don't think about it, just answer."

No. My entire body tenses up with a *fuck no, I'm keeping her—she's mine* response. But I don't say it out loud because I hear Cindy call out, "There she is!"

And there she is.

Vivian.

Walking down the main dock toward Cindy's open arms, carrying a big shoulder bag, and I can just tell from the way the bag's hanging that she's filled it with books. Such a nerd. I watch them hug. I watch her squint over at me, and I can see that she is just as surprised to see me here as I am to see her. If she's feeling anything more than surprise, she isn't showing it.

When I went into the guest bathroom before I left home this morning, the kitten was in her kennel, but she wasn't hiding in the back corner, she was right up front. She looked up and hissed at me, an automatic reaction, but there wasn't much fire behind it, and she just kind of stopped hissing after a second. She was still tense and watching my every move as I filled a bowl with dry kitten food, but it felt like progress.

That's how I feel right now. My initial instinct when I see Vivian—with her hair up in a ponytail, in her jeans and slip-on sneakers and that tight little T-shirt under a wool cardigan, carrying a hooded jacket—my automatic response is fear. To armor up. But when those walls are halfway up, I realize this doesn't make a lot of sense anymore. Not with this person. Not now.

And that fucking terrifies me.

"Well, look who's here. So glad you could join us." Larry doesn't even bother to act surprised. "I believe you know my colleague, Mitch," he says to Vivian.

"Oh now, let's not even try to pretend we aren't delightfully helpful wingpeople," Cindy calls out as she takes Vivian's hand and leads her down to the slip. "You know, even though we're in our lingam phase."

"Limerence," I correct her.

"Right. That too. Even though we're busy limerencing the lingam twenty-four seven, we do enjoy the company of other couples."

"Not a couple," I correct her again.

"Right. Not yet."

Larry holds out his hand to help Vivian onto the swim platform from the narrow walkway. "Come aboard, young lady."

I grab onto the dock cleat to pull the stern closer to the dock as Vivian takes his hand. She had plenty of experience climbing aboard boats when she lived on Mercer Island, but her hesitation tells me she hasn't been on a vessel for a while. Her shithead ex doesn't sound like the kind of guy who enjoys water-based recreation. My face heats up at the thought of the way that guy treated her. Or maybe my face is heating up because it spent, like, twenty minutes between her legs last night and it just wants to get right back up in there, but nope.

This is the opposite of my intention for the day.

I give Cindy a look, frowning at her, but it's not easy to maintain this expression when I'm so damned fond of that lady. I hold one hand out to her. "Step aboard, troublemaker."

"Oh, I'll just wait here a minute, hun."

Interesting.

"There's a full bar," she says to Vivian, pointing below deck toward the galley, "coffee and tea, sandwiches, cookies, protein bars. Lots of bottled water to keep you hydrated." She winks at her. "Oh, and the cabinets in both heads are fully stocked with anything our guests might need, if you know what I mean." She winks again.

Condoms. She clearly means condoms. Probably nipple clamps, whips, handcuffs, so many items I do not want to picture my clients using. Unless that client is Vivian. And even then, I don't *want* to picture it, but now I can't stop.

"You can call me anytime if you have questions," Larry calls out as he hops onto the dock. "About the boat. Or whatever."

"Wait, what?"

"You're captain for the day, kid." Larry unties the dock lines and tosses them onto the boat. "Me and my woman are going for brunch. You kids have fun. I set your course to Multnomah Channel on the Garmin," he says to me. "Up to you, though. You know yer way around."

For shit's sake. I start to coil the lines and stow them, muttering about meddling old people, and I don't care if they can hear me.

"You really aren't coming with us?" Vivian asks, still clinging to her shoulder bag and coat. She doesn't sound too disappointed, and that makes me very uncomfortable.

"I trust Mitch to take good care of both of you," Larry says as he wraps his arm around Cindy's shoulder and waves to us, like we're the teenage neighborhood kids and he's entrusting us with his luxury minivan that has condoms in the glove compartment. "Winds are light. Perfect day for cruising. Shoot me a text when you're back. Cabin key's on the hook," he tells me. "You can bring them to me at the gym tomorrow."

So casual. He has the ease of a man with so much money he knows he can just buy another gently used vessel if I sink or steal this one. And he knows I won't strangle him because I want him to invest in my business.

Cindy blows us a kiss. "Bye, babies! Have fun, y'all!"

I don't look over at Vivian when I'm done stowing the lines. I have to pass her to go up to the flybridge, but I am very careful not to bump shoulders with her.

"Make yourself comfortable, Vivian," Larry says. "Set your things down in the main salon. You can join Mitch up on the bridge. If you want. Plenty of seating and sleeping options."

"There's a deck of cards and some old board games in there," Cindy adds. "Plenty of clean towels, and well, anything you might need, I'm sure you'll find it. Stay outta trouble!"

"You're literally creating trouble for us," I mumble as I test the horn.

It works.

"Hold on!" I call out to Vivian. I have no idea where she is. "Backing out now!"

"All good!" she says from the main cockpit just below and behind me.

Way too close for comfort.

"Right. Here we go."

I reverse out of the slip.

"Looking good, Captain!" Larry shouts from the dock.

I motor north down the Willamette River, toward the Columbia River. It'll be about ten miles. Visibility is excellent from this elevated helm seat and because of the weather. I will concentrate on piloting this vessel and I will enjoy the views along the river. Most of the clear vinyl panels around the bridge are up and attached to the canvas canopy overhead, so I can enjoy the fresh air. There is more than enough space for two people on this yacht. She can have every room below deck. *This* is the captain's domain.

"O Captain, my captain…" she says in a singsong voice that is meant to scrape at the door to my soul as she takes the three steps up to my domain.

Shit.

"Mind if I join you?"

"I need to concentrate until we get to the channel."

"I get it," she says, sitting behind me on the wrap-around seat. "I won't distract you. I brought my John Green book."

"Mm-hmm."

"Did you? Bring the book?"

"I did."

"Good! We can chat about it later. When you're available to concentrate on something other than being the captain of this ship. How's the kitten?"

"Good, actually."

"Yeah? Have you decided to keep her?"

"Yes, I have."

"I knew you would."

"She sleeps a lot. That's normal, right?"

"Definitely. For kittens and senior cats. Hairy sleeps a lot now—it's nice. What are you going to call her?"

"Don't know yet." That's a lie. I'm going to call her Bella.

"You should call her Niall, since he was your favorite member of One Direction."

"He wasn't my favorite. I'm a guy. I don't have a favorite member of One Direction. I believe he has the most interesting personality of all the former members of One Direction."

She giggles. "Oh my God, you should call her Bella. Too soon?"

Fucking hell, get out of my head. "Like I said, I need to concentrate."

"Right. I'll go down to the cockpit until we reach the channel, then. If that pleases you, my captain."

"As you wish, First Mate." *Fucking nautical terms.*

"I wish I was your first." The sincerity in her voice is a jab to the heart.

To the back.

To the gut.

Who was *her* first? I don't want to know. I can't think about it.

"Well…as you were, Seaman." And we're back with our regularly scheduled sassy programming. "Keep up the good work." No reply from me. "Oh, do you want me to bring you anything from the galley? Water? Coffee? Protein bar?"

"Nope. I'm good—thank you."

"Okay. Well. I'll be in the cockpit if you need anything."

I need you to stop saying cock.

I hear her go down those three steps, settle into a chair, and I swear to God I can hear the breeze gently caressing her skin. I want to be the breeze. I want to be the late-winter sun planting a delicate kiss on her cheeks, with promises of spring and budding passion that is about to bloom. I want to be the surprise March snowstorm that encompasses and silences her with all of its weight and beauty, makes her feel warm and safe despite the cold and shocks her with its power. More specifically, I want to be the guy who wants those things without hesitation.

But I'm not.

And I can't concentrate on her.

I concentrate on piloting this vessel. *She's* a lot easier to handle. Completely under my control. She's a good girl.

I should be able to cruise comfortably at fifteen knots through the Portland area for fifteen to twenty minutes, then pick up to twenty knots on the Columbia River. Should reach the channel in forty-five minutes to an hour. I love being out on the water this time of year, as long as it isn't stormy, because it isn't overcrowded with wake-boarding assholes.

And thanks to the good weather, the cock-taunting asshole onboard isn't overcrowding me on this boat.

This might not be so bad after all.

Fuck.

Fucking unpredictable March weather patterns.

This could get bad.

Really bad.

An hour in, we've reached the Multnomah Channel. I've slowed to displacement speed so as not to disturb the waterfowl and the great blue herons. I watched eagles circling overhead and calmly enjoyed the pastoral scenery to either side of me, in total denial of the dark clouds rolling in.

Now it's raining.

There's a canvas Bimini top over the flybridge, so it offers protection from light rain. It's not a hardtop, but it's not pouring rain. Yet. I put her on autopilot since the waterway looks clear up ahead and lower the window panels nearby to keep the rain out. The wind is picking up a bit, but this narrow channel is buffered by the trees and vegetation of farmland on either side, so the water won't get too choppy. It's fine.

I am about to yell for Vivian to help me lower the panels that are farther away from the controls, but she's already bounding up the steps.

"Hi. Let me help."

I disengage the autopilot and take manual control again. "Can you put down the window panels and then cover up the upholstery with those seat covers?"

"You got it."

She does got it. She was always really adept at sailing when we went out on the water on Mercer Island. I knew I could count on her. I glance over at her when her arm brushes my shoulder as she reaches down to get the upholstery cover that's folded up on the floor by the companion seat, and fucking hell, she's just wearing her tight little T-shirt and it's white and it's a little bit damp and I can see her bra and she's the fucking devil.

"Never mind. I'll do it."

"What?!"

"Just go below deck—I'll take care of everything up here."

She totally disobeys me and continues to cover the seats. "Are you nuts? Find somewhere to drop anchor. It's going to start pouring rain soon."

"I'm sorry—are you telling the captain what to do right now?"

"I mean, yes. If your plans don't include piloting us to that cove up ahead and dropping anchor until the weather changes, then I am telling you what to do."

"You know what—why don't you go down to the galley and make us some hot chocolate."

"Seriously?"

"Yeah. They have an electric kettle. Do it now, please."

"Do you want me to bring up your jacket or a sweater?"

"I didn't bring one."

"Oh right, because of your overheated muscles."

"They aren't overheated—will you get down there and stay down there please?"

"That's what she said!"

I shake my head. "Vivian."

"Fine. I'm going. But you'd better drop anchor."

I don't respond to that because I am the captain and I decide.

When I hear her open and close the door to the main salon, I decide to pilot around the bend and drop anchor. This motoryacht has an electric anchor windlass, so once I've positioned her over the desired spot, I can deploy the anchor from the helm, but I go out to the bow to get a better visual.

While I'm there, Vivian opens the door and steps outside. "Everything okay?" she asks.

She sounds like she's wearing a tight, wet T-shirt, so I don't look back at her. "Yes. Go back inside."

"The water's boiled."

"Then enjoy a mug of hot chocolate by yourself. I'm going to stay up on the flybridge."

She huffs. "I don't know who needs to hear this, but you're being a stubborn assclown."

Man, oh man, she must have really enjoyed having her ass slapped last night because she is asking for it.

"Will you just come inside?" she continues. "There's so much room! I'll read in one of the cabins. You can have the rest of it to yourself!"

"I'll see you inside when I'm ready, Vivian."

She makes a guttural frustrated sound that is somehow sexy, and I don't turn around until I hear her close that door again because I am positive she didn't put her sweater back on over that damp white T-shirt.

I go back up to the flybridge, put the boat in Reverse to set the anchor, ensure that the anchor is holding, and then I take a seat in the captain's chair, taking a big, deep breath.

It's really coming down now.

The herons have taken shelter.

The ducks are still on the water, but they've paddled closer to shore.

The hawks and eagles have disappeared.

All the wildlife is taking shelter.

There's a light spray of water coming through the gaps of the vinyl panels and the metal frames, and fuck it—I'm going below deck.

Why shouldn't I take shelter too?

She's right. There's tons of room down there, and it's gorgeous. Why should she be the only one who gets to enjoy the climate-controlled environment and all that high-gloss cherry trim and the cozy beige ultraleather sofas? Why shouldn't I relax to the soothing, rhythmic sound of rain on the cabin roof? As I make my way down the steps to the cockpit and open the cabin door, I can't think of one good reason why I shouldn't get comfortable inside with my book and a mug of hot chocolate. I'm a grown man who's one hundred percent capable of not fucking a woman if I don't want to fuck a woman.

Even when that woman is Vivian Sparks.

Even when I take that last step down to the salon and look up to find Vivian standing in the galley, holding her T-shirt and jeans, wearing nothing but a bra and panties.

But fuck.

CHAPTER 21
BRAD

"Um...I was looking for the dryer," she says. "These are wet." Holding up the wet T-shirt and jeans, she exposes even more of her gorgeous tits in that sweet, white bra and the smooth expanse of bare skin between her bra and her pink cotton panties. She crosses one leg in front of the other, and I can see a wet spot right above where her upper thighs touch.

Fuck.

FUCK.

I have two choices.

I could run back on deck and fling myself overboard. Swim to shore. As long as Vivian doesn't follow me, I could make it through one more day without fucking her. Or I could accept my fate, open the floodgates, and let myself drown in my lust for this woman. Just for today. Let this fear die so I can be born again—again—as Mitch, the guy who's so badass he faced down the very woman he built a fortress to protect himself against.

A self-respecting man really only has one option in this situation.

And I have a lot of self-respect.

"Nuh" is all I have to say, apparently.

My clothes are also pretty wet. So I take hold of the bottom of my Henley with both hands and pull it off, over my head. I stand here, shirtless, for a second. Until I know for certain that all the blood that rushed to my cock is going to do me a solid and allow the rest of me to function, for about five more minutes at most. I also stand here, shirtless, until I know for certain that Vivian's pussy is clenching even harder around nothing and that she is aching for me, because this is going to be fast and dirty and one time only and she will come before I do.

Her lips part. She stares at my bare chest, my abs and bites her lower lip. I take a step toward her, confident now that my legs won't betray me. She stays exactly where she is. As I walk by her, I take her wet T-shirt and jeans from her. The tiny combination washer/dryer unit is stowed beneath a panel in the sole. I lift the access panel in the floor, toss the clothes inside the drum, and turn on the dry-only cycle.

Then I close the access panel and find Vivian standing right there, two feet away from me. Still in nothing but her bra and panties. I back into the closed door to the VIP stateroom. She has literally backed me into a tight corner. My entire body is so tense. She holds up her hands as if to say *I come in peace.* But she doesn't. This isn't peace. This is the end of the fucking world I tried to build without her. She has absolutely no intention of using those hands to bring me peace.

"God, you're so tense," she says, marveling at my

muscles, the veins, the vessel I built to carry around all my resentment and all the *no* feelings I was supposed to have for her.

She can't hear my heart beating over the rain on the cabin roof, so I still have a move or two left in me before she figures out I'm a goner. "And?"

"And I've decided to be flattered. By your resistance. Of me. I realized you wouldn't be so afraid of getting close to me again if you didn't find me so incredibly attractive and charismatic." She smirks.

Shit.

"If this is your attempt at reverse psychology…" I can't even finish that sentence to tell her it's not going to work, because we both know everything she says and does is going to work on me at this point.

She takes another step toward me. "It's not. This is my attempt at making you less afraid of getting close to me again." Her voice is so soft and unthreatening, but that expression on her face, that body, is hostile. Those curves —the upward one at the side of her lips and the luscious ones all over her body—they are designed to ruin my life. "Come on. What happens on the boat stays on the boat. We can be sex pirates."

"This is not the high seas." I place my hands on the slender strips of wall space on either side of me, bracing myself.

She takes one more step toward me. Shrugs her shoulders, puts her hands on her hips. So easygoing. Like we're seventeen and hanging out in my parents' basement. "Let's use each other for sex. See who's better at it. Let's start a two-person sex club."

I cock an eyebrow. "ASC? Asshole Sex Club?"

"*Other*holes Sex Club, for starters." I lock eyes with her as she reaches out to cup my face with both hands. She leans in, stands on her tiptoes, to whisper into my ear. "What's the worst that could happen if we have sex?"

I never want to stop having sex with you. I fall desperately in love with you. You meet some billionaire named Mitchell Brad who calls himself Rich Mitch, and I lose you all over again.

Her tits are pressed against my chest and I can feel her hard nipples beneath the thin fabric of her bra when she moves, and it's all over for me. I'm a dead man.

"Are you worried I won't have an orgasm because you aren't good with your penis?" Even when she's teasing me, her voice is warm and enticing.

"Oh, I'm good with it, Vivian. That's not a concern."

"Great, because I have a magical vagina and I really think your penis will enjoy being inside it." She catches my earlobe between her teeth and tugs on it, gently.

"Jesus, who says things like that?"

She flicks at my earlobe with her tongue, says, "I do. But only to you. For now." She kisses along my jaw, slowly, toward my mouth.

Meanwhile, she's massaging my erection over my jeans. So gently. She unbuttons and unzips me, reaches inside my boxer briefs. We both make a hissing sound when her hand wraps around the tight, hot skin of my hard cock. And she just holds it. Grips me. Waiting for me to give her the go-ahead.

Finally, her mouth is on my mouth. Those pillowy lips brush against mine, she pulls her head back a few inches, and then she kisses me. I press against the walls on either side of me as she pushes my pants down past my hips, fingertips grazing the underside of my erection, cupping the head and twisting, but so slowly, it's agonizing.

"Fuck. Vivian. You're driving me crazy—is that what you want to hear?"

"Yes. I want to hear everything."

I lean in to kiss her, but she leans back, gripping me a little harder, pumping slowly.

Devil woman.

"I can't stop thinking about you," I grit out. "You have no idea how much I want you. I have never wanted to fuck anyone as badly as I want to fuck you. I want to fuck both our brains out."

"Then do that. My brain is only good for thinking about you now too."

"You're killing me."

"I'm not. I learned about this from a podcast—your lizard brain thinks I'm a wild animal who's about to attack you. When really I'm just a woman who wants to touch you and feel you inside of her and on top of her and then stay with you after you've come, because, Bradley, Jesus, you need to come. Let it out. Let me be with you."

Fuck.

I reach around to grab her ponytail, arching her neck back so I can kiss it.

My lizard brain still thinks I'm going to be attacked by a wild animal, but my cock wants to die an angry, violent death inside that she-beast's magical vagina.

I kiss my way down to her tits, and she releases my cock to unhook her bra, and I have never been so frustrated and grateful at the same time. I take her heavy tits in my hands and her nipple into my mouth, and she wraps her arms around my neck, leaning back, giving herself to me. I fantasized about kissing her here, licking and sucking and swirling my tongue around her, so many times when I was a teenager, it feels like I'm time traveling back to the first time I let myself imagine it while jerking off.

But I am not teenage Bradley.

I'm a fucking man and I'm in control of this situation.

I am the captain.

I kiss her one more time and then straighten up, leaning back against the door, bracing myself against the walls again, and give her a little nod.

She knows what I want, and she complies.

Grinning, she slowly lowers herself to the carpet, on her knees, staring up at me. This view. This is the view I fantasized about, over and over again, until the hot water at my parents' house ran cold. My jeans are down around my ankles. Her face is directly in front of my boxer briefs and the erect, throbbing organ that wants to explode inside her mouth or all over her tits or in her hand or inside that magical pussy. Anywhere inside or on her—we don't care.

But instead of pulling down my underwear, she unties my shoes. I groan and bang the back of my head against the door. On purpose.

"Shhhh," she says. "Safety first. I don't want you tripping and hurting yourself before you fuck me."

My cock hurts more than she could possibly imagine, but sure, I will step out of my shoes and jeans if that means I won't fall on my face before fucking her.

She removes my shoes, my jeans, my underwear, finally, finally freeing my cock. I can barely see straight, but I can feel her staring at it, in awe, licking her lips as she grips the base, cups my balls, and then laps at me with her tongue. Kissing and nibbling and flicking and then taking me into her mouth. The noises she makes. Fuck, she's so hungry for me. She squeezes one of my ass cheeks, taking me in deeper, and I can't. I can't. Too good. I'm dizzy.

Groaning, I take her head in my hands, drag my fingers through her hair, pulling it out of the hair tie. It takes all the strength I have to tug her head back and say, "Vivian…"

She sucks on the head one last time before looking up at me and wiping the precum from her lips with the back of her hand.

Her face is flushed and her lips are swollen, and she is so fucking beautiful I ache all over.

Reaching behind myself for the handle, I open the door to the stateroom. "Wait for me on the bed."

I help her up from the floor. "Aye aye, Captain."

CHAPTER 22
VIVIAN

Finally.

Finally, finally, finally!

I climb onto the guest berth like a pirate wench claiming her treasure chest. It's queen size, with a high, wood base and two narrow carpeted steps leading to the head of the bed. This room is small and rounded, and I feel cocooned and safe. There are two small porthole windows on either side of the berth and one overhead, like a skylight. The sound of rain is a reminder of the world outside of this cabin while buffering us from it. It's nothing but water and farmland out there, and this is a sturdy boat, but if it starts rockin', I don't expect anyone to come knockin'.

And I am so, so ready for Brad to rock this boat.

The pressure has been building between my legs ever since he grabbed that cleat and pulled the stern in closer to the dock when I stepped aboard. He didn't hesitate, he just did it to keep me safe. And he was so, so strong, it seemed effortless. I wanted him to grab and pull me around like that.

I just want him on my skin and my bones. I don't care if he wrecks me and splits me in two or makes sweet love to me—I want him inside of me. I want to be able to see and feel and enjoy his body too, but first I want that big, hard cock to come on home. I don't care if it's Mitch who fucks me or Bradley or Brad. I need this more than I have ever needed anything in my life.

The door to the adjoining head opens, and Brad walks through it. Naked and stunningly beautiful in the most masculine, sexy way. A strip of condoms in one hand, his erection in the other. What a sight for blurry, heavy-lidded eyes. His jaw is clenched so tight as he stares at me, stroking himself. I'm on my back, totally naked, propping myself up on my elbows. My boobs are swollen so big they're probably affecting the tides.

He grunts.

God, I love it when he grunts.

He tosses the condom packets onto the ledge beside the bed, climbs up, crawls between my legs, and presses me down into the mattress with the full weight of his body and a punishing kiss that shocks me and takes my breath away. The hot head of his cock is at my entrance. I take it in, just the tiniest bit, and the way we moan into each other's mouths…it's the most erotic thing I've ever experienced.

"You're so fucking wet—don't tempt me." He grips his cock and teases my clit with it. "You trying to drive me wild, you animal?"

"I just want you to drive into me."

He grunts. I kiss him again. So deeply, with my entire

body and soul, offering him the most passionate, dirtiest parts of me, telling him with my tongue that he had better fuck me this hard and deep right now or he will never hear the end of it.

He pulls away, tears open a condom, dips down to kiss my breasts as he rolls it on himself. I arch my back, rolling my head around, writhing, bending, and stretching my restless legs, arms reaching for something, anything, and finally, finally, he presses into me. Hard. Just like I wanted. Crying out, I wrap my arms around his neck, brace my feet against the mattress. He's hovering over me, trying to control his breaths. Concentrating. I force my eyes open and we stare at each other, and even though we're both dizzy with very grown-up lust, I know we're thinking the same thing. We're pretending this is the first time. Not just the first time for us, but the first time for each of us. With each other. Because this is how it should have been.

He lowers himself to kiss me again, thrusts into me. He is so big, so stiff, it stings despite how ready I am to receive him. He is not gentle. Thank God. He isn't trying to hurt me, he's *taking* me.

And for the first time ever, I am giving myself to a man.

I always felt the pressure to perform with other guys. Trying to modulate their enthusiasm or control. Sometimes just trying to get it over with.

But Brad is so strong and so determined and so present.

I can just receive him. Not passively. With gasps and moans and clenching and releasing and rocking. "So good, Brad" may be the last sentence I ever utter. Over and over.

"This what you wanted?" he grits out.

"Yes!"

"This how you thought it would feel?"

"Better. So much better."

He stops thrusting, grabs my waist, and rolls onto his back, flipping me on top of him. "I wanna see you."

I straddle him, grip his muscular shoulders, lower myself down to kiss his mouth, so my nipples brush against his skin. When I sit up and bear down on him, clenching, and rocking my hips, he sucks in a breath and reaches for my breasts. Massaging them, stroking down my waist to my hips. Guiding my hips as we find a rhythm and I feel an orgasm coming on, deep and rolling. A thunderstorm in the distance.

"God, you're so fucking beautiful," he whispers. "You're a fucking goddess, you know that?"

And I had forgotten, but I do know it now. "Yeah," I say.

The storm, the big waves roll in, and Brad lets it ride. For how long, I don't know, but all of a sudden, he sits up and maneuvers my legs to wrap around his back and he's driving up into me, with so much power. To tempo. My tits are bouncing in his face, and he drags his fingernails down my back and slaps my ass, pulling me down onto him as he thrusts up with controlled ferocity. Converting all of the chemical energy inside of me into wild and unruly electricity. My orgasm becomes a tidal wave, and I let myself go because I know he has me. He's holding me so tight. Possessing and claiming and owning me in a way that I already know he won't admit to when this is over.

The rain is coming down above me and I'm coming on top of Brad, and he waits for me to release that final jolt before pulling out of me, moving behind me and pushing into me when I'm on my hands and knees. This bed is so solid it's not moving at all, but he is ramming into me with triumphant athleticism.

Very quickly, that athleticism turns primal. One big hand circles the back of my neck, tugs at my hair, grips my shoulder for leverage, and I would do anything for him. As much as I needed him inside of me before, I need him to come now. I want it more than he does, probably. Not because I want this to end, because I want to be the one who makes him feel so good he forgets about every bad thing that's ever happened to him.

The sound of him panting, his skin aggressively slapping against mine is filthy, beautiful music. That music is reaching a crescendo. I can feel him resisting, like he's trained himself to. I push back into him, hear him grunt ferociously, grip my hips so hard I hope I have bruises there, and when he slams into me and then freezes, I feel the heat of him inside of me. It's contained by the condom, but I feel it and it's so good.

He sighs, hitting a falsetto note that's so sexy, and it would drive him nuts to know that it makes me think of boy bands.

I wait for him to exhale, feel him start to relax, and slowly lower myself to the mattress, bringing him with me.

I love feeling the weight of him on my back, all spent and limber, pressing me into the comforter. He starts to lift himself up, but I clench around him, grab his hand, and say, "No. Stay." With a gentle urgency that doesn't scare him off. I know he'll want to clean up, so I tell him, "Just for a minute, okay?"

"Mm-hmm."

He rests on top of me again, staying as still as he can

while our breaths and heart rates slow. I would imagine his resting heart rate is normally much slower than mine, for workout reasons. But I bet mine will be lower than his while we lie here because I'm not anxious about what this means.

I know what it means.

It means I fractured his fortress and little by little, it will crumble at my feet.

He'll try to rebuild it, but he'll have to build it around both of us this time.

I guess I drifted off to sleep, just like I did last night.

Once again, Brad has covered me with the comforter. He is lying with his back to me, which is fine. I'm not big on spooning. Especially when the guy who has his back to me has such a magnificent backside.

And so, for the aftercourse, which is what follows the intercourse, I take a very dainty, ladylike bite of his right butt cheek as he sleeps.

He must be sleeping very soundly, or perhaps I should have bitten harder. He doesn't clench or move, so I kiss my way up that friendly gluteal slope, down to the small of his back, all the way up to his very powerful shoulders, and over to a part of him that I'm very fond of—the back of his neck.

"Kissin' my back," he mutters, to the tune of "As It Was" by Harry Styles. *"Somebody's kissin' my back."*

I growl-sing like Eddie Vedder into his neck. *"Heeyyyyy, IIIIIII, ohhhhhh, I had to bite."*

"That was a first," he says.

"Was it? You didn't even flinch." There's no way to tell time in here, so I reach around to find his dick to see if it's bone o'clock again.

He grabs my wrist—not in a rough way—and says, "It stopped raining. I'm gonna go back up there. Pull up the anchor and get underway… Okay?"

I release an exasperated sigh. "One time? Once?"

"Not enough for you?"

"I'm afraid it won't ever be enough." I'm not being a drama queen—that's just the truth. I am a fucking goddess who is speaking her truth. I take my hand back and stare up at the porthole above me. "Is it enough for you?"

"It will have to be."

"Why? Gym policy? Or Mitch policy? Is there specific wording in your employee handbook? Is there a formal code of conduct? About not dating clients?"

Now he's sighing and staring up at the porthole above us, running his fingers through his hair. "It's not in the handbook. It's an unwritten policy…I think."

Aha. There it is. Another fracture. "Get me a copy of all of your corporate documents and the handbook. I'll read through them to make sure there's nothing in them that would get you into trouble." He starts to speak, but I continue. "Assign me to another trainer. If necessary, you can have your lawyer change the wording."

"Won't that create suspicion?"

"You can either relieve yourself and your employees and possibly other gym members of paranoia and angst and blue balls, or you can run the risk of creating suspicion. Those are your options. Personally, I doubt that your lawyer or his or her paralegal has enough time in his or her schedule to wonder whether or not you're boning your gym's members. Unless, of course, he or she has eyes and can see you with them."

He scrubs his face with the palm of his hand. I am exhausting him—I know it—but he wants me to wear him down—I know it. "I don't want this to change the way I run my gym. I didn't set out to open a nightclub with exercise equipment. This isn't Crunch Fitness."

I cover my mouth, but I can't suppress the laugh. Oh my God, he's such a nerd.

He gives the side of my butt a slap, under the comforter, sits up, and says, "All right, that's it. The clothes should be dry by now. I'm going back up to the bridge. We'll keep cruising up the channel, but I probably won't do the full loop around Sauvie, okay?"

"Whatever you say, Captain. I'll read down here for a bit and then go back up to the cockpit."

He swings his legs around and takes the weird steps down off the berth. I hike myself up onto my elbows again to watch him walk out. That man really knows how to make an exit. He shuts the door behind him. Which is fine.

I stare out the side porthole. I wish I had my phone with me in here so I could take a picture to send to Aubrey. She'd lose her mind. And then she'd tell me exactly what I already know—that I can't sleep with him again until he's read the emails.

I need to have an unwritten code of conduct too.

CHAPTER 23
BRAD

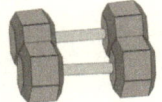

The sliding doors from the lobby open again, and once again, someone who isn't Vivian walks through them.

The amount of disappointment I feel is...disappointing.

"Christ on a cream puff, Mitch." Larry's doing seated leg curls and I've lost count of his reps, and even though this isn't a training session, that is inexcusable. "You've gone way beyond Pussy Face. You've got Pussy Soul, my friend. What exactly did she do to you on my boat?"

I made sure to leave no trace of anything we did on his boat before we disembarked. Not that we did that much. Once was enough. For yesterday. That's a lie—it wasn't anywhere near enough. Today is a new day, and I'm ready to negotiate terms with Vivian. But I will never be ready to talk to Larry about what we did on his boat or anywhere else. "I think we can add another weight plate" is my reply.

"Fair enough, bruh," he says, shaking his head.

And then, across the gym, the sliding doors open and Vivian does walk through them. She is somehow more beautiful today than ever before. Her dark hair is billowing around her shoulders, which is not appropriate for working out, but I don't even care because she's hot and I want her mouth on my cock again.

She doesn't do the usual friendly scan of the room as she enters. She probably knows that Cindy and the girls aren't here right now. She's on time for our session and heading directly toward me. As much as her directness pains me, I have come to expect and desire it. I'll think about what that means later.

"Good evening, Captain," she says as she stops in front of me. She's wearing workout clothes that are not as revealing as the ones she wore last week. Loose T-shirt over her tank top, joggers instead of leggings. But that does nothing to hide the curves that taunt me from under those layers.

She smiles over at Larry. "Hi, Larry. Thanks again for the use of your yacht. It was a really lovely day."

"My pleasure, darlin'." He winks at her. "She's all yours whenever you feel like going for a cruise."

She looks back over at me. "Shall we have a chat in your office?"

That is a different tone for her, but I'm into it. "Yes, let's have a chat in my office."

We both gesture for the other to lead the way, probably because we want to see each other's butts. I end up going first. My gift to her. She shuts my office door behind us and opens up her giant shoulder bag.

She hands me a printout of the weekly questionnaire. She's filled it out already.

What is your ultimate goal for these personal-training sessions? To continue boning Brad Mitchell.
Why? Because he enjoys it.
How much water did you drink today? Barely enough to replenish the fluids I lost over the weekend from not-working-out reasons.
What are your strengths? Fellatio.
What are your weaknesses? Too good at fellatio.

I fold up the paper, tear it into twenty pieces, and drop them in the recycling bin. "Ms. Sparks. If you aren't going to take these training sessions seriously…"

"Oh, calm down and check your email. I sent you my real answers when I was at the office."

"That was a waste of paper."

"No, I think it was worth it to see the look on your face while you read it." She removes two manila envelopes from her bag and hands them to me.

"What's this?"

"One contains some notes on wording for your employee handbook. I haven't seen what you've got in your current handbook, but I had some ideas and did some research on my lunch break. Don't worry—I won't bill you for it. The other envelope contains an affidavit stating that I, Vivian Sparks, will not sue or threaten to sue you or write any negative reviews online, that any intimate activity between us is consensual and in fact was initiated by me. I had my friend notarize it."

"Okay…"

"And I would like you to assign another trainer for my one-on-one sessions here. Whoever you're most comfortable with."

"Okay... That would be Gwen. She's actually free right now."

"Great."

"Good. So, do you want to come by my place later tonight?"

She looks down and sighs.

I don't like that.

"You still haven't read my emails, I take it?"

"No."

She shakes her head. "Bradley...Mitch...what's the worst that could happen if you forgive me?"

"That is not an appropriate topic of discussion while I'm at work."

"Right. Okay. Look, I'm not going to go by your place later tonight." She fiddles with the zipper on her shoulder bag, and it reminds me of her unzipping my jeans yesterday, and I can't focus and this is bad.

Did she just say she's *not* going to my place? "Huh?"

"This has been really fun and...stimulating, but I'm tired of pretending."

"Pretending what?"

She won't look at me. She shrugs, as if she isn't saying things that are totally devastating to both of us.

"That it doesn't hurt." She's tearing up and her voice quivers, and it hurts my heart. "I know I hurt you, and I know you've built this new life around the anger you have about the way people treated you in high school. I get it. I don't want to disrupt your life in a bad way. But at this point it's just *you* hurting yourself and blaming me for making you feel things. I say this as your former best friend—you're gonna have to feel the feelings."

She takes a deep breath and finally looks up at me.

"You have to. And I don't want to see you outside of the gym until you're ready to do that. I don't want to have to keep missing you when you're right in front of me...or on top of me or under me or behind me, depending on...you know what I mean."

"Yeah." I place the manila envelopes in a locked drawer and tap on the desktop. "Lemme go talk to Gwen. You can wait for her in the private room."

She sniffs and dabs at the corners of her eyes with her finger. "Are you okay?"

"Yep." I do the only thing I can think of doing right now. I hold out my hand to shake hers. "Good luck with the rest of your training. Keep up the good work."

She blows out a laugh and takes my hand.

It takes all my strength not to pull her in and kiss her.

"Thanks. Same to you."

I go talk to Gwen, fill her in on what we did in the first three sessions, and I don't even watch her walk into the back room because I don't want to risk seeing Vivian in there if I can't go in myself.

This was not my intention for the day.

But I will make the necessary mental adjustments.

I find myself wandering back over to the leg-press machine, where Larry is working on his quads. "Keep your back flat against the seat pad," I mutter.

He glances over at me, exhaling as he pushes the platform away. Pausing at the top of the movement, he says, "Yeesh." As he returns the footplate to the starting position, he says, "What happened in there?"

"Nothing."

"Certainly looks that way, Scorp." He pauses his set, staying in the same position as he continues talking to me.

"Listen. You don't have to give me any details. I don't need them. I can guess what's going on here. She wants you to open up somehow, and you're reluctant. I get it. Here's the thing. Are you listening?"

I crouch down so he doesn't have to yell. I don't really want to hear any more of this real shit today, but Larry has a way of dishing things out that I can handle. "Go ahead."

"*Love* is a verb. You make a choice every single day when you're in a relationship, whether you're married or not: Do I want to love this person and make the relationship work? Yes or no. Proceed according to your answer. Do you want to verb Vivian? Don't think about it, just answer."

"I want to verb her so hard it terrifies me."

"Sounds like a *hell yes* to me, bruh."

"That is incredibly insightful…"

"For someone who's been divorced four times?"

"I mean."

"Two of my wives chose not to verb me any longer. I eventually chose not to verb any of them anymore. The biggest lesson I learned after my first company and my first marriage ended was that you only fail if you decide to give up when something doesn't go the way you wanted it to. You don't want to get hurt? Roger that. Nobody really wants to get hurt. Are you willing to feel the pain of loving a woman so much that it feels like you're dying when you lose her?" he asks. "Man, you got your journal to keep track of gains and personal records when it comes to muscles and lifting. How about a journal that tracks being brave when it comes to loving someone who's explicitly told you she wants to love you? That kind of strength is undervalued in a man. Why don't you challenge yourself to set some *emotional* PRs for a change?"

I have to grip the headrest for leverage when I stand up. This is all too much. I feel bullied and beat up, and no one has touched me or said one mean thing. They're just scraping away at my ego with every sentence. I don't even know what to say.

"Like I said, Cindy told me about what happened to you senior year," he continues, "but don't you see how lucky you are? First of all—it's a gift to have your heart broken for the first time. A broken heart is an open heart. We're all the same when we're in love—there's nothing easier than falling in love for the first time in your life. It's how we respond to getting our heart broken that first time that defines who we become as adults. I'm not saying what you did was wrong, not at all. But do you know how rare it is to have the opportunity to be healed by the person who broke your heart? For that person to be willing to heal you and grow with you, as the new people you've both become?" He shakes his head, then stares up at his feet. "That shit is priceless, bruh."

Even if I didn't have a huge fucking lump in my throat, there isn't one thing I could say in response to that.

I go home early. Before Vivian's session is over. Partly because I don't want to see Vivian and partly because I want to spend some time with Bella. Mostly because I need fresh air and zero humans around me while I enjoy my remaining hours as a free man.

I kitten-proofed the condo last night. Covered up any spaces under furniture and between appliances that a tiny cat could hide in. I don't want to rush her, but I have a feeling Bella's ready to leave the guest bathroom and do a little exploring.

Leaning against the door, I say, "Hi. I'm going to open this door, give you your dinner, and leave the door open. And then I'm going to walk away to heat up my dinner. Okay? You can come out and wander around if you feel like it and then come back in here whenever you want to. You will have this room to retreat to for as long as you need it. But you're welcome to come out if you want. Cool?"

I open the door and leave a bowl of kitten food on the floor by the kennel. Bella's in there, near the opening of the kennel, watching me. I don't tell her this, because I don't want to pressure her, but I've decided that if she comes out tonight, then I will open that archived folder and read Vivian's old emails. If she isn't ready to come out, well, I'm not ready yet either.

Not even half an hour later when I'm in the kitchen, finishing up the ground-turkey taco bowl I prepped yesterday morning, I hear a bold, high-pitched little meow from the living room.

Fuck.

CHAPTER 24
THE EMAILS

From: viviansparksisawesome@gmail.com
To: thesmartbrad@gmail.com
Subject: WTAF Bradley?!

Jun 18, 2017, 10:15 a.m.

Okay. You have clearly gotten a new phone number.

Baller move.

And you deleted your Facebook account? Or maybe you blocked me, I don't know. But I can't find you online, and it's making me anxious. I tried to give you space to process your feelings (which is a weird sentence to write and I probably would never say it out loud, but it's the kind of crap people say on TV all the time). And now we've graduated.

And yeah, as you probably know, I went to prom with Brad Turner. I didn't have fun. I didn't make out with him. At all. I just wanted you to know that. He wasn't nice about it, but whatever.

It's not like I liked him or anything, it just seemed like a good idea to follow through with the prom date since you were so mad at me anyway.

Okay, that's not exactly it.

I was scared of what would happen if I told him I had changed my mind.

And Aubrey thought it would be a bad idea to back out. Path of least resistance, blah blah. So I didn't.

If it bothered you that I still went with him even though I knew how upset it made you, I'm sorry.

I'm very sorry.

I don't know how to write it so it comes through in an email, but I am really, truly, forever sorry.

In my defense, I am not the only teenage girl who did something dumb because she thought it was a good idea to say yes to the popular guy. It's not an excuse for hurting you by saying yes to Other Brad. Although I really didn't know how badly he had treated you over the years.

This isn't an excuse, or maybe it is, but...it's hard being a girl.

There's obviously stuff you didn't want to tell me and there is also stuff that I don't talk to you about. Girl stuff. I don't expect you to understand it or to want to. And I don't blame you for not understanding. But some part of me knew that for the rest of my life I'd be asked about my prom experience and I decided I should actually have a prom experience. It didn't occur to me when Other Brad asked that you would want to go since you had seemed very vehemently against it up until that point.

I don't know what I'm trying to say here, other than you are my best friend, but you're also a guy. An extremely stubborn and kind of moody guy. And I didn't feel like I could talk to you about everything. Especially prom and other guys. Not that there were other guys. I mean, there were guys I made out with before I moved here, but only ever in closets at parties or spin the bottle or when we were drinking or whatever.

Ugh.

I'm rambling.

Well. Happy graduation! Friends forever!

I can't believe you're icing me out, Bradley. That's such a thirteen-year-old girl move.

Please write back. Please. Just so I know you're okay.

From: viviansparksisawesome@gmail.com
To: thesmartbrad@gmail.com
Subject: Gone Boy

Jun 27, 2017, 4:35 p.m.

Hi.

I went to our spot at the beach today.

I was doing some magical thinking and thought maybe I'd find you there. Spoiler alert: I didn't. It was so weird, being there by myself. It used to be a place where I knew I could feel good and calm and not think about anything outside of the tide beating against the shore and the breeze and whatever book I was reading and you. Today it was the loneliest place on earth.

Where are you?

Where did you go?

I don't understand how you can just disappear like this.

Your parents too?

Gone.

You're just gone.

My family went to Orcas Island for a week, and when we get back your house has a For Sale sign and a Sold sign in front of it and it's empty. None of your neighbors know where you guys moved to, they just know that you're all fine.

What the hell, Brad? How can you just disappear like that? Did our friendship mean nothing to you? Does me doing one thing that you didn't like negate every other thing? Really? Is that how relationships work? Is that how you work?

I'm so confused and so hurt and just shocked.

And okay, I'm just going to say the thing that people never say out loud.

You're acting like I broke your heart. Even though you never told me it was mine to break. I'm not saying I didn't have some idea that you were into me. But also, I'm seventeen, so what do I really even know? I don't understand guys yet. Maybe I never will. But I thought I understood you. I thought we had a silent agreement that we would never ruin our friendship. I thought it was more important to both of us to always hang out with each other. Like, always always.

I'm also not saying that I didn't think about it. About things being different between us. More.

There were moments when you looked me straight in the eyes. When you stood so close to me, asking me about a book, so intense. You have gorgeous eyes. I hope you know that. I've stared at your hands. There's been moments when I've imagined those hands on my body. Exploring me. I've seen you look at my boobs. I've thought about you touching them. I didn't really let myself think about it before, but now I can't stop thinking about it.

I've stared at your mouth. You have a beautiful mouth, Bradley. I am 1000% sure no one else has said that to you. Yet. But you do. You look like you'd be a good kisser. And there were moments when I imagined you kissing me. Now I think about it all the time.

And fuck it, I might as well tell you this now: I had a sex dream about you. Back in February. We didn't actually have sex in the dream. Neither of us was naked or anything. There was just this…I don't know…intention? The way you looked at me. And I felt something. I was so attracted to you. In the dream. I woke up feeling all hot and bothered, as they say in the books. That was the day I kept my headphones on and refused to talk to you when we walked to school. That was why. You assumed it was my time of the month, but it was so much more than a monthly thing. It was the only time that's ever happened to me, and it freaked me out.

I've never wanted anyone like that. Not someone I actually know, I mean.

And you were planning to go to Princeton, so we only had a few more months together and I didn't want to ruin them.

Right now I'm really wishing I'd ruined things by grabbing you, just once, when you were grumbling about how you thought Pride & Prejudice is overrated and people should be talking more about Persuasion. I mean, if there was ever a moment when a guy should be kissed it's when he's ranting about how underrated his favorite Jane Austen book is.

And I wish you'd kissed me that time I came back from family vacation. Or when I'd fallen asleep on your shoulder. Or those times we were watching literally anything in your basement and your parents weren't home. I would have kissed you back. I would have liked it.

I'm not saying that to be mean. I just want you to know.

Or maybe I am saying it to be mean because I want you to feel as tortured about it as I do.

Maybe I'm only telling you this because I have a terrible feeling I'll never get to say this to your face. Maybe one day I'll forgive both of us for not trying harder.

I miss you.

I miss you.

I miss you.

You better miss me too.

From: viviansparksisawesome@gmail.com
To: thesmartbrad@gmail.com

Subject: Blech

Jul 7, 2017, 5:17 p.m.

I am so sick of summer and I am so mad at you for getting me started on binge-watching Lost and then abandoning me partway through Season 3. I have so many thoughts and no one else I know IRL has watched this show and I refuse to go online to discuss this with strangers. I have been missing you every day, but I have never felt lonelier in my life until now because I can't talk to anyone else about what a bunch of assholes these people are! Like, I wouldn't want to be friends with or date any of them!

Write me back. Please. Don't be an asshole. Don't make me go on Reddit.

From: viviansparksisawesome@gmail.com
To: thesmartbrad@gmail.com
Subject: Hi

Jul 30, 2017, 10:35 a.m.

Okay, so you're being an asshole.

It's been over a month and I can't believe I haven't heard from you.

I just can't believe you would ghost me, Bradley. I'm going to keep writing to you because I do believe you're still reading these emails and that maybe one day I'll say the thing that you need to hear in order to even consider the possibility that we can talk about maybe being friends again. If friends is what you want to be, that is.

I am saying to you now—and please believe me when I say that I have never said this to anyone else before and never thought I would—if you want me as more than a friend...if you want me in all the ways that a boy wants a girl, then I want you to understand that I want that with you too.

I am open to this.

I am open to talking about where we went wrong and how to get better at being each other's best friend and how to feel safe enough to love each other and fall in love and do awesome things to each other's bodies.

And if we aren't good at doing those things at first, then we will allow each other to get better at it until we are experts at making each other feel good in all the ways people can make each other feel good.

I want that.

I didn't know I wanted it until it was too late, apparently, but I want it and I want it with you.

If you want this with me and you're reading this, please, please, please write me back.

Just say hey.

I will take it from there.

But don't take advantage of my guilt. Don't try to make me feel worse than I already do about what happened. I don't even know that what I feel is guilt, to be honest. I feel so bad about what happened and I wish things had happened differently, but neither of us had all the information.

I feel like this is the most mature email I will ever send anyone, so I really hope it gets a response. If not,

I'll probably just go back to being how I was before. Whatever that was. Or who knows, maybe I'll go down a totally different path. But this is how I feel now. This is what I want. So there is no confusion.

Even though we're going to different schools in different states next month. Even though we have hurt each other. Even though I made you read Twilight and you read it even though you hated it.

From: viviansparksisawesome@gmail.com
To: thesmartbrad@gmail.com
Subject: I guess I'm an email stalker now?

Sept 15, 2017, 10:46 p.m.

Okay, now I am genuinely, actually mad at you. I can't believe I haven't heard from you at all. Are you even reading these emails? I don't think you are. I believe…I have to believe that if you read these emails you would at least respond in some way. Maybe you're just deleting them. If you are, it's because you're still hurt. I get it. But I'm not giving up until you tell me to.

I move into my dorm room next week, so I'll be busy. I'm going to limit my emails to you. I'm not giving up and if you reply, then I will, of course, respond. But I'm going to get on with my life now. I wish I could get on with it knowing that you're out there somewhere, not hating me.

You should have started classes at Princeton by now. I tried calling the registrar, and you'll be pleased

to know that it got me nowhere. I wasn't able to find out anything online. I still can't find you on social media. You're just gone. And yet Mrs. Chen says she's heard from your mom and that you're all fine. It's weird. But I believe everything Mrs. Chen says, so…
I'm glad you're fine, I guess.

From: viviansparksisawesome@gmail.com
To: thesmartbrad@gmail.com
Subject: ABC

Oct 7, 2017, 11:13 a.m.

So, I'm a college student. Are you? I have decided to continue Asshole Book Club.

I'm reading that book you told me about. S. by JJ Abrams and Doug Dorst. I had always planned to read it this summer when I could really enjoy it. But I thought I'd be able to talk to you about it while I read it. And then I didn't want to read it while I knew I couldn't talk to you about it. But now I just want to read it in the brief moments when I'm not studying or doing homework or being this amazing new college student version of myself that you're totally missing out on. Not that it feels like reading so much as scanning the pages.

Oh my God, I despise you, Bradley Mitchell.

I don't know why this is the thing that makes me feel your absence more than anything else. More than when I walked to school by myself. More than you icing me out. More than finally watching the last

season of Lost and not being able to vent about it with
you. There is literally no one else I can talk to about
how much I love this book. I love that it smells like an
old library book even though it's new.

I wish we had a book we had written notes in.

I love the entire physical experience of reading the
handwritten notes in the margins and unfolding the
letters and finding the postcards and everything that's
tucked between the pages! The mystery and the
puzzle of it.

I love the collaborative detective work between Jen
and Eric in the notes.

It's like an archeological dig. I'm obsessed. I stayed
in last night, stayed up way too late with this book.

I know I have to say something I hate about it. The
gimmick does overshadow the narrative, but I also
don't really care?

And I absolutely hate that it will always remind me
of you.

Wait, that's not right.

I hate that it will always remind me of how I
hurt you.

And how you won't forgive me for it.

From: viviansparksisawesome@gmail.com
To: thesmartbrad@gmail.com
Subject: Turtles

Dec 10, 2017, 3:27 a.m.

I finally got a chance to read the new John Green
book.

I stayed up all night.

I don't even care if I ever hear from you again, I just need you to read this book.

I say this as the only person you know, probably, who would ever encourage you to read a novel about two teenage girls. Or, idk, maybe you've started a whole new book club at Princeton with some skinny rich girl named Suzan with a Z, who has straight blonde hair and wears plaid skirts and headbands. If so, I hate her even more than I hate you.

But I still want you to read this book.

It's just a beautifully written portrayal of anxiety and OCD and the patience needed in order to have a lasting friendship and how people struggle to connect with each other. There's a mystery element that I just know you would say is underdeveloped and I also know you'd complain about how neatly things were wrapped up in the end. But the mystery gave it a structure. It's really just about the characters.

Maybe I loved the missing person piece of it because of, you know, you being missing. So since you aren't missing yourself, you might not be quite so intrigued by this. I also read Where'd You Go, Bernadette, but I knew you wouldn't read that one even if I really wanted you to now. You would have a year ago, though.

That makes me sad.

But anyway.

Hi.

I wonder if you'll be going home for the holidays.

I wonder where home is for you.

Now I'm getting mad at you again.

Read Turtles All the Way Down by John Green, you asshole.

I like UW well enough, but I still hate not talking to you and I hate you for not talking to me but I also miss you.

From: viviansparksisawesome@gmail.com
To: thesmartbrad@gmail.com
Subject: In the Woods

Mar 25, 2018, 8:17 p.m.

In the Woods by Tana French. Have you read it? I just tore through it. It's another missing person book. Missing child. Unsolved mystery. I should probably stop reading these, it's kind of depressing. But I guess it's comforting to me, knowing there are others who have to deal with unresolved stories.

Asshole commentary: I did figure things out before it was revealed. The ending was somewhat unsatisfying. But so is life, apparently!

I loved the way it was written. Those Irish authors, they really have a way with words.

I genuinely think you'd like this one. I don't think it would blow your mind or anything, I just think you'd enjoy reading it.

Or not.

I just don't know who else to recommend it to.

Hope you're well.

God, I hate writing that.

I do hope this email finds you well, though, and it's

kind of hilarious to me that I'm writing that at the end of the email.

From: viviansparksisawesome@gmail.com
To: thesmartbrad@gmail.com
Subject: Welp…

May 17, 2018, 10:37 p.m.

Okay. It's been a year. I'm done.

I hope you're alive.

I hope you're happy.

I am so, so mad at you.

Still.

It's a muted kind of anger, but it lingers.

I'm keeping you alive in my heart by being mad at you.

I wish we could be friends.

Or at least friendly.

Or at the very least I wish we could be two people who read the same books and email each other about them once in a while.

But I kind of hate you for hating me like this.

If you don't even hate me and you're just being a dick, then I hate you even more.

Regardless of what's going on with you, the way you just blew me off…it's not okay.

I don't deserve that.

But if it's what you need, then okay.

Fuck you, but okay.

But I also want to say this just once, because we never said it to each other: I loved you.

It makes me sad to be saying it in the past tense.

So, fuck it, I'll say it in the present tense, because I think if you really love someone then the love never really ends even though the relationship does.

I love you.

I love you as a friend.

I always thought you were great.

I never cared what anyone else thought about you.

I could have loved you in all the ways a person can love another person, I think. I wish you'd tried harder to love me. And I don't know if I'll ever forgive you for not giving me a chance to make things up to you. I hope I forgive you. I hope you forgive me.

I still have hope, but I'm letting you go.

I'm going to make a real effort to stop thinking about you now.

I just wanted you to know.

Goodbye, Brad.

From: thesmartbrad@gmail.com
To: viviansparksisawesome@gmail.com

Mar 10, 2025, 9:17 p.m.

Hey.
I'm coming over.

CHAPTER 25
BRAD

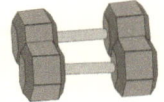

I t's raining.

It's raining, and my heart is racing as I drive to Vivian's house like I'm racing to the airport. She isn't about to board a flight, as far as I know, but I am absolutely running late. Eight years late. Maybe nine. I can't tell if my heart's racing because I have no idea how to say what I need to say to her or if it's because I just want to see her. *Need* to see her.

I am so fucking mad at myself. At eighteen-year-old me anyway. I was so hell-bent on protecting my ego that I forgot to protect *her* feelings.

I felt bad about putting Bella back into the guest bathroom after she'd been brave enough to emerge on her own and explore the condo, but she didn't fight me when I picked her up to take her back to her kennel. Her fortress. She seemed kind of relieved. That's probably how I'll feel when I go home after tonight. But maybe not. Maybe making Vivian feel good will be my new fortress.

I am equal parts relieved and annoyed that there is

plenty of parking on her street tonight. I pull up right in front of her little house. The front porch light is on. I haven't even checked my phone to see if she wrote me back. But I see a light through the part in the living room curtains and a shadow moving behind a curtain. As I park my car, I realize two things. One: I forgot to bring a jacket. Two: I haven't felt like this since the morning I walked to school with sparkles on my face. I wasn't even nervous when I was walking to school—that's the thing. It didn't even occur to me back then that anyone would come between us. When I slam the car door shut, Vivian's front door opens.

It is the strangest feeling, seeing her open her door to me like this. The way she did hundreds of times when I'd walk to her house back when we were in school. There's hesitance in her posture now, the way she rests a hand against the doorframe, but she doesn't look much different. Her hair is down. She's barefoot, wearing loose-fitting wide-leg pants that sit low on her hips, and a cropped sweatshirt. Much like I did when I was a teenager, all I want to know now is whether or not she's wearing a bra under there. Will I get to see her boobs? I am a lot more confident about seeing her boobs tonight than I ever was back in Seattle, but I feel like I'm coming home.

I stride up the path, and by the time I take the stairs up to the porch, she's opened the door wider and stepped through the doorway with the confidence of a woman who knows she's about to get what she wants. And nothing's stopping me from giving it to her. Not even me.

I wrap my arms around her shoulders, she wraps her arms around my waist, pressing the side of her face against my chest. I hold her so tight, kissing the top of her head, stroking the back of her neck with my fingers. "I'm so sorry," I exhale into her hair.

She grabs onto the back of my shirt, tilting her head back in a silent invitation to let me show her how sorry I am.

I kiss her forehead. Her cheek. I cup her beautiful face in my hands and kiss her mouth. Once, twice. Soft and slow with my lips parted just a little, stroking her jaw. And then I claim her with my mouth, my tongue, confirming her teenage suspicion that I am a good kisser. Pushing her hair aside, I kiss across her jaw and down her neck. "I'm sorry. I'm sorry. I'm sorry." Something sticks to my tongue. Her necklace. That pretty little gold necklace. She tastes clean, which means she wore the necklace in the shower, and that makes me so happy on top of all the other things I'm feeling. I kiss back up her neck, her cheek, her forehead, her mouth, her forehead again.

She sighs, her knees give out a little, she rests her forehead against my chest. We settle back into another long hug. Rubbing her back, I say, "I had no idea I'd hurt you that much, Sparky. I didn't think you'd miss me the way I missed you."

"Well, you could have just read the emails..." she mutters. Still sassy even as I cover her with kisses and apologies.

Thank God.

But also—fair. "I thought you were mad." My arms circle her waist. She's already more toned than she was a week ago, and it makes me proud but also achy. Partly because I'm not her trainer anymore and partly because I like her soft spots. "I only saw the subject line of the first one, and then I set it up so your emails would go to a hidden folder."

I let one hand wander up her back, under the bottom of her cropped shirt.

"I didn't know how many you sent. I was determined to move on, and the only way I knew how to do that was by not engaging at all."

God dammit. No bra.

I stroke the sides of her waist and kiss her before saying, "I was so crazy about you, Vivi. I hid it really well back then, but you would not believe how much I like you now."

"Come inside and show me how much," she says, tugging at the bottom of my shirt. "No jacket…," she says as she glides her hands up my wet shirt sleeves to my wet face.

"No bra…" I take her hand and pull her through the front door. "Thank you," I say as I close the door behind her, because I am about to forget everything I need to tell her about eight years ago. "For what you wrote. For writing to me even when I didn't write you back."

She looks up at me, slow-blinking, sliding her hands up under my shirt.

I cup her sweet, beautiful face in my hands, groaning and kissing her all over. I'll never be able to look at this face and not kiss it. "I hate everyone who ever hurt you, but I was the worst. Why do you forgive me?"

"I've met a lot of guys, and you're the only one I've missed. I haven't found anyone else I like as much as you," she says, without hesitation. Pulling back to look me in the eyes, she adds, "Although I could run off with

Cindy and the girls at any moment, so don't fuck up again, all right?"

She studies my face, and I must be too horny to hide the fact that I have zero confidence in not fucking things up again. "Hey," she says, holding my face. "Hey. You don't have to change who you are now. I just want you to be real with me. Okay?"

I nod. It is okay. My body has known for God knows how long what my brain is finally ready to accept—that this thing I've been so afraid of, loving Vivian without limits, will be my life's work and my salvation. "You are the most perfect woman who ever lived."

"I know."

Lowering my forehead to rest against hers, I say, "There is so much I need to tell you."

"I'm not going anywhere, so you can tell me later. Talk to my body first."

My. Life's. Work.

"You got it. I also hated the way *Lost* ended, by the way, but we can talk about that later too. Turn around and put your hands against the wall."

Her kind brown eyes flash with excitement, but she turns around very calmly and slowly, leaning forward to place her hands flat against the wall above her head. Her gorgeous round ass is sticking out toward me, and when I tilt my head, I get a satisfying glimpse of underboob. *That's my girl.*

But right now, I am focusing my attention and adoration on the expanse of bare skin between the loose waistband of her pants and the bottom of that cropped sweatshirt. I wrap my hands around her waist and stroke upward, letting my thumbs trace the heavenly curves along that valley of the small of her back. "You have excellent lumbar alignment, you know that?" I push my groin up against her ass, keeping my words and hands controlled even as things get rough from the waist down. "Your lumbar curve is perfect and so sexy."

"Thank you." She pushes back into my growing erection, wiggling around. Playing dirty in the most innocent way and driving me wild.

"Your hips." I massage her luscious hips. "I get dizzy thinking about your fucking beautiful, round hips."

"Brought to you by banana cream pie and weighted hip thrusts."

"Yesssss." Untying the drawstring of her pants, just below her belly, I discover that the sides of her panties are extremely thin. Thin straps. "What have we here?" Pulling back as I lower her pants, letting them drop to her ankles, I find raspberry-red-colored ribbons creating a V across the back of her waist and disappearing between two magnificent globes.

And my brain has stopped working.

"It's called a lace adjustable V-string panty. Do you like it? I ordered it the day after I first saw you at the gym."

I make a sound that could unfairly be described as a whimper. A very masculine whimper. In my defense—this is the best ass I have ever had my hands on. I grunt, lowering myself to kneel on the floor so I can simultaneously fondle those two magnificent globes and let my mouth and tongue and teeth do all the insane things they need to do to them for, like, thirty uninhibited seconds.

Her gasps are felt more than heard over my moans.

Remembering there is so much more of her to explore, I take a steadying breath before standing up again and get myself out of these stupid shoes and pants and boxer briefs. "So, that would be a yes, I like it... Walk me through your evening."

She's squeezing her thighs together. I use my knee to spread them apart, stroke my cock a couple of times, bend my knees as I close the space between my chest and her back. And then I let my erection inhabit that warm, wet space between her legs. She's still wearing that tiny strip of fabric she calls panties. She rocks and rolls her hips. Stroking her outer thighs and up, up, up, I say, "You get home from the gym. I'm at my place, being emotionally devastated while reading your emails. You walk through that door, take off your workout clothes, get in the shower..." Finally, my hands connect with boob and I can't speak anymore.

"I fed Hairy Styles his wet food first."

I groan. "Fuck, your tits are amazing."

"Thank you. How's your kitty doing?"

I play with her nipples and then massage her breasts. "Bella. She's great. I let her out of her room for a little bit."

"Oh my God," she exhales, for not-cat reasons. "Brad." She clenches around my cock, and it is pure heavenly torture. After a minute, she continues. "Are you really calling her Bella?"

"I am... So, you took a shower, dried off your silky smooth skin, and then thought to yourself, *I'll just put on these V-string panties and a crop top in case my old friend Bradley shows up all in his feelings and I can punish him by being the hottest woman he's ever known*?"

She blows out a laugh. "Pretty much."

"See, this is one of the main reasons I like you so much." I pull away from her, my cock bouncing up as I spin her around to face me. "You are diabolical." Pressing my hands against the wall on either side of her head, caging her in, I lean in to kiss her. She does the best, friendliest thing ever and reaches down to stroke and cup the parts of me that really need to be handled right now.

Then she does a mean thing. She stops stroking and cupping and kissing me so she can pull my shirt up over my head and run her hands all over my pecs and abs. "You are so beautiful, Bradley."

"Yeah, yeah."

"No. You are. You know that, right?"

I wrestle her sweatshirt off over her head and stare at her tits. "Yeah." I dip down to kiss them. Suck her nipple into my mouth, because that is exactly where it needs to be. In my mouth. I need to figure out a way for us to have productive lives day-to-day while her nipple is in my mouth. This is exactly what I was afraid of—this over-whelming need to be in her and on her and with her all the time. And I'm just gonna lean into the obsession.

"Bradley, I want to make sure you understand how amazing it is that you did this for yourself. Do you?"

I can't think or see straight, much less use my mouth for talking about my body. I give her other nipple some attention, because I like both of them equally and I want both of them to like me. I feel drunk. I feel like a teenager. I am so in love.

"Condoms?" is all I can say right now.

"Bedroom. I ordered those the same night I ordered the panties," she says.

You are so, so perfect is what I'm thinking as I lift her up and carry her to the bedroom, folded over my shoulder. Vivian squeals, and that is perfect. I drop her onto the mattress and her tits bounce and they are perfect. She lies back, resting on her elbows. The curves, all of them, from her collarbone down to her toes...they're perfect, and the lace front of those raspberry-red panties are perfect, and I pull them down her legs and place them at the end of the bed, because they are tiny and special and must not be lost, not ever.

And then I find a condom packet in the drawer of her bedside table, roll it on, ask, "Where's Hairy Styles?"

"Probably under the bed in the guest room."

"Ah." And then I grab her ankles, yank her closer to me and the edge of the mattress, flip her onto her stomach, grip her hips, pulling her up onto her knees and elbows, and push into her. Hard. We both cry out from the sudden shock of it. So tight. So perfect. I wait for her to exhale a loud sigh, accept the way I fill her up, before pressing on her back, encouraging her to lie flat on her stomach, and then climb on top of her. Holding myself up, caging her between my arms, I can be closer to her as I plunge in and out. In and out. Her amazing ass beneath me. She is languid and receptive and humming. She presses up on her elbows, arching her back, tilting her head so it's closer to mine. I can lean down and say into her ear, "You're mine, you're mine, you're mine."

"Yes! Bradley, yes." She tilts her hips, puts more weight on her knees, thrusting back to meet my thrusts, so I can penetrate her at different angles, so deep, and get her screaming. This is so good for her core and her entire lower body.

"Good, baby, so good."

Everything accelerates.

I maintain this frantic rhythm, fucking my girl and

somehow maintaining my sanity because I am so focused on making her come. On feeling those spasms around my cock, hearing her scream my name, the name she wants to call me—Brad. I am the only Brad, the only Brad who gets to fuck her and make her come, the only man, ever, ever, ever.

Her orgasm is bold and stunning and forgiving.

She melts into the comforter, and I rock my hips gently, giving her a moment.

When she's humming again, I grab her wrists and pin her down with my entire body weight. My legs wrap around hers. I engulf her. Dominate her entire body. She is mine, mine, mine.

She turns her head, moaning, begging for a kiss.

I kiss her and circle one arm under her neck, gripping her shoulder, pulling her closer, squeezing her tit with the other hand. "I want you in every way a man can want a woman, Vivian."

"Yes."

"I'm gonna take you in ways you didn't know you could give yourself to me."

"Good."

"I spent a lot of years imagining all the ways I can have you, even when I didn't want to."

"You always wanted to."

"Yes. Fucking yes, I never stopped. I'll never stop." I'm not going to lie—there's still resentment there, with each possessive thrust. So much resentment at her for owning me so completely, so much anger at myself for wasting so much time not having her. It's a savage love in this moment, and I'll own it and surrender myself to it. Now and over and over.

I kiss her shoulder, her cheekbone. She presses herself up to meet me, that beautiful round ass welcoming and taunting me and driving me wild with desire. Over a decade's worth of lust for this woman is bursting forth. She clenches around me and sends me over the edge. Even when I'm pinning her down, she is in total control of my cock and my life. I feel her bracing herself so I can give it all to her, and I do.

All the heat and the blinding white light and the blackness and all the stars.

Every inch and every ounce and all the fire and everything that makes me *me*...I give it to her.

Surrendering to this, to her, is the bravest thing I've ever done, and the relief is better than anything I've ever known.

CHAPTER 26
VIVIAN

"I just have to say that I'm really, really proud of you for having a perfect penis. I mean it. It's really good. Ten out of ten, no notes. And you really know what you're doing with it too."

"Wow. Ten out of ten, huh?"

"You sound disappointed. I was negging you because you're pretty. It's actually twenty out of ten."

"Thank you. That feels more accurate."

"Never neg the peen, am I right?"

"Probably just don't call it a peen, ever."

"Okay, but full disclosure, I already texted Aubrey about your marvelous peen yesterday and we started calling it Captain Peen." I grimace at him. Brad. Bradley. Mitch. Brad Mitchell. My best friend from high school that I'm friends with and having sex with and a lot of feelings.

The cutest smile spreads across his handsome face. "I will allow it. Because I can do this all day." He still does an amazing Captain America impression.

"Yay. I got you to dimple-smile."

We're lying in bed—or on the bed, rather. Still on top of the comforter, facing each other. We are deep into the after-course. We've already passed out, cleaned up, fell asleep again, woken up again, put on our undies. I put on a real pair of panties because the V-strap thing is ridonkulous. It's, like, ten thirty or eleven. I want him to sleep over, but I also want him to be a good cat daddy and go home to keep her company. Things are so complicated already. My biggest problem right now is that I cannot stop touching his hot, hot body.

"I also have to know how you got these V-lines." I trace the muscles between his lower abs and his hips. "They are top notch and very hot, and I'm wondering how I can get them too."

"Well, first of all, thank you. I prefer to call this my Adonis belt. Mine aren't all that well defined, but I have twelve percent body fat and I have been doing consistent core work for, like, seven and a half years, three to four times a week. V-ups, hanging leg raises, Russian twists."

"I can do Russian twists!"

"Yeah you can. More importantly, though, very disciplined eating. Defined abs are made in the kitchen."

"Okay, never mind. I don't want them. But I'm really glad you have them."

"Thanks. Planks are also good—you can do those. Did you have a good session today? At the gym?"

"Oh my God, yes! I made Gwen almost laugh twice, and we spent extra time on stretching at the end."

"No wonder you were so limber. Might have to give Gwen a raise."

I start to stroke Captain Peen over his boxer briefs, because it's about to be an all-hands-on-deck situation down there, but I realize Hairy Styles has just jumped onto the bed.

Which is amazing, because Hairy used to hate Brad and the only guy he ever shared a bed with before was Jeremy. And he really didn't like Jeremy all that much either. But he swaggers right on over to Brad, sniffing his leg, as if he recognizes him. Brad holds his breath and doesn't move. Hairy turns around a couple of times and then curls up right between Brad's legs and mine.

I carefully move my hand away from Brad's body and cover my mouth because oh my God, this is amazing. Brad's mouth is open, and he still won't move or breathe. We look at each other and silently mouth *Oh my God!* This is a sign. Hairy Styles is giving us his blessing. This is the best thing that has ever happened to us since Brad and I had amazing sex just now.

"Good boy, Hairy!" I say.

Brad shushes me.

"He's not going to leave—look at him."

"This is very cool."

"It's so good."

"He looks great. Do you think he can tell I'm a cat guy now?"

"I mean, I think everyone can tell. You had cat hair all over your shirt."

"I wish."

We just lie together smiling at each other, barely breathing.

All because I'm such an amazing email writer and Brad finally stopped being an idiot.

"I have to tell you something," he says.

I start touching his pecs and biceps again, very gently, so it doesn't disturb Hairy Styles or Captain Peen.

"Are you listening?"

"Yes. I'm listening with my ears, but my hands aren't paying much attention to what you're saying."

"That really fucking works for me. So, the reason I was extra pissed off about what happened with Brad Turner and prom is that I was planning to stay in Seattle so I could be with you."

"When?"

"After we graduated. I mean, at the end of April I deferred my spot at Princeton. I was accepted to both schools, remember, and you seemed so sad that I chose Princeton."

"I never blamed you for wanting to go to Princeton—"

"I know. But it was too late to register at UW, so I was going to take a gap year and then go to UW in 2018. I was gonna surprise you. But it seemed kind of intense, giving up Princeton for you."

"Wow."

"Yeah."

I put my hand over his heart. "Bradley." Now I'm tearing up. "I wish you'd told me."

He shrugs. "Anyway. I didn't need a degree from Princeton to become a personal trainer, so…"

"Wow. I mean. Everything happened for a reason, I guess, right?" It's so easy to say those words, but the thought of him deferring his spot at Princeton so he could be with me before all that happened with Other Brad…it's just too much. No wonder he was so mad. But also, he should have told me. It would have changed everything.

"Don't cry, baby." He wipes a tear from my cheek with

his thumb. "I didn't want to make you sad. I just wanted you to know how much you meant to me." I make a happy-sad little kitty-cat sound and rub my cheek against his hand. "How much you *mean* to me. So much."

"Oh my God, your parents must have been so upset."

He exhales. "They were not happy about it."

I have this realization all of a sudden. "Oh my God. Did your parents make you stay away from me because you gave up Princeton for me?" This is so much more romantic and acceptable to my brain.

"I mean…no. That was all me."

"Oh."

"My mom was actually pretty upset that I didn't want her talking to you or your mom at all."

"Oh. Well, that is nice to hear. So can our parents be friends again now?"

"Yeah. I look forward to giving mine the good news."

I'm about to mention how happy my mom will be to have two more people to talk about Aubrey's wedding to, when I realize I still haven't got a date to that wedding yet…

He slowly reaches down to touch Hairy's neck and Hairy doesn't move, so he strokes his fur, as sweetly as he stroked my cheek just now. And I know I need to lock this guy down, like, yesterday. I clear my throat and say, "So, I have this event on Orcas Island in June…"

"Aubrey's wedding?" he asks without looking up.

"Yeah. How are your weekends looking that month?"

"If you want me to go as your date, Vivian, I am available to go as your date."

"Yeah? That was easy."

"Yeah, well. I'm easy."

We both laugh at that, because it was so *not* easy to get to this place with him. "Okay. Well, I'll tell Aubrey I'm bringing you as my date, then." I roll over onto my back and look up at the ceiling. "Brad Mitchell is my date…"

He sighs, stops touching Hairy Styles, and strokes my arm. "Hey. I meant what I said—I do want you in all the ways a man wants a woman, Vivi. I have no idea if I'll be good at this. But I want to be good at it."

And because I would like to think that *I'm* the one training and challenging *him* now, I look him in the eyes and whisper, "Be good at what? Exactly?"

"Relationship-type stuff."

"Serious-relationship-type stuff?"

He smirks. "Boyfriend-type stuff. Too soon?"

Grinning, I say, "Bradley, you are right on time." I sit up, because it feels like I should sit up to say this. "If we do this, I can't promise that I won't hurt you again—I can only promise that I want to learn how to love you in a way that you will always know I never want to hurt you."

He sits up too, very carefully, checking to make sure he's not disturbing Hairy. "Okay. Same."

"Okay." I lean in to kiss him.

He kisses me softly, touches my face. "I should go home and check on Bella."

I nod. "Yeah. We can stay at your place next time."

He nods, kisses my forehead. "Let's do that tomorrow. I had fun tonight."

Laughing, I ask, "What should I call that sex position we did when I text Aubrey about it as soon as you leave? Lazy doggy style?"

"Excuse me? That was called Captain Peen: Brave New

Dog. Between the two of us, I was definitely not the lazy one."

We're so cute.

Beaming at him, I wrap my hands around his bicep and say, "I love us."

I only feel him tense up a little bit. I want to tell him I love him, because I know I do. But love is a muscle. We've already worked our love muscles pretty hard the past few days. And I've learned that we need to take rests, so our torn love-muscle fibers can repair themselves and grow stronger.

What I do say to him is "In case it wasn't obvious, I forgive you for being a dick and ghosting me. I forgive us for being young and scared of what other people think."

"I forgive you too," he says, nudging my shoulder with his. "I don't forgive Other Brad and his shithead friends, though."

"Oh, me neither. They're forever the worst. Everyone else from high school is still an idiot. It's just you and me out here being awesome, mature grown-ups who have muscles and cats and great sex and talk like adults."

He stares at me, his eyes travel all around my face. My eyes, my mouth. He lifts up my chin with two fingertips and says, "I love you, Vivian. I knew I loved you that summer you went to Orcas Island with your family. I know now that I never stopped loving you even when I hated you." He exhales, as if he just lifted his weight in words.

And then he kisses me, and I say into his kiss, "I love you too."

And then I let him go home so both of us can give our

racing, broken, healing hearts a chance to repair themselves some more.

CHAPTER 27
BRAD

Emotional Fitness Journal—March 24

Today's Intention: *1. Continue being a relentlessly awesome boyfriend. 2. Try not to text her every ten minutes.*

The Four F's of Good TransFORMation

FLOW: *I'm working on letting my feelings flow through me instead of burning everything to the ground. Every time I open up to her, instead of stoking the old fire, I feel relief. There is passion without limits. There is a powerful charge from desire, even without the conflict of trying to control it. Aside from the obvious restraint from tearing her clothes off and fucking her senseless in public. I have so far been successful at waiting until we're mostly alone before turning into a savage beast with my cock out.*

Also, I can actually feel my heart expanding every time I hold Bella. She fell asleep in my lap last night, and I didn't move until she woke up. It was the longest I'd stayed still while being awake in eight years. Literally. I loved it. I spent the entire time talking to Vivian on the phone. When I called her, she answered in a panic, because apparently it was the first time I'd phoned her without texting first. She thought maybe something was wrong with Bella. But I just wanted to hear her voice. It was the first night we'd spent apart in over a week, and I missed her. It was crazy how much I missed her. Even while I was talking to her on the phone, I missed her. But it felt good because everything she makes me feel now is good.

FOUNDATION: *I can feel myself creating a life built on love and trust, not fear and control. I like it. It works. People need emotional nourishment too—I get it now. Her love and acceptance isn't conditional upon my performance or the way I look. It never was. Although I'm not gonna lie and say that I don't like how much she likes the way I look now. This is some kind of cosmic fuel that's going to get me through everything as long as I'm doing it for and with her.*

FREEDOM: *My boundaries are strong enough to be vulnerable and secure enough to let her in.*
I've been very honest with her about how she's turned my professional world upside down. Not literally in a chaotic way, but the new identity I created when I killed off that part of me that hurt too much...I don't know what to do with that guy anymore.

I still need the fire and the fuel and the fortress and the fractures for my brand to work. I think. It's going to be about integrating all these new things. Reintegrating the parts I didn't think I could handle. I don't know. Just admitting that I don't know, to myself and to her...that wasn't something I could even think about doing a month ago. But she doesn't push me to do anything one way or another. She just listens. Validates me. She is beautiful in a million different simple and astonishing ways, but in this way, she is breathtaking and without equal.

I used to think freedom meant not needing anyone. Turns out it means trusting the right ones.

FUSION: *Where we come together and I don't fall apart.*

All those places where I thought I was broken—that's exactly where we fit together. And I will spend the rest of my life making sure she never feels abandoned again.

YOU: *Today is your birthday. You are special and worth celebrating every single day of the year, but today is the day we celebrate your birth. That's why I'm sharing the first entry of my Emotional Fitness Journal with you. Because this is also a day to celebrate my re-rebirth, thanks to you. It's all pretty fucking cheesy, but I don't hate it.*

I transformed myself because I thought it was the only way I could get over you, and now you're transforming me, just by being you. And by being really good at fellatio. It took me eight years to build up my resistance to you, and it took you seven days to break me down. I'm not mad about it. I'm not mad about anything anymore because I'm so fucking in love with you. I mean, I still contain within me a sufficient amount of rage in order to aggressively remove your clothing by any means necessary, because fuck that clothing for trying to create a barrier between my eyes and mouth and hands and cock and any part of you.

I can't stop thinking about last night with you.

I can't stop thinking about any time with you. For instance, the time before last night when I was going down on you and you came so hard you kicked a lamp off your bedside table and bruised your hand when you flung it against the head of the bed. To be clear, I do not regret making you come that hard, but I am sorry you broke your very cool lamp and I'm sorry you bruised your very pretty and very capable hand.

However, I am very pleased that after you responded by holding back when I inevitably brought you to orgasm with my mouth and fingers last night, we agreed that a better way to prevent such accidents from happening again would be to tie you up. So you could be unrestrained in your restraints. So I could do all the things I love to do to you that force you to work your core and tense every muscle in your body until they release with a jolt and a loud sigh and my name on your lips.

The way you give yourself to me, Vivian. Your love, your trust, your body, your light. Every day it is and will be my intention to give back to you. With more trips to Powell's Books so we can walk hand in hand down the aisles. With as many hikes as you'll allow me to take you on. As much Cheat Day artisanal ice cream as you can handle.

You are my Aries queen, and I can't wait to ram into you tonight. Cindy said this is "peak Aries fire season." She said you were born when winter dies and everything comes back to life. She said that's what you've been doing to my heart. She is not wrong. About anything, it seems.
I have eight birthday presents for you, not counting this one.

They don't make up for the time we lost, and that debt will never be cleared, even when you say it is, but I do look forward to giving these presents to you.

I can't wait to see you at the gym later and then drinks with Larry and the girls, and then I will finally, finally have you all to myself again. I honestly don't know if I have the strength to wait that long.

You were always the strong one, Vivian. I see it so clearly now. It was always you.
Vivian Elizabeth "Sparky" Sparks.
Happy birthday to you.

PS: I think we need to introduce Bella to Hairy Styles soon. We're all going to be spending a lot of time together, going forward.

CHAPTER 28
VIVIAN

June

Granny Sparks keeps laughing at me, but I haven't even said anything funny yet.

I think she's just giddy about my dreamy boyfriend and she's trying to steal my date.

She is also amused by me standing up here with a glass of champagne in one hand and a microphone in the other, because everyone who knows me knows that I hate public speaking. Unless drunk-singing "Summer Nights" counts as public speaking. And I might have to start telling everyone about what a blast I had last summer, because I don't have a maid-of-honor speech prepared.

My mom, who is at least two and a half sheets to the wind, is visibly crossing herself, praying that I don't fuck this up and embarrass the whole family—and she isn't even Catholic.

This is all Brad's fault. By "all Brad's fault" I mean it's all thanks to him being a personal trainer who's good at motivating people, because he convinced me I should just wing it. He said I'm so good at speaking from the heart and no matter what I had planned I would probably just end up winging it anyway. And then he distracted me by doing magical mouth things to my clitoris and entire vulval region, so my brain never got back around to stressing about how I had to compose the perfect speech.

I look over at Brad, frowning at him. But he is so damn handsome in that navy-blue suit that makes his green eyes pop. And his dark hair is just so...*unh.* And I love it when he has stubble, but he shaved, so his jawline is just...*hoo-ah!* And his butt in those suit pants is just...*wowza.* And I mean everyone has been ogling my date today, but he is *mine.*

And he's widening his eyes at me, reminding me that I am supposed to say words about my sister the bride up here.

"Um. You're probably wondering why I've summoned all of you here..." I say into the mic. *Classic.*

"Tell me more, tell me more!" Granny Sparks hollers from the seat next to my date.

"*Uh-huh, doo-doo, uh-huh!*" I glance over at my sister, who looks so beautiful and...damp...and happy...and only slightly impatient with me. "Yes. Aubrey. This is a toast to the beautiful bride, my big sister, Aubrey. Looking around, it's nice to see all the people Aubrey cares about gathered here under one deluxe heavy-duty wedding tent. This way it will be so much easier for her to tell each of us what's best for us. And let us all, truly, be glad for this, because the thing about Aubrey is—she isn't just telling us what's best for us because she thinks she's right about everything. It's because she really does care for us and really does want the best for us. And also because she's right about everything. Which is why she keeps track of the weather where we live. She thinks of everything for everyone she cares about. It just somehow never occurred to her that it might rain on Orcas Island during her outdoor ceremony on her wedding day…"

I wait for the loving laughter and cheers to subside before continuing. "Seriously, though, I'm sure you all agree that it was the surprise thunderstorm that made today especially memorable. But another thing I will never let my sister forget is that *I* was the one who thought to bring rainboots for her and everyone else in the wedding party—just in case."

Aubrey holds her champagne flute up to me. "Well played, sis."

People applaud for me, and I actually receive it. I'm still not sure that I deserve the title maid of *honor*, but I'm working on the whole feeling-worthy thing. I did carry the train of her beautiful wedding gown as she walked out of the hotel and down the very wet lawn path to the arbor for the ceremony. And I did rock the bachelorette tea party last weekend by bringing penis-shaped teaspoons. And whiskey. In a penis-shaped decanter. Her on-again, off-again BFF Jenna is rooting for me to fail, but I am, unfortunately, nailing it.

"And well played to you as well, sis." I raise my glass to her and Eric, immediately regretting it, because I have raised it way too early in the game. Now I'm going to have to hold it up like this for a very long time. Good thing I have such strong biceps. And the iron will to make my sister cry. "I think about all the times I've had the pleasure of being around Aubrey and her *husband*, Eric. How when they're with a group of people, like today, they always make sure everyone feels included. Seen. Heard. Told what to do. But even when they're talking to other people, they're always connecting with each other. Eric always somehow has his hand on Aubrey's leg or on her hand or he's rubbing the small of her back if she's nearby. Aubrey's always looking across a crowded room to make eye contact with him for a second even when she's busy making someone else feel like all of her attention is on them.

"My sister knew she wanted to marry Eric after their first date, around three and a half-years ago. And she wasn't impatient either. She was perfectly happy to spend years getting to know him while she waited for him to get his act together and finally propose. And I remember being kind of in awe of that. Not the patience, but that *knowing*. Because at the time, I hadn't experienced it myself."

I look over at Aubrey, who is clearing her throat, and her eye makeup is still a bit smudged from the rain, but she is definitely not crying. *Nice try*, she mouths to me.

"I owe so much to Aubrey and Eric. Through them, I met Eric's friend Jeremy..." Silence befalls at least half the people under this canopy. Not total silence, because of the pitter-patter of raindrops on the polyester fabric above us, but more silence than I was expecting. I suppose not everyone here got the memo that I'm not *Poor Vivian* anymore, that I am in fact super happy Vivian with the extremely hot and literate boyfriend, the one they've all been staring at.

I glance over at Jeremy, whose jaw is almost always tight, but it looks like he's grinding his molars to dust.

Duckface is seated at a nearby table and looks like she wishes she could disappear under it, and not for fun reasons.

"What I mean is I had the great good fortune of meeting Eric's handsome, charismatic friend Jeremy, we started dating, and I moved with him to Portland when he got a great job there. And at the end of last year, he decided to move back to Seattle to be with his lovely fiancée, Duck..." I look over at Aubrey, who is covering her mouth because she's laughing at me.

"His lucky duck...beautiful face...Langley. They're here tonight and they're such a wonderful couple, yay!" I slap the inside of my bare arm repeatedly, with the hand that's holding the microphone, making loud humping noises and encouraging people to applaud for Jeremy and Duckface. While they applaud them and Jeremy nods at me from his seat at the opposite end of the head table, I take a quick sip of champagne because *yeesh*.

"So, after Jeremy left Portland, I stayed there. And I had the opportunity to meet so much delicious pie and artisanal ice cream and tacos and wine, and well...as much as I loved getting to know myself and all those carbs again, I wasn't doing as great as I thought I was.

"And Aubrey wanted the best for me. So she tracked down the person she knew was the best person for me. Someone I hadn't seen in a long time. It's only a little terrifying that she hired a private investigator to find him..."

Aubrey grimaces, reaches over to squeeze Eric's knee, and I realize she never mentioned this to Eric.

"Super chill and low-key, though, Eric! I just want to emphasize how loving and generous a big-sisterly act this was. Because it changed my life. For the better. For the best. In so many ways. And his too." I smile at Brad. But I can feel my eye twitching because *God dammit, Granny Sparks, get your hand off his shoulder.* "I know who I want now. I remember who I am now. I know what I deserve. And it's all because of you, Aubrey. Let's raise our glasses to my sister, who is always right—except for that one time when I was in high school when she sort of ruined every-thing—and her husband, who gets to acknowledge how right she is forever and ever, amen. I love you, Aubrey! Cheers!"

Finally, I gulp down my champagne, hand the micro-phone to my dad, who pats me on the back and says, "Thanks for not saying the F-word," and I go over to Eric to give him a hug.

Then Aubrey stands up and gives me a hug, and I stage-whisper into her ear, "I just realized you totally planned for it to rain on your outdoor wedding so no one would be able to tell when you were crying."

She pulls back and frowns at me. And then she smirks. "No regrets. My hair looks amazing when it's wet."

"It really does. And don't worry." I take her hands in mine. "Your secret's safe with me, you witch."

She looks behind me and sighs. "You should see the way he looks at you, Vivi," she says, clearing her throat. And that's when I know for sure that she is going to cry. "He's always watching out for you. He loves you so much. You know that, right?"

"I do."

"I'm so glad." She touches my face as mascara-stained tears stream down hers. "I'm so glad you got this second chance."

"It's all because of you—don't cry. How is your mascara not waterproof?"

She waves her hand dismissively, sniffling. "I don't even care. You're really for-real happy now, aren't you?"

"So happy." I reach for a napkin to dab at her cheeks.

"It's all I wanted. You deserve to be so happy."

"I know. Stop crying. I don't like it."

"Okay. Is my face a mess now?"

"No, you look so beautiful." I dab beneath her eyes one more time. "This is how the kids are wearing eye makeup now, so as always, you are right and perfect."

She inhales and sighs. "Yeah."

Eric's best man taps at his glass, so Aubrey and I take our seats.

I stare across two tables, at Bradley. Granny and her boyfriend are talking his ear off, and he's nodding and laughing but smiling at me. He's doing that thing where I always feel like he's with me, even though we have to sit at different tables during dinner. He does make me feel so comfortable. We're still in the blissful new part of dating, but since we knew each other for years when we were teenagers, despite all that time apart, it still feels very cozy when we're alone together.

I even tooted once after eating a breakfast burrito a couple of Sundays ago, and instead of being mortified like I would have been around Jeremy for the entire two years we lived together, I thought of what Aubrey had said about being comfortable with Eric and I looked directly at Bradley and laughed. He also laughed. So far he has not tooted around me, which makes me angry. The good news is we know a lot of fun ways to work through our anger.

When the toasts are over and Aubrey is dancing with

Dad to "Steal My Girl" by One Direction, because she didn't want to cry, I get up to join Brad at his table. As I pass by Jeremy's end of the head table to get there, he nods at me again. I nod back. This has been the extent of our conversations this weekend, and it's really all we need to say to each other at this point. Before I reach my destination, I feel a tap on my arm and turn to find Duckface looking at me.

I had only ever seen her in pictures before, and in every single one of them she was making a model-y duckface. Apparently that's just her face. "Hi. I'm Langley."

"I figured—hi. Nice to meet you." I hold out my hand to shake hers, and she takes it.

Her hand is smooth and cold, as expected, but she seems nice enough.

In my peripheral vision I can see Brad sauntering over, slowly, staying slightly out of the way, just being nearby in case I need him. Or in case he decides I need him.

Langley keeps glancing over at him, because of course she does. But she says to me, "I just wanted to thank you for saying what you said in your speech. It was kind of you. I was really nervous about coming to this event. I almost didn't."

"Oh, well, I'm glad you did. I hope you're having a good time."

She scans my expression, because my tone suggested I wasn't only asking about the wedding. Blinking, she lowers her chin and tucks her hair behind her ear and says, "Of course. Everything's perfect."

"Okay. Great. Well, enjoy the rest of your night." I give her arm a little consoling rub, because I actually kind of feel sorry for the lying, cheating duckface.

Brad takes two strides and he's by my side with his arm around my waist. "She definitely looked like she wanted to run away screaming."

"Huh?"

"Because you're so hot."

"What are you talking about, you nutjob?" I wrap my arms around his neck and kiss his neck.

"You don't remember?"

"Nuh-uh."

"Your first day at the gym. I asked you for your motivation for getting in shape." He leans in and whispers into my ear. "You said you wanted Jeremy to jizz in his pants and his fiancée to run away screaming because you're so hot."

My jaw drops. "I would never."

"Oh, but you did, when pressed."

"Isn't it funny that I don't even care? I guess being happy and in love is the best revenge."

"Happy and in love and strong and hot." He kisses the top of my head. "Fantastic maid-of-honor toast."

"I know! I slayed."

"You did... Oh, hang on." He pulls his phone out from inside his suit jacket. It's vibrating. "It's Larry FaceTiming me. We should take this."

"Oh no." We hustle over to a corner of the tent, away from the speakers. Larry and Cindy are checking on Bella and Hairy Styles while we're out of town. Both cats are staying at my place because we thought it would be better than leaving Bella alone for three days. Brad accepts the video call, and as soon as I see Larry and Cindy's faces, I say, "Are they okay?!"

"Oh, calm down, y'all, nobody died," Cindy says, laughing at me.

"Phew! Are you at my house?"

"Yes, darlin', we're here, and would y'all look at this?! Turn the phone around, Larry!"

"I am. Gimme a minute, woman!" Larry turns the phone around, and eventually the lens finds two cats curled up together. My skinny black-and-white old man is wrapped around that little black kitty, and it's so cute I want to cry.

"Did you get pictures?" Brad says, before I get a chance to.

"Yeah, we only took about a hundred—don't worry," Larry says.

"That little Bella is giving such Capricorn energy!" Cindy tells us off-camera. "I mean, not right this second, but she's very bossy and independent."

"That she is," Brad concurs, a little rueful, but with pride.

"I tell you what, though, when a Cappy decides they can trust you, they are loyal for life."

"I feel that," I say, smiling at Brad.

"Well, you kids look absolutely gorgeous. You havin' a good time up there?"

"He cleans up pretty good, doesn't he?" I straighten Brad's tie. "Yeah, we're having a great time."

"She just gave a real corker of a speech."

"That's my girl. Well, we'll let you get back to the party. Bye, babies. We'll take good care of your babies!" I see a flash of red hair, and then Larry ends the call before we say goodbye.

I look at Brad. "Well, that was promising."

"That was the cutest thing I've ever seen."

"That's because you never saw yourself sleeping with Bella asleep on top of your head."

"I will never forgive you for not having your phone with you."

"It'll happen again—I'm sure of it. Aww, and remember how scared you were of her that first day?"

He frowns at me as he leads me over to the edge of the dance floor so we can watch Eric and his mom. "I wasn't scared." He maneuvers me in front of him and then wraps his arms around me, like we're posing for a prom photo.

It's hard to believe there was ever a time when I didn't know who I'd bring as a date to this wedding. Even harder to believe there was ever a time when Brad and I weren't talking to each other. As I stand here, swaying to "What a Wonderful World," in his arms, I find it hard to believe there will ever be a time when we aren't together. I don't think there will be.

Out of the corner of my eye, I see Granny Sparks approaching, in her sequin dress and cardigan, and I say, laughing, "I swear to God, Granny, if you touch my boyfriend one more time, I will cut you."

CHAPTER 29
BRAD

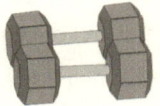

"*Tell me more, tell me more, like, does he have six abs? Uh-huh! Doo-doo, uh-huh! Mm-hmm, bop-bop, yeah!*"

"*She ran by me, to the wrong dooooor!*" I sing to the tune of "Summer Nights," and I *do* do a mean Travolta impression.

Hah!

Doo-doo.

I've only had one vodka tonic and half a glass of champagne, but I feel amazing and hilarious and horny as a motherfucker.

My girlfriend is gorgeous and barefoot and waving her key card in the air as she approaches the door to a hotel room that does not currently house our belongings. This is the first time I've had the pleasure of her company while she's tipsy on champagne, and I have no complaints, other than the fact that she is still wearing clothes.

"Wrong door, Sunshine Sally."

"What?! No, it's not." She holds the key card up to the

scanner, and it doesn't unlock the door, because as I told her, it is the wrong door. "Hang on, hang on."

"Oh, you wanna try again? Okay, sweetie." I'm holding her shoes and her handbag, and I have exactly no patience left because I haven't been alone with this woman all day, but I would fucking love to stand here and watch her try to open the wrong door with that key card.

She flips the key card around. Not facing the other way, she turns it upside down, presses it against the scanner again, and then looks back at me, frowning, because of course it's my fault. "Did you switch key cards on me?"

"No, I came back up here and switched the doors during the reception. That's how much I wanted to stand here in the hallway tonight"—I lower my voice—"instead of fucking you blind in our actual hotel room!"

She lowers her chin the tiniest bit, but my girl is not willing to admit defeat, even at the risk of waiting longer to get fucked blind. Like a stubborn toddler, she flips that key card around, maintains eye contact with me while attempting to hold it up against the scanner.

"You're aiming about two inches too low," I tell her.

"That's what she said," she quips, literally without batting an eyelash.

Before she can raise the card to the wrong scanner, I scoop her up into my arms and carry her to the end of the hall. "You are a pain in the ass, and I am so fucking in love with you, it's stupid."

"Ha! Yeah, you are!" She starts making out with my ear lobe. It feels really, really good, but I put her down on the floor, take her hand with the key card in it, and hold it up to the scanner on the door.

The handle clicks, and I kick the door open, guiding

her inside, dropping her shoes and handbag to the floor, walking her back up against the opposite wall. Her bridesmaid dress is shiny and smooth and the fabric hugs her curves and the color is apparently called quartz, but it is the exact color of her labia and that has made things very difficult for me today. "I don't know who needs to hear this, but you look stunning tonight," I tell her.

"I know."

Finally my mouth crashes against hers, starving for connection. Her tongue tastes like chocolate and strawberries and champagne and sass. She's humming the tune to "Summer Nights," and my cock is wide awake now, remembering how it feels when she hums as it's touching the back of her throat. I groan at the thought. "Turn around so I can unzip you."

She catches my lower lip between her teeth, tugs on it the tiniest bit, and then turns around like a good girl. Only she's doing little dance choreography moves like hip bumps and arm scoops, and I can't grab the little zipper pull to unzip her.

"Stay still so I can get you naked," I say in my most commanding voice.

It works. She goes still. I unzip her, letting the dress cascade to the floor, around her ankles. She isn't wearing a bra, only a pair of black lace panties that accentuate the curves of her ass in a way that makes me forget words.

I grunt and start to remove my suit jacket.

She turns to face me and says, "Keep your suit on! I want you to fuck me in a suit."

I nod, staring at her amazing tits while unbuttoning my pants.

"Wait, no, I want you naked!"

Nodding, I start to pull off my jacket again.

"Wait, no, suit on!"

"All right, that's it." I scoop her up into my arms again and carry her to the very comfortable bed, dropping her onto the mattress and watching her astonishing boobs bounce so rhythmically I am awestruck. For a moment. And then I grab the silk scarves I placed on the bedside table before I left for the ceremony. Because I knew my girl would be frisky when we got back tonight.

She rolls her eyes. "Just don't rip these panties. I like them."

"Oh, I like them too—trust me."

The wood headboard is not helpful to me, but there are light fixtures with brass arms attached to the wall on either side of the bed and they will do nicely as long as Sparky doesn't come too violently and rip them from their base. I'll have to go easy on her, I'm afraid.

She is still, even lying on her back, doing fifties dance moves and humming. "I can't believe my sister's married —can you?"

"Sit up," I say.

She does. I let the end of one of the silk scarves caress the skin of her breasts, her face. She sighs, closing her eyes as her head falls back. She holds her wrists together behind her back for me; I don't have to ask. I quickly, carefully, loosely tie the scarf in a figure eight around her wrists. "I always thought she seemed like the kind of girl who'd like being married."

"Oh yeah?" she says, her brows knitting together. "Do I seem like that kind of girl?"

"You didn't used to," I say, honestly. "I put a pair of scissors in the drawer, just in case."

She nods. "And now?"

I take a seat on the edge of the bed beside her, kiss her bare shoulder. "Do you feel safe and cherished, baby?" I ask her this every time I restrain her now.

"Yes."

"Good. I always want to make you feel that way. And yes, you do seem like a girl who'd like to be married. To me."

"Good."

This hotel is filled with Vivian's relatives, and I don't need them hearing her scream my name while I rail her. I hold up the other scarf, silently asking her if she's okay with me covering her mouth with it. She nods. I tie it loosely behind her head, covering her closed mouth. She won't be very quiet without a gag, but she'll be quieter. She lies back, wriggling around until she's comfortable.

I stroke up her outer thighs with my fingertips and pull down those black lace panties, and then I nearly choke on my own tongue. I can see from her eyes that she's smiling.

"Fucking hell."

The little minx. She shaved. All of it. Everything.

"Well, well. What have we here?"

Her muffled giggle is music to my ears and her gorgeous naked body is a feast for my eyes and I am so in love it actually makes my skin hurt all over.

I'm not going to last a full minute.

Standing up, I remove my jacket, my tie, my shirt, my pants. She watches me the entire time, and I am staring at her beautiful, glistening pussy. She's trying to keep her legs relaxed so I can see what she knows I want to see, but I can tell she's dying from all the pressure between those legs. She wants to squeeze those thighs together.

I drop my boxer briefs to the floor and climb onto the bed, crawl between her legs, kiss up the inside of her thigh, and lick the sweet center of her. Long and tender and slow, gently teasing her opening with my fingertip. I have spent a lot of time down here and gotten to know her so well. I know how she'll react to firm tongue strokes and which parts of her like gentle nibbles. I know that when I circle her clit and then flick at it with the tip of my tongue I have to be careful because her hips will shoot up. I know that when I grab her ass and fuck her with my tongue, she will writhe around like a maniac and swear like a Marine, but fuck me, neither of us has ever known how fucking good this would feel with absolutely no friction.

Unbelievable.

She is silky all over and I will make her come first, but fucking hell, I need to get up in there.

She's doing a not-very-silent scream into the scarf, bucking her hips, and I keep that steady, punishing rhythm until she goes stiff and then totally still, breathing so heavily, I sit up to make sure her nose is uncovered.

She's good, all good.

And I am so good to go.

"You ready for me, baby?"

She nods, but her neck is like taffy.

I kiss her over the scarf. "You taste so good, and I'm dying to be inside you."

She nods again, murmuring.

I get to fuck her without a condom, because we are really all good, have been for a month, and sweet mother of God, the warm, wet, tight, delicious slide in…it almost kills me.

She makes a high-pitched whiny sound, quivering, and

then she bends her legs and rests them on my shoulders. Either side of my head. My fucking dream girl. She's even tighter around me, and so, so silky smooth. I wrap my arm around her thighs, making things tighter still. Rocking into her, I groan, dig my fingernails into the flesh of her thigh, her ass. "God, I love you."

She whimpers.

"I love you so fucking much, baby. So good. I am so fucking in love with your pussy. This pussy is mine."

She makes a muffled, affirmative sound.

I'm not going to last.

She clenches and releases around me.

She wants me to come.

I watch her tits bounce as I fuck her, and this is five billion times better than anything teenage me could ever imagine.

I drive into her, hard and fast. She's high-pitched panting, and there's the joyful slapping of skin against skin, and I'm grunting so loud I probably should have gagged myself, but it feels better than anything I have ever, ever felt. It feels like all the years we spent apart and all the hurt and anger, all the tension has been erased. It's all smooth sailing, and there's nothing between us except her magical elixir and so much love.

She's screaming yes and my name over and over into the silk scarf, and I come. I explode into her. Every good thing that I am, it goes to her. On the big screen behind my shut eyes I picture myself coating the inside of her. All of her with all of me.

I want to make little people with her and build an empire with and for her and a home and more muscles and everything she wants. I want to be the one who gives it to her.

She spreads her legs and lowers them, circling them around my waist, pulling me into her with her feet. I rest against her heaving bosom and listen to the heavy beat of her heart. Hands up in her hair. Burying my face in the curve of her neck, I am about to tell her I love her again and again, when there's a confident knock at the door.

"Helloooooo? It's Granny Sparks!"

We both freeze, and then we both shake with laughter.

"Are you in there? There's no Do Not Disturb sign on the door, so I thought I'd see if you'd like to join me and Wally for a drink downstairs? Vivi? Brad?" She knocks again.

I pull the scarf from Vivian's mouth. She licks her lips and calls out, "Hey, Gran! We're kind of tied up at the moment! See you at breakfast in the morning—love you!"

"Okay, honey, we'll be at the bar if you change your mind!"

"She is relentless," Vivian whispers.

I kiss her neck and sit up. "Be right back, okay?" I say quietly and then go to the luxurious bathroom to clean up and bring back a hand towel to clean up between Vivian's legs.

She's able to sit up without help because she has excellent core strength. Untying her, I ask, "You feel okay?"

"Yep. Slightly better than okay."

I bring her a glass of water, hold it for her to drink from it, place it on the bedside table, and then cup her face in my hands and kiss her, deeply, tenderly. "Thank you."

"For shaving my hoohah?"

"Yeah."

She giggles. "You're welcome."

After we've showered together, when we're wearing matching hotel bathrobes, Vivian turns on the TV and gets comfy in bed with her paperback novel. I go to the closet and unlock the in-room safe, thinking about how much I love that she's almost always got a book in her hand when she's at home. I love being at her place, with all her pink Himalayan salt lamps and throw pillows and Hairy Styles. We also love being together at my place, with Bella and my bookshelves, and Vivian really loves it when I fuck her standing up against those bookshelves like Keira Knightly and that guy in *Atonement*.

I take out the velvet box, close the safe as quietly as possible, put the box in the pocket of my robe, and get into bed with her. I just love being around this woman. I love watching her do her thing while I'm doing meal prep for the week. She'll have *Clueless* on her iPad while she walks around with a paperback copy of whatever we're reading for ABC that week, singing some ABBA song, and doing Kegels. She thinks I can't tell when she's doing Kegels, but I can tell.

Fluffing up the pillow behind me, I tell her again how great her toast was, how beautiful she was, standing there next to Aubrey, and how mad I am that she made me do the chicken dance with her. Even though I loved it.

I tell her she was the perfect maid of honor because I know she has always had that little-sister syndrome.

"I guess I always will," she says.

"You know where you've got her beat?"

"My boobs have always been bigger, and my booty is objectively more wowza than hers now. It's more wowza than most people's."

"Yes, yes, and absolutely yes. And…she dated Eric for how long before he proposed to her?"

"Over three years."

"Well. Guess how long you dated me before I proposed to you?"

Her face lights up. "Less than three months?"

I pull the box out of my pocket, like I'm offering her a midnight snack. "Yeah. Less than three months." I'm not going to get on one knee because I know Vivian would rather I just stay by her side. I open the box, revealing the diamond engagement ring.

Cindy told me that the Aries birthstone just happens to be a diamond.

I wrote about my intention for today in my journal this morning: *Lock that girl down.*

I spoke to Mr. and Mrs. Sparks before the end of the reception and told them of my intentions. Mrs. Sparks burst into tears and hugged me, thanking me. Mr. Sparks asked me how much I spent on the ring.

Their daughter is just smiling at me, her eyes welling with tears and filled with all the love I can handle, maybe more.

"Vivian Elizabeth Sparks. I love you more than I have ever loved anyone in my entire life. Will you marry me, so I can love you for the rest of my life too?"

She nods. "Yes, sir. I'm going to marry you, Captain Coach Brad Bradley Alexander Mitch Mitchell. I'm going to love you forever and ever."

Sliding the ring onto her finger, I say, with all the sincerity of a sparkly teenage vampire, "And so the lion fell in love with the lamb."

She blows out a breath and says with a smirk, "Stupid, stupid hot lamb with womanly curves."

"What a sick, masochistic, hot, physically fit lion."

EPILOGUE - VIVIAN

My husband sparkles when he steps into the light.

And so do I.

It's early evening in the middle of May. Almost exactly ten years since the day our friendship suddenly ended the first time around. This time around, we are best friends, lovers, workout buddies, Cheat Day artisanal-ice-cream enthusiasts, Asshole Book Club members, cat parents, housemates, and partners in marriage.

If only miserable eighteen-year-old me knew how happy Bradley and I would eventually be together and that we would have—objectively—the most perfect wedding ever.

Bradley had to talk me out of doing a destination wedding in Forks, Washington, or any of the filming locations for *Twilight*, which by the way, includes towns in Oregon, in and around Portland. But I have no complaints about the location of our *Twilight*-themed wedding in Portland. At an evergreen-filled botanical garden wherein we recreated the forest-wedding scene in *Breaking Dawn: Part One*, and my dad walked me down the aisle to a quartet playing "A Thousand Years" by Christina Perri. My dress is a not-exact replica of the one Kristen Stewart wore in the movie, because that is still the prettiest damn wedding gown I have ever seen, but I am a grown woman with curves. My neckline plunges. My hips stretch the fabric like round yet firm divas. And speaking of asses—the open lace back of my crepe satin gown was tailored to ensure maximum booty sculpting.

My goal was to make Bradley *almost* jizz in his pants in front of all our invited family and friends, while also making him proud because he locked me down *and* continued to oversee my hourglass-shape workouts after we got engaged. If a bride can't torture her groom with a boner-inducing dress on their wedding day, is it really worth *not* eating banana cream pie for an entire month just so she could fit into said dress? I think not.

My husband wore a tux with a long jacket like the one Robert Pattinson wore in the movie, and he was not happy about it, but he did it. Because he loves me. And because I promised to let him do unspeakable things to me on our honeymoon if he did. Granny Sparks had a lot of complaints because she couldn't see his butt while he was standing up there, and honestly, I get it.

But for the reception, we've recreated the *Twilight* prom.

Our millionaire friend Larry, who is now officially Brad's investor in the new senior-focused gym location *and* officially Cindy's husband, pulled a few strings. We were allowed to have a big white gazebo built in the event area, covered in lights and vines, and that is where my husband

and I are now standing. It was my idea, of course, because prom is an important rite of passage. I didn't want him missing anything.

Brad has changed into a regular black suit and tie, his dark hair swooping up to the heavens with Cullen-like broody verve, his gluteal curves visible in those pants and a shorter suit jacket. I did not go so far as to wear a cast boot, but I am wearing a very pretty cardigan over my blue prom dress and Converse sneakers.

We've both got glitter makeup all over our faces now and amber-colored contact lenses, but we didn't for the ceremony.

The DJ starts "Flightless Bird, American Mouth" by Iron and Wine, and my supernaturally handsome husband smirks at me and says "Shall we?" as he holds up his hands.

I do my best to look all quivery and demure yet also bold and confident in my love for him as I say, "You're serious?"

"Oh, why not, wife? Why not?"

We slow dance, just the two of us, under hundreds of little white light bulbs, as eighty of our guests stand around the gazebo, drinking and watching us, among hanging paper lanterns. Our first dance together as husband and wife. With all the hopeful energy of our youth, all the experience from our time apart, and all the love and trust that can only come from choosing to verb each other every single day since we came back together.

"I want you," I whisper to him. "Always."

"Forever?" he asks broodily.

"Forever."

He dips me, staring deep into my intense doe eyes. The

flash of the wedding photographer's light bulb goes off as he gently kisses my arched neck. There is cheering. There is whooping and hollering. There is very loud sisterly sobbing.

I've got the most badass ragtag team of bridesmaids, with a combined age of around a thousand and fifty years old. Aubrey, who is pregnant and cries almost nonstop, Marlo, my friend from work, Cindy, Mabel, Dolores, and Gwen. Because I finally won her over, as I knew I would.

When Brad lifts me up again, we're smiling, but the joy is laced with the bittersweet. What if we had actually gone to prom together ten years ago? Would we have gotten married sooner? Would we have a kid by now? Would we have dated and then broken up for good?

As if reading each other's minds, we both shake our heads. Because what is the point of thinking like that? It is the bitter that makes this joy so sweet. We have each other now. We might not live forever, but we will grow old together. Old and hot, with joint mobility and excellent bone density.

Part of me wishes we would go to our ten-year high school reunion in August, just so we could rub it in everyone's faces how hot *my* Brad is now. But neither of us really enjoyed high school so much as we enjoyed each other in high school. So, we've already had the reunion that really matters. Good Form has agreed to be a sponsor of the event, though. The image that will accompany his ad in the memory book is a photo of us in our sexiest gym clothes, flexing as we flip off the camera. Because *fuck you, high school dicks*.

A week before Brad proposed, Aubrey had already sent me twelve options for small houses within our assumed combined budget, in a neighborhood that was exactly halfway between Good Form and my office. We ended up buying the perfect little house, which is where Hairy Styles and Bella are probably curled up with each other right now. And we have custom-made floor-to-ceiling bookshelves along two walls of our living room. Our books intermingle on those shelves, and Brad Mitchell, who goes less and less by Mitch nowadays, bangs me against them at least once a week.

At dinner, for the toasts, the Asshole Wedding Club rules were that everyone had to name at least one thing they didn't like about us, even though they loved us. Criticisms ranged from way too good looking to not very good at being illiterate. The one thing I don't like about us is that I still haven't figured out a way for both of us to see each other's butts at the same time, except in pictures.

But every single day, it's my intention to get to the bottom of this.

ACKNOWLEDGMENTS

The author would like to refer to herself in the third person in order to thank her very enthusiastic and helpful beta readers, Michaela and Michelle S.

The author would also like to thank narrators Emma Wilder and Jason Clarke for performing the voices in her head while she wrote this. They didn't really perform inside her head, but the audiobook is now available and you can hear them voice the characters in your ears!

ABOUT KAYLEY -
PRINT VERSION

USA Today bestselling author Kayley Loring spent many years as a screenwriter (under a different name) in Los Angeles before moving to the Pacific Northwest to live out her childhood dream of being a Disney heroine who talks and sings to woodland creatures. Still waiting for the woodland creatures to clean her house, though.

Read or listen to Kayley's books when you want humor, heat, and heart. You'll enjoy top-notch banter, strong heroines, lovable characters you'd want to know in real life and you'll swoon over perfectly imperfect book boyfriends. All Kayley Loring books are steamy open door romance. Be sure to check out her next-level audiobooks!

For more about Kayley and her books,
visit kayleyloring.com.